The Closing Door

Deborah lay back upon the grass, dimly aware of her daughter and her friends frolicking out of sight amid the trees, and of the very close presence of the Duke of Harwood kneeling over her.

"I . . . should get up," she said, yet made no move to match her words.

"Not just yet. Relax." Harwood gently combed her hair from her face.

His hand was so soothing as it brushed her hair, smoothed her brow. Deborah let her eyes drift closed. It registered on her that his hand was sinking oh, so gently into her hair, his fingers curling around and behind her head, his thumb stroking her neck and ear.

It was a caress, she realized, and she knew she ought to stop it, but it felt so good.

"Dee," he breathed, moving his thumb forward to feather a caress across her lips. "Dearest Dee."

Then Harwood began to lower his head—and Deborah knew that unless she escaped now, she well might lose her beloved freedom forever. . .

The Duke's Desire

June Calvin

A SIGNET BOOK

SIGNET
Published by the Penguin Group
Penguin Books USA Inc., 375 Hudson Street,
New York, New York 10014, U.S.A.
Penguin Books Ltd, 27 Wrights Lane,
London W8 5TZ, England
Penguin Books Australia Ltd, Ringwood,
Victoria, Australia
Penguin Books Canada Ltd, 10 Alcorn Avenue,
Toronto, Ontario, Canada M4V 3B2
Penguin Books (N.Z.) Ltd, 182–190 Wairau Road,
Auckland 10, New Zealand

Penguin Books Ltd, Registered Offices:
Harmondsworth, Middlesex, England

First published by Signet, an imprint of Dutton Signet,
a division of Penguin Books USA Inc.

First Printing, March, 1996
10 9 8 7 6 5 4 3 2 1

This book is dedicated to Nancy Berland, who also writes as Nancy Landon. She has unselfishly shared her knowledge of the art of writing and her business expertise with me and countless other writers. Her unfailingly cheery voice on the telephone has been a lifeline to me on many occasions. Thanks, Nancy!

Chapter 1

An unfamiliar sound caused Justin Stanton, the fourth Duke of Harwood, to look up from his struggles with the estate books. Unrestrained weeping expressive of the deepest feminine grief echoed across the vast tile and marble entryway of Harwood Court. The duke sprang up, realizing that his usually cheerful daughter, Sarah, was the source of the distressing sounds. He could hear her sobs as she raced across the entryway, past the library, where he was barricaded by his bookkeeping.

His long stride carried him to the door before she had mounted half a dozen steps up the massive central staircase. "Sarah? What is it?"

Sarah whirled around and reversed directions, a blur of golden curls and frothy pink muslin. "Oh, Papa, Papa, I shall die. I shall simply die." She flung herself into his open arms, weeping uncontrollably.

Harwood looked over her head into the sympathetic eyes of Timmons, his elderly butler. He gave a nod, which Timmons easily interpreted, and swung Sarah up in his arms as the old retainer opened the door to the front drawing room.

"Now, Sarah, can you tell me . . ." he began, depositing her on a sofa. "No, obviously you can't." He studied her features, usually so prettily arranged in a dimple-punctuated smile. Her chin was trembling and tears drenched her cheeks. She was attempting to speak over her sobs, with distressing results. Harwood crossed to a large cabinet. He turned the key, already in the lock, and extracted a decanter of brandy and one glass.

"Drink this." He put the glass to her lips. "Sip it—that's it—slowly."

In spite of his cautions, Sarah almost choked on the fiery liquor. He persisted until she had downed a sizeable dose.

The brandy calmed her, or numbed her. Her sobs gradually faded away into her father's lapels. His large comforting hand rubbed and patted her back while she regained control of herself.

"Now let me hear it, Sarah, for I may be imagining even worse than you have to tell me." He lifted her chin and looked into the grey eyes so like his own.

"Y-yes, Papa. It is quickly told. I drove out with Gregory this morning . . ."

Harwood's mouth firmed. "And?" His voice was ominous.

"He sent word that he must speak to me. I thought . . . I thought . . ." Her chin began to wobble again. ". . . he was going to propose at last. But he didn't. He explained to me why he couldn't, why he doesn't want to . . . oh, Papa, he's going to marry Amanda Greenwood."

The duke drew his daughter into the circle of his arms again. He wasn't surprised. He'd long suspected Allensby wasn't as eager for their union as Sarah. Though his heart bled for his daughter, he couldn't help but feel a certain relief. Allensby was a very ordinary young squire, with little to recommend him in terms of intellect or prospects. He was also burdened with a mother and three young sisters and an estate that was little more than a farm.

The duke had insisted Sarah go to London for the season before allowing her to be betrothed to her childhood friend. He had hoped she would find some more worthy suitor. When she'd come home a month ago still determined to wed Gregory, Harwood had bowed to what seemed to be the inevitable. "Allensby is a great fool to pass up such a bride," he whispered into Sarah's golden curls.

"Oh, Papa, he said he wasn't worthy of me. He claims that is why . . . but he can't love me, or he wouldn't let our difference in rank matter, would he?"

"Not everyone would agree with you. Some might say it is a sign of his unselfish love."

"Well!" Sarah sat up, her tears drying in a flash of indignation. "I don't think it's unselfish; I think it's foolish. But anyway, he lied. Gregory could never fool me when he was lying. He always looks every which way. He was just trying to let me down kindly, I'm sure."

Justin studied her bright hair and lovely features. Sarah was petite and pleasantly rounded. She was blessed with perfect skin, thick-lashed grey eyes, a short, slightly retroussé nose, and a rosebud mouth. Her frequent smiles brought enchanting dimples into play.

"Surely that young fool couldn't prefer Amanda Greenwood to you!"

"Oh, Papa, you are biased. She is tall and . . . and sturdy." Sarah's eyes filled with tears. "He said that she knew how to be a farmer's wife and wouldn't pine for a place in the fashionable world, as I would. But I wouldn't! Not if he loved me. I wouldn't!" She sought the comfort of her father's shirtfront again.

"No, of course you wouldn't. I never saw a young girl less affected by the fashionable *monde*."

"Indeed, I missed the country terribly. My season would have been unbearable if Davida hadn't been there with me! I know I would be a good wife to him."

"I wonder if I should speak to him. Perhaps he thinks I wouldn't approve the match?"

"No." Sarah let out a long, hopeless sigh. "He spoke as if it was all settled between them. In fact, I got the impression that while I was in London—"

She stopped abruptly and was silent so long her father pushed her away and looked at her face. It was beet red.

"She's increasing?" At his daughter's nod, Harwood stood up. "I've a mind to horsewhip him. He's been here visiting you any number of times recently. What kind of a rig was he running?"

Sarah stood up, too, catching her father's arm in her

small hands. "No, Papa, you mustn't. He was trying to find a way to tell me. I can see that now."

Despondently, she worried the ruffles on the front of her sprigged muslin. "I shall just stay here and keep house for you. I've no wish to marry, after all. Why, I am just now getting the rose garden and the succession houses the way I want them."

Harwood put out a hand and smoothed back the golden curls that tumbled over her cheeks. "That will make an excellent project to occupy you this fall and winter. By next spring when I go to London, you'll be feeling much more—"

"No!" Sarah bounced away. "I won't go. I won't ever go through a second season, stared at and measured like a beast offered for sale at the county fair. I never would have endured this last one if I hadn't thought I had someone who loved me, truly loved me, to marry when it was all over."

The duke nodded sympathetically, but his mind was racing. Somehow he had to prevent his daughter from burying herself in the country. "I quite understand how you feel. And of course you must do as seems best for you. But you will help me, won't you? As I explained to you after my five-minute betrothal to Davida, I am weary of my widowed state. I plan to go to London to seek a bride; surely you'll go with me and lend me your assistance?"

Sarah tilted her face up, perplexed. She had never quite believed that her father had wanted to marry her best friend. Surely he had just been acting out of kindness when it seemed Davida needed a way out of an unfortunate betrothal. "But Papa, if I am not to marry, I will be here to keep house and be your hostess. Why should you marry?"

Mastering the impulse to laugh at her naïveté, the duke slid his arm around his daughter. "There is a bit more involved in marriage than that, my dear."

Once again Sarah turned beet red. "But you are forty!"

Harwood lost his battle for control and laughed outright. "I realize I have one foot in the grave, but still, forty is not dead, Sal."

Chagrined, Sarah turned away, not quite able to deal with the implications of that pronouncement. "Well, then, I expect I must go with you, for it would never do for you to select a wife I could not deal well with, as I will be living with you."

Passing his hand over his mouth and emerging sober and serious from behind it, the duke nodded. "An excellent point."

"And you won't push me to marry? Or arrange—"

He held up both hands. "Pax, daughter. You know my feelings on marriage. I would never push you to marry, and certainly would never arrange a marriage for you. Though I do believe you will change your mind sooner or later. You are only eighteen, far too young to think you can never love again. Nor do I think you will relish being called an ape leader."

Sarah's lower lip jutted out. "That is what they will call me, but I don't care! I won't give my heart to be trampled on again." With dignity she stalked from the room, leaving her shaken father to stare after her.

Dear God in heaven, I hope she can change her mind, Harwood prayed. The duke was less likely than most men to dismiss his daughter's fascination with young Allensby, which had begun at fourteen, as calf-love. He had fallen in love once and only once, at eighteen, and had waited until he was of age so that he could marry Eleanor Gresham, a farmer's daughter, without his father's permission.

The duke paced back and forth the length of the drawing room, remembering his utter indifference to all the lovely females his father had paraded before him in the intervening three years, in the hope of securing a more eligible bride for his oldest son.

If Sarah, like him, could give her heart but once, she was destined to be lonely all her life, a fate he did not want for his sweet, loving daughter.

His own decision to remarry was a pragmatic one. After five years of grieving for his beloved wife, he recognized his increasing vulnerability to the pangs of desire.

He did not approve of illicit liaisons, so he had now decided to select a suitable mate, to save himself from repeating the kind of folly that had very nearly resulted in his marrying a girl his daughter's age. He would hope for regard, perhaps even affection, on both sides in his second marriage. But he never expected to be able to love again. How terrible for her if Sarah were similarly constituted.

The Duke of Harwood stopped his pacing and looked up at the painting of his wife, Eleanor. *I will do my best to find a husband for her, my love. I will see that she has every encouragement to meet eligible young men.* He bowed his head, remembering the clumsy efforts his father had made to distract him from his love for Eleanor. *I shall be much more subtle than my father. Pray God I shall be more successful.*

Deborah Harper Silverton, Dowager Viscountess Cornwall, suppressed a shudder as she seated herself on a backless sofa in the Egyptian Drawing Room. Merely changing the decor, as the new viscountess had done, could not cleanse the room for her. Nothing could wipe out the memory of her unhappiness in this house when her husband was alive.

She sat as stonily erect as if she were wearing a backboard and looked her brother-in-law in the eye, her own large brown eyes narrowed in an attempt to hide her alarm. It was unusual for her to be summoned in this way.

"Thank you for coming so promptly, Deborah." Vincent smiled a quick, insincere smile as he took his place in a fragile-looking chair opposite her.

Deborah bowed her head briefly in acknowledgement and waited for him to come to the point.

"I asked you to come today to discuss Jennifer's marriage."

Deborah gasped. "What can you mean? She is only sixteen."

"Yes, but before the season ends next year she'll be seventeen, *n'est-ce pas*?"

"Only just." Deborah opened her mouth to rush into protestations, but Vincent held up his hand to silence her.

"I've been giving the matter a great deal of thought, and Winnie and I feel it would be best if she was wed before Lettice makes her come-out, which must be year after next at the latest. And then there is Patience right behind her."

"Could . . . could not Jennifer make her come-out with Lettice? After all, she is only three months older. Or even with Patience? Indeed, would not the most economical way be to bring them all three out together, perhaps two years from now?"

Deborah knew that economy was important to Vincent, especially as it bore upon his own purse; she was surprised he was proposing a plan that did not allow him to charge some of his girls' expenses to Jennifer's account.

A brief widening of Vincent's light blue eyes told her she had scored a hit. He hesitated, his mouth pursed in thought.

Deborah rushed on eagerly, hoping to convince him. "I mean, that is quite acceptable to me, and that way she would have another year at least to grow up. She is too young to marry."

Vincent eyed her suspiciously. "I think, madam, given your attitude, you would not see her married at all."

It was Deborah's turn to hesitate. "True, but I know it is inevitable . . ."

"Yes, it is. Your hints to the contrary, Jennifer must marry. I cannot spend the rest of my life tending to her affairs without compensation. I'll be glad enough to hand them off to a competent husband. As for economy, the most economical way to manage the matter would be for me to select a husband for her."

"No!" Deborah stood suddenly, fists clenched.

"Calm yourself, madam." Vincent leaned forward, pointing with an imperative finger to the sofa, indicating that she should return to her seat. "I will not insist on doing so, providing you can find an acceptable candidate yourself during this next season. Winnifred and I will put the town house at your disposal, and I will see that Jennifer is provided with sufficient funds from her trust to make a creditable entrance into society.

"If the season ends without your having selected a husband, I will then take matters into hand. Do I make myself clear?"

Deborah nodded, clenching her fists against her sides to keep from lashing out at him. He had that haughty look he took on when he was being Lord of the Realm.

"Good. See you purchase some respectable gowns for yourself, too. You look a veritable dowd." Vincent leaned back in the chair, considering his sister-in-law's appearance.

"Perhaps you will take the opportunity to seek a second husband." With the title, Vincent had inherited his brother's enormous debts; he considered it a great burden to have to support his relict also. Seymour had spent his wife's portion, however, leaving only her dower rights, which Vincent must honor. His wastrel brother had not been able to get his hands on the fortune Deborah should have inherited through her mother from her grandfather, Lord Knollbridge. To keep it from Seymour, Mrs. Harper had passed over Deborah, leaving everything to Jennifer.

Vincent looked at Deborah hopefully. She was still a beautiful woman, with those large, liquid brown eyes, a perfect oval face, and hair the tawny color of old honey. Her figure was lush without the slightest hint of avoirdupois. Neither her thirty-eight years nor her many unhappy days were written in lines on her face, which was remarkably as it had been when she had married at eighteen. Surely she could attract an eligible *parti*, perhaps an older man.

His sister-in-law's response to that suggestion did not surprise him, however. "Certainly not! Once was quite enough!" Deborah's full lips firmed with determination.

"Ah, well." Vincent, embarrassed, skirted any discussion of her marriage. He was ashamed of his late brother's cruelty to his wife. So far they had managed to prevent it from being generally known, and pride demanded that he keep it thus. Such behavior, while lawful, was frowned upon by the *ton*. Fortunately, Deborah hated scandal as much as she hated her husband's memory, so she could be counted on to continue to say nothing.

"Then our business is at an end. Will you stay to nuncheon?" He stood.

It was a pro forma invitation, as both knew. Deborah avoided her in-laws whenever possible, and they were content to have it so. Making a polite excuse, she escaped to the hall, where Croyden dispatched a footman to bring her mare around. Deborah fled the butler's company, pacing the front portico until Buttercup arrived. Croyden had been an avid observer of her tumultuous, unhappy marital struggles at Woodcrest too many times for her ever to be comfortable in his presence.

How would she tell Jennifer? Deborah felt the tears sting her cheeks as she made the short ride to the dower house. Her daughter abhorred the idea of marriage; though Deborah had tried to reassure her that not all men would behave as her father had done, the child had seen too much not to dread putting herself into any man's power.

She was relieved that Jennifer was not in the house when she arrived. She washed the tears from her face and changed from her heavy black riding habit into a cool summer morning gown before seeking her daughter in the most likely place, their garden.

Her heart rose in her throat as she saw Jennifer romping about with her King Charles spaniel puppy. Her light brown curls were bouncing, her cheeks flushed from her pleasurable exertion. She was a child, just a child. To have to marry so soon!

But they would have to do as Vincent commanded, of course. He was Jenny's guardian. He was not deliberately cruel as his brother, Seymour, had been, but he had little true feeling for women's sensibilities, and such as he had was quite used up in concern for his two insipid daughters.

A few minutes of thought had brought Deborah to the

conclusion that it was not dislike of administering Jenny's fortune that caused Vincent to hurry her toward marriage. No, Jenny must marry while still a child so that Lettice and Patience would not have to compete with their beautiful, well-dowered cousin in the marriage mart.

"What is it, Mother?" With her usual sensitivity, Jennifer rushed up to Deborah as soon as she caught sight of her. "Why are you so Friday-faced? Does Uncle Vincent want you to play at some party or something?"

"No, Jenny, it is much more serious than that." Deborah led her daughter to the bench beneath the willow tree, where it was marginally cooler on this warm summer day.

When she had explained her brother-in-law's edict, Jenny threw herself on her mother's breast, weeping. "I don't want to. I don't want to marry, ever!"

"Now, Jenny, we have discussed this."

"Yes, but . . ."

"Just because I had an unfortunate marriage does not say that you will. We shall just have to choose your husband with great care. At any rate, you don't wish your uncle to choose. He would focus upon a title and a fortune, without regard for whether his candidate and you would suit."

Jenny sat up, her lower lip trembling. "I'm afraid, Mother."

Deborah nodded, staring off into the distance toward the magnificent outlines of Woodcrest, where she had been brought as a young, innocent bride a little more than nineteen years ago. She had been afraid then, too, and with good reason. Her parents had chosen Seymour for her. He had seemed a good choice—handsome, titled, wealthy, witty, sophisticated. They had forgotten to inquire if he had a heart.

"If you will allow yourself to be guided by me, Jenny, I do not despair of finding a man who will treat you well. I believe I have gained some insight into the sex." *Dearly won,* she thought. *Oh, so dearly won.*

Jenny nodded fervently. "I will, Mother."

Deborah patted her hands soothingly. "I will make it my

first concern to know whether he is apt to be kind and gentle, and no gamester. But in case we are deceived, or he should change, I will insist that the marriage settlements be structured in such a way that he cannot waste all of your portion, so that you do not have to live on the charity of your in-laws, as I do!"

"Yes," Jenny agreed, nodding her head until her soft curls bounced. "And one who will agree to let you make your home with us."

"That may be asking too much," Deborah cautioned, but her brown eyes kindled with hope. This was an idea she had not yet contemplated. *Was it possible? Oh, to be free of Vincent and Winnie, and out of sight of the towers of Woodcrest!*

I shall look in the peerage, Deborah thought. *And study the papers. I must find out who is available, sufficiently wealthy, and yet likely to be kind to a young wife.* Reluctantly, but with a grim determination born of necessity, she began laying plans for finding a suitable husband for her daughter.

Chapter 2

" 'Tis a great mistake to have one's ball so early in the season, do you not agree, Your Grace?"

Before the Duke of Harwood could respond to the plump woman by his side, he was interrupted by a dignified matron, Lady Penton-Smythe, another member of the cluster of females surrounding him.

"Do you say so, Amelia? I was just thinking how fortunate she is to have it all behind her. With her daughter's ball out of the way, she can just relax and enjoy the season."

"But only consider, my dear Adelaide. This early in the season, some of the best people are not yet in town. And then, with so few on hand, and so many yet unknown to one, one is forced to include someone who simply won't take. Such as the Cornwall chit over there." Amelia Gracemont so far forgot herself as to point briefly with her fan.

"Who?" Lady Penton-Smythe turned to stare.

"Jennifer Silverton, daughter of the late Viscount Cornwall. See her there with her mother? All arms and legs and eyes. She has no conversation and can barely dance for stumbling over her own feet, though it hardly matters, for who would ask her to dance, except for fortune hunters and men hoping to curry favor with her mother? Such a shame to bring a daughter to town so ill-prepared. I've been preparing my Hermione so that she knows how to conduct herself in society. *She* won't detract from a man's consequence, no, even if he should be a duke, do you not agree, Your Grace?"

The Duke of Harwood, thus appealed to, turned his cool grey gaze upon the young woman standing by Mrs. Gracemont. Though only slightly taller than her mother, and scarcely less rotund, she had somehow mastered the trick of looking down her short nose upon the world in a supercilious manner.

"Oh, I absolutely do agree, Mrs. Gracemont. Indeed, your daughter has so much consequence of her own, she scarce needs to marry a man with any. Coals to Newcastle. She will be the making of some plain mister of no social pretensions. I know a very wealthy ironmonger whose son requires just such a wife to establish himself in society. Shall I arrange an introduction, ma'am?"

Mrs. Gracemont froze in horror, torn between the fear of offending the duke and the absolute necessity of disavowing interest in pledging her daughter to a Cit. The other ladies in the group were equally stunned, though one nervous giggle was heard. In the rare conversational vacuum thus created, the duke was able to free himself from the cluster of matchmaking mothers.

Excusing himself, he glanced around the Penwickets' ballroom, first locating Sarah, who was dispiritedly trudging her way through a country dance. Then he began examining the fringes of the ballroom, seeking the object of Mrs. Gracemont's scorn. He located her quickly, a coltish young woman in a gauzy white dress, identifiable to him by her close resemblance to her beautiful mother, who was wearing a striking gown of deep coral satin.

"All arms and legs and eyes," he whispered to himself. Yes, she was that. Antelope eyes, Byron would have called them, and very like those of her mother. She would be a beauty, too, one day, just as Lady Cornwall was. Tall, perfectly proportioned, and graceful, Deborah had always been a woman no man could ignore.

Harwood's eyes swept over the dowager viscountess, pleased to note that his wife's friend had kept her looks. She must be—what—thirty-eight? And looked young enough to be the sister of the child by her side, not her mother.

But why bring so green a girl to the Penwickets' ball, or any ball, for that matter? She was obviously still too young to face society, and sadly frightened at that, as well she should be with harpies such as Mrs. Gracemont and Lady Penton-Smythe about to rend her limb from limb for the sin of being prettier than their daughters.

Well, no matter. She was here, and Harwood saw a chance to repay a very old favor.

The duke worked his way around the ballroom floor, still managing to keep Sarah in the corner of his vision. He ignored several feminine attempts to catch his attention and detain him.

Lady Cornwall became aware of the tall, dark-haired man bearing down on her with firm purpose in his stride. She mentally braced herself, preparing to repel the enemy as politely but firmly as she could. The silver at his temples made him ineligible for Jennifer, and she herself had no interest in masculine attention.

When he drew near enough, the duke saluted Lady Cornwall by name. Surprised, for she did not think she knew him, she looked up at him blankly.

"Justin Stanton, Lady Cornwall. We first met some nineteen years ago at another ball. You were kind enough to take my very frightened young duchess under your wing."

The wary look in the viscountess's eyes abated somewhat. "Can it be . . . ?" She recollected him now—remembered his narrow, high-bridged nose and wide forehead above penetrating grey eyes, his thin face and firmly molded chin and jawline. Lines radiating from his eyes and deep creases at the corners of his mouth were the main visible changes in the duke's appearance. He wore his hair long, pulled back in a queue in the old fashion, though now there was no powder, nothing beyond nature's silver tracery at his temples to lighten his raven-dark locks. His perfectly cut evening clothes underscored his sleek yet powerful build.

"Harwood?" Memories flooded her. Memories of a tiny, nervous young girl with this tall man hovering near her, so anxious that she not be hurt by bristling matrons who felt it their duty to let the new duchess know she'd married above her station. Deborah smiled welcomingly at the duke, offering her hand.

"At your service." He bowed formally over her gloved hand. "And this must be your daughter. So very much like you, and promising to be as beautiful."

Lady Cornwall nodded, retrieving her hand swiftly. "May I present my daughter, Jennifer, sir?"

"*Enchanté*." The duke took the young girl's hand, smiling what he hoped was an encouraging smile. "The first ball of the season. A momentous occasion, *n'est-ce pas*?"

Jennifer gave the duke a deep, respectful curtsy, and then wobbled so on arising that her mother had to steady her by taking her elbow. Lady Cornwall flashed an apologetic look at the duke.

He did not allow any flicker of evidence that he noticed the young girl's bobble. Instead, he looked toward the dance floor. "I want you to meet my daughter as soon as this dance is over."

Lady Cornwall's smile reached her eyes for the first time. "Is she here? I can't wait to see her."

The duke gave a small bow of acknowledgement. "Takes after her mother, as you shall see." The dance had ended. He lifted his head a little, signifying that Sarah, who had been seeking him with her eyes, should come to him. She all but pulled her partner from the floor. The unfortunate young man stumbled behind her, chagrined awareness that he had not managed to charm Lady Sarah showing on his face.

Introductions being made, they all stood rather awkwardly for a moment. The duke took his daughter's hand to be sure he had her full attention. "Lady Cornwall was extremely kind to your mother in her first season. You may recall her speaking of her friend Deborah."

Sarah's face, heretofore fixed with a social smile, lit up.

"Are you Dee? Mama often told me the story of how terrible she felt, the first few times she went among the *ton*. You always joined her in the drawing rooms and made her feel welcome when the old biddies snubbed her."

Lady Cornwall smiled reminiscently. "She was a very dear person. Harwood, you certainly spoke true—Sarah is the image of Eleanor! Except for her eyes, which are the same grey as yours, where Eleanor's were a brilliant blue."

"Is this your first season, Lady Sarah?" These were the first words Jennifer had managed. Her large brown eyes were fastened eagerly on the young girl before her.

Sarah sighed. "No, it's my second. And I'd far rather be at Harwood Court, I can tell you."

Jennifer nodded her head vigorously. "Me, too. That is, I'd rather be anywhere but here!"

"Jennifer." Lady Cornwall's voice held a warning tone, but Sarah suddenly came alive.

"Oh, I'm so glad I'm not the only one. Let us promenade."

The young man who had been hovering on the fringes of the group, not sure how to leave but not particularly wanting to stay, brightened and offered Sarah his arm.

"No, Geoffrey, we mean to have a comfortable coze. Go away, do!"

It was Harwood's turn to remonstrate. "Sarah . . ."

But Sarah's bright head was already lifted eagerly to her taller companion as the two walked away, chatting excitedly.

Geoffrey gave Lady Cornwall and the duke a sketchy bow and retreated hastily. Harwood chuckled as he watched the boy go. "I'm afraid my daughter has deplorable manners sometimes."

"At least she has self-confidence." Lady Cornwall watched her daughter's progress around the floor with worried eyes. "Jennifer is so overwhelmed by everything."

Harwood's smile faded. "She must not be but . . . Let me calculate . . . fifteen, sixteen?"

Lady Cornwall bristled at this reference to her daughter's age, feeling defensive. "She will be seventeen in June."

She relaxed a little as she saw that the duke's expression lacked any hint of condemnation. Instead, he nodded his head sympathetically. "Ah, I see. It is awkward when their birthdays fall just at the end of the season. I sent Sarah to my sister to be presented last year when she was seventeen. She wasn't very interested in the *ton* then, but I thought it was partly her youth. However, she is even more disdainful of the season this year."

Deborah's curiosity was aroused, but she could not well pry into his comments, for fear he might return the favor. Pride, which had kept her going and kept her prisoner so often, prevented her from explaining why she had brought Jennifer to the marriage mart so young. Instead she offered, "Then you know how difficult it can be, getting a young girl to overcome her shyness. And I have so few acquaintances, having been from town so many years . . . but I do not mean to bore you with my problems. Doubtless you will be wanting to dance."

"By all means." A waltz was just beginning. Harwood held out his hand to Lady Cornwall. She drew back, almost in horror.

"Heavens, I didn't mean with me. I mean, that wasn't a hint. I don't intend to dance. I shall need to keep an eye on Jennifer."

The duke took her refusal in good part. "Just so. I must needs watch Sarah, too, lest she insult every eligible *parti* in the place."

Lady Cornwall's questioning look was so devoid of malicious curiosity, so sympathetic, that the duke, not normally a confiding man, found himself explaining about Sarah's disappointment, and her determination not to marry. He offered Deborah his arm and she, caught up in his story, took it absentmindedly. They trailed after their daughters in a companionable coze that was observed with interest by a goodly number of people in the ballroom.

Dolphus Heywood, Lord Morton, watched the progress of the young girls and their parents around the room with intense interest. He had already begun to harbor proprietarial feelings toward Seymour's daughter and widow. The girl, with her fine dowry, would do very well for either of his sons. Perhaps better for the second, Newton, who was in need of an heiress, as he would inherit nothing from his father. Though to be sure, Harvey would get little enough other than entailed land and debts if Dolphus did not come about soon.

Another rich wife was what Lord Morton needed, but of course Deborah wasn't eligible, as Seymour had thoughtlessly spent every sou of her money, leaving nothing for a second husband. But she would make an admirable mistress and doubtless be glad of the opportunity, for hadn't she been a widow for two years now?

It did not occur to him that Lady Cornwall might have remained in the country after her husband's death, and even long after she was out of mourning, because she had no interest in a lover. Nor did it occur to him that his powers of attraction left anything to be desired. He did not see the watery, bloodshot eyes when he looked into the mirror, nor the parti-colored grey and yellow of his hair, except to preen himself that it was more abundant than that of most men his age. He did not notice the fine varicose veins that threaded his nose and his fat cheeks. And the only time he acknowledged his embonpoint was when he struggled into his corset for nights such as this.

No, Lord Morton's mirror still showed him the golden youth he once had been, with the clear, smooth peaches-and-cream skin any girl would envy, the bright yellow hair, and perfect teeth. When he looked in the mirror he saw, essentially, what his two handsome sons, both in their twenties, saw in theirs.

Well he knew that both boys were fortunate in taking after their illustrious sire, not their plain, mousy mother, a Cit's daughter whom Dolphus had wed and then scorned while eagerly spending her fortune. His sons were alarmingly remiss in seeking out heiresses of their own. The older, Harvey, was more interested in carousing, while the younger was mad for sport, especially coaching.

Damn the lads, why were they not here? He could have presented them to Lady Cornwall's child and let one of them charm her into wedlock before any serious rivals could appear on the scene.

It would be as well to go and renew his acquaintance with the beauteous widow and begin charming her daughter, to lay the groundwork for their arrival. But he would wait until she was away from Harwood. Something about the duke set Lord Morton's teeth on edge.

Lydia Smithfield fluttered her ornately painted chicken-skin fan idly as she watched with glittering sapphire eyes the progress of Harwood and that Cornwall woman around the room. She scarcely heard the buzz of gossip around her as she considered the duke.

He had only improved with age, she thought, sensuously measuring his length, the strength implicit in those long legs and broad shoulders. His black hair was only slightly frosted at the temples. She shivered a little as her eyes caressed his person. She had always desired the Duke of Harwood, had often daydreamed of the havoc those firm lips might work upon a woman's body. More than once she had imagined those cool grey eyes darkening with desire for her.

But it had never happened. She had been a young chit in her first season when he turned twenty-one and abruptly married his rustic bride. Lydia had, perforce, to accept Smithfield, without a title to his name, nor much in the way of looks, but with a comfortable fortune which was now hers.

She had attempted to interest the duke in subsequent years, when it would have been reasonable to assume he had begun to be bored with his wife and would be looking for a mistress. But he had always treated her with aloofness that was barely polite, just because she had snubbed his precious Eleanor.

But that was long ago. Doubtless, he had forgotten all
that by now. He was here, and single, though there would
be intense competition for his interest. An unmarried duke
was a magnificent prize in the marriage mart. He had
hardly been able to move around the ballroom for matchmaking mamas throwing themselves and their daughters in
his way.

Lydia doubted that such tame fare would interest the
duke now. No less assured than Lord Morton that her
youthful looks were untarnished, she meant to entice Harwood as she had so many other men in the years since her
boring husband had taken himself off to the country and his
coin collection, leaving her to enjoy herself in the *ton*.

Her flawless creamy complexion had not suffered over-
much through the years, and she had kept her lush figure.
That her red tresses owed more to her hairdresser now than
to nature was not, she believed, easily discerned.

Yes, she would have him! Now that Smithfield had finally condescended to stick his spoon in the wall, she fancied herself a duchess. That her husband would be a
handsome, virile man was icing on the cake.

Mrs. Smithfield was not at all pleased to see the Dowager Viscountess Cornwall on the duke's arm. Competition
was to be expected, but Lydia realized uncomfortably that
Lady Cornwall was looking remarkably fine. She began to
scheme on ways to separate the two.

There was a third very interested observer of the duke
and Lady Cornwall's promenade around the ballroom behind their daughters. Henry Fortesque, only son and heir of
Baron Egerton of Sandhill Close, studied the two young
girls carefully. His hostess, eager to deflect his attention
from her own daughter Penelope, had told him about them.
Two heiresses at the first ball of the season! How wise he
had been to skip the cock fight to attend the Penwickets'
ball.

Of the two, the taller one appealed to him most, partly
because she was so obviously a green girl that she would be

easy to attach, and partly because the little blond beauty was Harwood's child. Henry shook his head. He would not care to tangle with that father, should the duke set his mind against the match.

But the Cornwall chit had no father, and her guardian had not come up to town with the mother. Henry couldn't wait to brag to Alexander about his discovery. Wouldn't Alex regret having disdained the Penwickets' ball as likely to be a paltry affair?

The two young men made bachelor's quarters together, though they were as much rivals as friends. How chagrined Alex would be to learn that Henry had not one, but two pretty birds in his sights on this very first night of the season!

Deborah had listened sympathetically to the duke's recital of his concerns for Sarah and now felt called upon to make some reciprocation.

"I have been taken by surprise by Jennifer's awkwardness. You would not credit it, but at home she seemed so poised. She has suddenly taken a notion to be self-conscious of her height. Of course, I can understand that, being something of a Long Meg myself."

"And rightly self-conscious, too. For what young man would wish a tall, graceful female at his side whom he needn't stoop to partner in the dance, when he can have a chit half his size to add challenge and spice to the endeavor?"

Deborah tilted her head to one side, trying to decide if she had received a set-down. The duke was unsmiling, though his eyes sparkled. Then she remembered that Harwood was given to odd and occasionally sarcastic humor. Eleanor, she recalled, had never seemed the least intimidated by his remarks, and he had always seemed to delight in her spirited retorts.

Surprising herself, Deborah responded to his teasing in kind. "What you say must be true, Harwood, now I recall— for Eleanor was scarcely taller than your Sarah." Suddenly aware of the flippant nature of this reference to his deceased wife, she held her breath as she braced for an angry response.

"Yes, and we did not even have the waltz to contend with then. Today's youth have so much more cogent reasons for despising a lovely girl who can look them in the cravat."

Deborah shook her head, relief making her a little limp. *He wasn't offended.* "You . . . you *are* roasting me?"

"No, am I?" But he smiled and patted her gloved hand where it rested on his arm. "Your daughter will come about. Mayhap there is somewhere a likely young man of Sarah's height who will desire Jennifer of all things, out of the sheer perversity of youth."

Deborah giggled. It surprised and charmed her to realize that the duke, who seemed so aloof, was savoring quizzing her and watching her response. "Well, I hope you know such a one, sir, for I am sadly out of touch. I have been wracking my brains as to how to help Jennifer meet eligible young men when I have so few acquaintances left in the *ton.*"

"I do not think that will be a problem any longer." The duke winked at her and nodded toward where Sarah and her new friend were just coming abreast of a cluster of exquisitely dressed young men.

Chapter 3

The moment Sarah had been dreading for months was at hand. When her father had insisted she accompany him to London, she knew that she must face her friends and acquaintances of the previous season. There would be everything from teasing to pity to be endured as they realized that the "understanding" she had used last season to discourage suitors had not resulted in marriage.

How she yearned for the support of Davida Gresham, her best friend, now that the embarrassing moment could no longer be postponed. But Davida was still in Yorkshire with her new husband.

Sarah was grateful to have her new acquaintance, Jennifer Silverton, by her side as she approached the cluster of young men. Jennifer's shyness and lack of ease seemed somehow to help Sarah feel more poised.

She quickly assumed command of the situation, introducing her new friend around with a sprightly patter that prevented any questions from being posed. She was aided in her object when a spirited competition broke out between the two tallest young men, Lord Threlbourne, and the slightly shorter Mabry Ventner. They immediately began to vie for Jennifer's hand for the next set. Sarah ended the dispute by linking her arm through Gilbert's, as being the least likely to seek to embarrass her.

The red-haired young viscount willingly allowed himself to be commandeered. Sarah fleetingly wondered where his fiancée was, the one he had spoken of so often last year as being still in the nursery. The family-sponsored match was expected to take place this year after Threlbourne's cousin had made her curtsy and enjoyed a season.

Of course, Sarah was the last one to bring up the subject of a missing fiancé. Instead, she turned around to introduce all four young men to Lady Cornwall, who was quickly importuned for dances with Jennifer.

Harwood stood back a little from the lively group, smiling and breathing a deep, inward sigh of relief. It was going to be all right. His Sarah was naturally gregarious. Once she got past this first evening in the *ton*, surely she would be fine—especially with a new friend to confide in. Unless he missed his guess, his daughter and Jennifer were going to be close friends in no time.

"Justin! Justin Stanton. How wonderful to see you again!"

The duke turned at the sound of his name and found his arm under attack by a buxom redhead who seemed suddenly to have attached herself to him.

Harwood had a strong aversion to being physically accosted in this manner, but he could hardly shake this woman off in a ballroom with the icy disdain he might have shown her had she thus approached him on the street, like the *femme de nuit* whose behavior she seemed to copy. Instead, he drew himself up to his full, imposing height, gave her his most repressive stare, and murmured, "I apologize, ma'am, but I do not recall your name."

"But surely you must! We were once such good friends." Lydia was actually pleased that he didn't remember her. That meant perhaps he had forgotten her behavior toward his precious Eleanor.

"I am sure we must have been, for you to feel free to destroy the sleeve of my coat in this manner; however, I do not recollect you."

"La, Justin." She swatted at his chest with her fan. Belatedly becoming aware that his attitude had passed reserve and gone to outright anger, she lifted her hands from his arm. "I shall give you three guesses. Or perhaps . . . here is a Langler beginning. I shall give you until we have completed it to remember. Doubtless it will come back to you as we dance together; we were ever a most delightful pair."

"I beg to be excused; I do not dance this evening, as I am chaperoning my daughter."

Nothing if not persistent, Lydia laughed. "She has taken the floor with a most acceptable young man, so I doubt she is in any danger, sir." The widow moved so she was between Harwood and the dance floor, quite as if she had been asked to dance and was positioning herself to be led out.

"I have taught my daughter not to dance with young men to whom she has not been properly introduced—"

"I am sure she has been introduced to Lord Threlbourne, for she was often seen in his company last season."

"—and thus I must set her an example. Whatever would she say if I could not introduce my dance partner to her?" Harwood made as if to bow to her in dismissal, but she clapped her hands as if delighted by his cleverness.

"There, you have taken the trick. I yield. I am Lydia Smithfield, but you knew me as Lydia Green. Come, we must hurry and take our places."

Harwood even more strongly wished to give in to his urge to strangle this encroaching woman, for her name was indelibly engraved on his memory as one of the women who had tormented his young duchess. She had reduced Eleanor to tears on her first evening in the *ton* by snide comments she made when the ladies withdrew to leave the men to their port after dinner. It had been Deborah who had rescued her; now Harwood looked around, hoping against hope that his wife's friend might rescue him.

What he saw caused him to abandon Mrs. Smithfield without a qualm, for it turned out to be Dee Cornwall who needed rescuing.

Lord Morton had been pleased to observe Lydia Smithfield drawing Harwood off. He quickly moved to Deborah's side when the swarm of young people began to dance. She saw him coming and recognized him all too well. Frantically, she turned back to Harwood, only to find him deep in an intimate conversation with a ravishing redhead.

"Lady Cornwall, how very pleasant to see you come to town at last."

Reluctantly, unable to avoid him, Deborah turned to greet her husband's good friend. "Lord Morton." She sketched a curtsey, finding that no social banality sprang to her lips.

"Ah, but let us be less formal, for after all, we are old friends, Deborah. You must call me Dolphus. Will you honor me with this dance?"

Deborah froze. "No, indeed, sir, I do not dance. My daughter . . ."

"Ah, yes, I have seen her. Lovely! Lovely! She quite puts me in mind of you at her age, but you, my dear, are even lovelier."

"Too kind," Deborah murmured.

"Not at all. Every word the truth. Have always admired you, one of many, as your husband well knew, else why did he keep you so shut up at Woodcrest? But now you are here, and we shall enjoy getting to know one another all the better for our coming together having been delayed so long."

"I beg leave to tell you, sir . . ."

"Now this nonsense about not dancing. You should put that aside. Your daughter is safe with young Ventner." Dolphus reached out to take Deborah's arm. She was the type who required physical persuasion, indeed, desired it, Seymour had told him.

Instinctively, Deborah drew back, but Morton tightened his hold on her arm, preventing her retreat. "Now, my dear, I will indulge your taste for rough treatment all you want in private, but you shan't want to make a public spectacle of yourself, surely."

Deborah blanched. What tales had her odious husband told on her? "I do not want to dance with you. Take your hand off me!"

"You do that so very well." A wolfish grin spread over

Morton's fleshy face. "I can scarcely control my anticipa-
tion. Come, now." He began pulling her onto the dance
floor, only to come abruptly against an obstacle.

Harwood had turned toward Deborah, hoping for rescue,
at the very moment that Morton had first grabbed Deborah's arm. The look of horror on her face propelled him
into action. Instantly, he disengaged himself from Lydia
and in two strides was standing just behind the baron, preventing his further progress toward the dance floor.

Morton's indignation quickly turned to unease upon
finding himself confronted by the duke's cold stare. "Oh,
it's you, Harwood. You're in our way, old man. Taking
Lady Cornwall for a spin about the floor."

Harwood looked inquiringly at Deborah, who shook her
head vehemently. "I told him I was not dancing."

"Been from town quite a while, Dolphus, but I don't
think manners have changed so much that it is acceptable
for gentlemen to drag ladies onto the floor against their
will."

Morton took out his handkerchief and wiped his forehead. "Not that at all; Deborah just seemed to feel she must
watch her daughter dance and miss all the fun herself. Not
necessary, not necessary at all."

"No, of course it isn't, unless she says so. But she does
say so. Said so to me, as well as to you. Queer, these rules
of society, but there it is: A gentlemen must honor a lady's
wishes in these matters."

Morton wished himself out of there. Harwood was too
tall, too stern-looking. Memories of his legendary prowess
with a pistol and small sword suddenly superseded Dolphus's interest in Seymour's beauteous widow. "Well, of
course, if she's already refused you. Should have said so,
my dear, Couldn't dance with me afterward, could you?
You'll need to relearn these little rules, else you'll commit
some social gaffe. Be glad to assist you. I'll call on you tomorrow. My sons will be eager to meet your lovely Jennifer."

He looked hopefully at Deborah, expecting some encouragement, but the widow Cornwall remained utterly silent, so he made a hasty bow and a judicious retreat, offering his arm to Lydia Smithfield, who was standing at the duke's elbow.

As for Lydia, she accepted it gratefully. Harwood's response had not been encouraging, and though Lord Morton was in no way as appealing as the Duke of Harwood, he, too, was a widower and had a title, didn't he?

The duke took one look at Deborah's pallor and steered her quickly to the chairs set up for the chaperons.

"Wait here; I will bring you something to drink," he commanded.

Deborah nodded, hiding her trembling hands in the folds of her gown. She pretended to watch her daughter dance, but her mind was too jumbled with unpleasant thoughts to concentrate on anything.

By the time Harwood returned, she had recovered herself somewhat and was beginning to be embarrassed by her loss of self-control. The duke distracted her and put her at ease by a running commentary on the dancers as they whirled by. She listened, smiling, until he pointed out a young woman she knew.

"See the short, heavy creature at the head of that set," he asked, indicating with a nod which group he had in mind.

"Miss Gracemont."

"Yes, that's the one. Would you believe her mother hinted that her child would make me a fine duchess."

Though Mrs. Gracemont had snubbed her and Jennifer, Deborah felt pity for the unattractive young woman whom the duke was mocking.

"She may very well be a lovely person, but I collect you require a diamond of the first water," Deborah responded in a repressive tone.

Harwood shook his head. Surprise at Lady Cornwall's implied criticism lifted his brows. "That was not my meaning. Her mother should have better sense than to look for her daughter's husband among the greybeards."

Deborah surveyed his beardless chin and shining black

hair, so lightly tinged with grey. "One would not think to put you in *that* category, sir."

"I assure you the young girls do! And their mothers had best look for young men to keep up with them, instead of greedily seeking the highest title they can obtain for their children."

Again Deborah felt the prickles of rebellion. How dare he condemn women out of hand? What did *he* know of the fears and anxieties that drove women?

"A mother seeking a kind husband for her daughter may well be painfully aware that a man in the first flush of youthful strength and vigor may not be the best choice." So saying, she rose. "I see the dance has ended, and Jenny is looking for me."

The duke followed her, looking thoughtful. He certainly hadn't changed his mind about the advisability of May-December marriages, but the viscountess's strictures made him think he should perhaps take a more charitable view of the mothers' motives in arranging them.

In response to an almost invisible signal from his daughter, Harwood suggested that Sarah sit out the next dance rather than accept Arnold Lanscombe's invitation to join him on the floor. "I think you are looking a bit flushed, my dear," he suggested.

"I am rather winded, Father," Sarah sighed, turning toward the chairs. "Do ask Penelope to dance, Arnold. She is without a partner now, and that is not at all the thing at her own ball."

Arnold's smirk as he bowed his acceptance suggested that the dandy was well aware of Sarah's reluctance to spend any time with him. She knew that in pushing him away she only delayed the hour of reckoning, for Arnold was an avid gossip who would keep on until he had the truth of her presence in London without her "farmer-fiancé," as he had designated Gregory at her coming-out ball last season. She could almost hear the limerick he would compose, ridiculing her. Doubtless it would sweep the *ton*, giving vast amusement to all.

Still, she would put Arnold off as long as possible, she vowed. Avoiding the question in her father's eyes, Sarah turned to Lady Cornwall. "Does Jennifer ride?" she asked.

"She does indeed. It is one of her chief pleasures, and we have brought mounts with us for that very purpose."

"Will she ride with me tomorrow afternoon, then?"

Deborah queried the duke with her eyes. He nodded his assent, but added, "I cannot accompany you tomorrow, Sarah. You will have to make do with one of the grooms."

"Perhaps I could accompany you?" Deborah was pleased to offer her chaperonage. Like Harwood, she was aware that Sarah was scheduling a ride when she might have been expected to remain at home to receive calls from those who had danced with her at the ball. And like Sarah, Lady Cornwall found very appealing the idea of being "not at home" the next day to callers such as Lord Morton.

"I should like it above all things," Sarah declared.

"With your permission, Lady Cornwall, I will still send a groom. I do not like to think of the three of you riding in London unaccompanied."

"Thank you, Harwood. That would be most welcome."

To forestall another approach by Arnold Lanscombe, Sarah began a campaign to convince her father to leave the ball early. Sensing that he had pushed her far enough for this first outing, Harwood agreed, and was not surprised to learn that Deborah was also ready to leave. They went down the steps to their carriages together, again eliciting several stares and pointed, envious comments from some observers. None were more chagrined than Henry Fortesque, who had failed to gain an introduction to either heiress.

"That's impossible! Tell me again who they were?" Alexander slammed both hands on the table on hearing Henry's news the next day as they broke their fast around noon.

No less than Henry did his friend Lord Alexander Meade, youngest son of the Marquess of Hanley, need to marry an heiress, though for a different reason. "What is so useless as a third son?" Alexander had often moaned. A tiny estate, hardly worthy of the name, was his total expectation. If Alexander hoped to marry, he must marry well.

Unlike Alexander, Henry had brought his status as a fortune hunter upon himself. He had gambled away his allowance and borrowed extensively upon his inheritance in the form of post-obit bonds. Be his unloved sire's demise ever so timely, he would still be a pauper. Fortunately, this was a fact he had thus far managed to keep secret from everyone but his bondsmen, and even they were ignorant of each other, and hence of just how much more he owed than he could ever hope to repay.

"I was told they were Jennifer Silverton, daughter of the previous Viscount Cornwall, and Lady Sarah, daughter of the Duke of Harwood. Why is that impossible?"

"But is not Lady Sarah married? She was very definitely promised last year. It was my understanding that she would be wed to a young squire from her home county by now."

Henry frowned. "I was told that she was single and an heiress. Unfortunately, before I could find anyone to introduce me to either of them, they left."

"It just couldn't be. I couldn't be so fortunate." Alexander strode up and down the small room, thrusting his hands through his thick blond curls, which required little such encouragement to adopt the windswept style.

"So, you know this Lady Sarah. Do I take it you have an interest there? That is as well, as I have set my sights on the other one."

"Yes, it certainly is as well, for if Lady Sarah is unwed, I most definitely intend to court her! I found her enchanting last year and would have tried to fix my interest then, but her heart was already engaged."

"Sounds alarmingly like a dangerous case of lovesickness, Alex!"

"I could love her with very little effort," Alexander readily agreed.

"I don't envy you, a penniless, titleless third son, seeking to court the Duke of Harwood's daughter. If you must know, that is the chief attraction of the Cornwall chit. Not that she isn't lovely, for she is, though a green girl and a true Long Meg at that. But she has no stern father hovering around her. I for one would not care to brave Harwood's wrath."

"Why should I brave his wrath? I have at least as much to recommend me as that Appleby or Allensby or whatever—that young rustic with whom she had an understanding last year."

"Perhaps that is why she is not married?" Henry examined his fingernails, covertly enjoying Alex's sudden grimace at this possibility. "Harwood does not look the sort to let young love dictate his choice of a son-in-law."

Alex sat down suddenly, frowning. "Yes, and he is a subtle man. He doubtless found a way to break it up without his daughter being aware . . . but no! I won't let myself be defeated without at least trying."

"I am extremely glad to hear you say that, for it is my hope that you will introduce me to the Cornwall chit."

"Your wits are going begging, Fort. Never laid eyes on her."

"But she and Lady Sarah are as thick as inkle weavers. And you *do* know Lady Sarah!"

Alexander looked at Henry Fortesque with chagrin. Not for the first time he regretted the economic necessity that had forced him into sharing quarters with his fellow equerry. Service in the Prince Regent's retinue, while a high honor, was not a well-paying proposition. Economy had forced him into an intimate association with a young man whose morals occasionally made Alex uneasy. He certainly hesitated to introduce him to a green girl with no father to protect her.

An exceedingly handsome young man who had a great deal of appeal to the opposite sex himself, Alex was often outflanked by Henry, whose dark hair and fair complexion, thick-lashed dark brown eyes, and muscular physique made him virtually irresistible to women. Unlike Alex, Henry had no qualms about bedding other men's wives, or maidens of the lower classes. Such behavior made Alex hesitant to bring him into Sarah's circle.

Still, as long as Fort's intentions were honorable, and as long as he did not attempt to engage Sarah's affections, Alex decided that it doubtless would be unexceptionable to introduce him to the Cornwall heiress. After all, he *was* heir to a title and, if he could keep his demanding sire happy, a considerable fortune. As such, he was a very eligible *parti*. Doubtless the chit would thank him for it.

"Well, Alex? You can't be thinking of refusing!" Henry stood and meticulously brushed his clothing free of any possible crumbs from their breakfast. The two young men shared one servant, a former army batman whose skills as a cook exceeded those as a valet, so to keep up appearances they both had long since learned to look carefully to their own grooming.

"If you are quite sure your intentions are honorable . . ."

"I can't mend my finances by mere seduction!"

"And no abducting an unwilling female!"

"Bah! For all my loose ways, I've no taste for forcing myself on a woman! Indeed, I can think of nothing more miserable than being leg-shackled to an unwilling wife. No amount of money would be worth that!"

"Well, then . . . as long as you keep to your Long Meg, and leave me to my little pocket Venus."

"Agreed!" Henry offered his hand, and Alex slowly but firmly closed his own strong fingers around it.

Chapter 4

The Duke of Harwood restlessly paced the thick carpeting of the blue salon, where he awaited his visitor. The sound of his daughter tripping down the steps brought him to the door in time to see her check her appearance in the mirror strategically placed for that purpose in the entry hall. She looked like spring itself in a light green riding habit with a daffodil yellow habit-shirt very nearly the same color as her hair. But her eyes were shadowed, her expression somber.

Had she been crying? The duke hastened toward her. His hopes that her melancholia of the last several months would have dissipated at her first ball had not been realized. Not even making the acquaintance of Jennifer Silverton had put the roses back in her cheeks.

The months since Gregory had wed his Amanda had seen Sarah lose weight and acquire an unwonted air of gravity. This morning at breakfast she had been as subdued as at any time since last summer. *Still breaking her heart over Gregory Allensby!* The duke grimaced angrily.

"Why are you looking so fierce, Father?" Sarah had completed her inspection and turned, arrested at the expression on her father's face.

"I was thinking of suitable means of torture for ignorant farmers."

Sarah laughed, the sound a little forced. "Entirely unnecessary, Father. I am sure Amanda Greenwood will accomplish your revenge. And at any rate, I don't think of Gregory anymore, I assure you."

"No, doubtless those red eyes were caused by tears of regret for the napkin you shredded at breakfast this morning."

"I was just thinking . . . I can only avoid Arnold Lanscombe and his cruel limericks for so long. Then everyone will know I've been jilted."

"Ah! Pride." The duke truly smiled, his relief evident. "Hurt pride heals much sooner than a broken heart."

"Yes, Papa." But Sarah looked doubtful. "May I invite Lady Cornwall and Jennifer back to tea?"

"I insist. Oh, and John will be here by then."

Sarah perked up at the mention of her second cousin. "He is returning today?" John Warner was her father's very efficient secretary. He had been in Scotland for a fortnight, attending to his recently deceased father's affairs.

"Yes. It was a near-run thing. I greatly feared he might elect to stay with his mother."

"Pooh! She would not appreciate it. Old tartar! She doesn't deserve a kind, considerate son like John."

Harwood nodded his agreement and watched his child dash out to her waiting horse and groom. He yearned to protect her from the spiteful tongues of the *ton,* but knew he could not do so, not completely, any more than he had been able to protect her mother. Eleanor had learned to cope, indeed to give as good as she got, and soon Sarah would have to learn to do the same. But it grieved him to think she must surrender some of her sweetness in the process.

Standing on his front steps to watch his daughter ride away, Harwood surveyed the skies, which were grey but did not look immediately threatening. He wished he could join Sarah, but duty called. Preston Tarbridge, his man in the House of Commons, was calling on him today with what the tiresome old place-holder had insisted was urgent business.

"What incredible luck!" Abruptly, Alexander drew up Cavalier, his rangy roan gelding, causing Henry's mount to bump into its flank.

The resentment this caused in both high-spirited horses kept Henry from learning the reason for Alex's excitement for several moments as they both struggled to control their mounts. When Henry's black, Demon, had finally been convinced not to savage Cavalier, and Cavalier had been convinced not to bolt, both young men were red-faced with exertion and embarrassment.

"What the devil brought this on?" Henry demanded.

"After our fine display of horsemanship, I regret to inform you that we have an interested and very interesting audience." Alex tapped Cavalier lightly with his heels and sprang away toward a group of four horses that had stopped to avoid colliding with them on the bridle path. He drew the roan up smartly and took off his hat, sweeping it forward in greeting.

"Lady Sarah! What a breath of spring you look on this grey day!"

"Lord Alexander!" If Sarah had not already realized her heart was healing from Gregory's rejection, the way that formerly blighted organ raced at the sight of the handsome blond man's approach would have told her. Introductions were made all around, and her pleasure grew as Alexander made it clear he had eyes only for her. Since Jennifer, looking very fine in a severely tailored black riding habit, had attracted no small amount of masculine attention on their ride thus far, Sarah was flattered and relieved at Lord Alexander's attentiveness.

Indeed, he wasted no time, but as soon as he could politely abandon the general conversation, maneuvered his horse alongside hers to engage her in a tête-à-tête. There was nothing remarkable about the words they exchanged, the mere commonplaces that a well-bred gentleman might safely offer to a gently bred young lady. But all the while the two of them were exchanging remarks about the weather, and town being thin of company as yet, their eyes, their bodies were speaking eloquently in another language, the language of lovers.

For quite some distance they rode thus, often in silence,

the innumerable sights and sounds of the park fading into obscurity, in their absorption with one another.

Meanwhile, Henry was having heavy going with the two women who rode beside him. Jennifer was painfully shy before this dark, curly-haired Adonis, and Lady Cornwall was studying him in a cool, measuring way that bespoke a most cautious parent. Not terribly propitious, but still, the chit's very silence might indicate he'd made a strong impression.

After a few commonplaces about the weather and last night's ball, Henry asked Jennifer if she would enjoy watching a military review. "Parades are few and far between with the Prince unwell and so often in Brighton," he told her. "You should seize this chance to see us in all our glory."

"Are you a soldier, Mr. Fortesque?" Jennifer asked timidly, because Henry and Alexander were both dressed in civilian riding attire.

"I am one of the Prince's personal soldiers, if you will, one of his equerries, as is Alex, there. We have quite impressive uniforms, I assure you, and can show to much better advantage on horseback than we did a few minutes ago."

Jennifer giggled, while Lady Cornwall lifted her eyebrows in amusement. "That is an exceptionally fine horse, Mr. Fortesque."

Henry leaned forward and patted the black stallion's neck. "Demon is Arabian, you know. Won him off of Eberlin. He breeds the best cattle in England," he bragged expansively. Jennifer looked suitably impressed, but as Henry's gaze swept past her to her mother, he realized he had made an error. Lady Cornwall's mouth was primmed in disapproval, and he could almost hear her thinking, "A gamester!"

Demon chose this moment to live up to his name. Caught up in their idyl, Sarah and Alex had slowed almost to a walk, allowing Demon the opportunity to express the grievance he still felt for the encounter of a few minutes ago. A sharp nip to Cavalier's flank set the gelding to kicking and jibbing sideways. This caused Sarah's mare, Lorelei, to break into a jerky canter from which she fought her rider for the opportunity to gallop.

Sarah's alarmed groom yelled out as he spurred his mount to pass Henry, hastening to aid his mistress, "Here, now, sir, if you can't control him . . ."

"Mind your manners, man, and keep to your place," Henry snarled, much vexed. "I've my mount under control, though I can't say the same for Alex."

But Alex had firmly settled Cavalier and quickly moved forward to catch Lorelei's bridle, ending her attempts to bolt. Sarah was glad for the assistance, for though she was a competent horsewoman, she had a healthy fear of a runaway. She flashed him a grateful smile.

Alex then turned on his friend, his concern for Sarah making his tone harsh. "The groom is right, Fort. That ill-tempered beast isn't fit for riding alongside ladies. He's hardly a park horse, you know."

Already regretting his burst of temper, Henry did not take offense. "Right you are. He's best suited for racing. Eberlin may raise beautiful animals, but their docility is far from guaranteed."

The group had come to a standstill, or as close to that as could be managed on six high-strung animals. "I've even greater need to redeem myself now, ladies," Henry asserted. "Please do attend the review tomorrow. I'm to carry the Prince Regent's colors."

"And you do *not* intend to ride Demon, I take it?" Sarah's dimples flashed.

"No, indeed, Lady Sarah. I've a fine bay who'll carry me as steady as you please."

Agreeing that she would seek permission to attend the review, Sarah bade Alex a reluctant good-bye, for he was urging his friend to get Demon out of the park before the stallion could contrive more mischief.

Henry noted with chagrin that Lady Cornwall very reluctantly agreed that she and her daughter would make one of the party to watch the review. But a glance at Jennifer raised his hopes again, for that damsel pinked beneath his gaze and breathed a fervent "Thank you," when her mother agreed to the outing.

By the time the three ladies had made their way back to the Harwood mansion for tea, a fine mist had begun to fall. "We must go upstairs and do something about our hair," Lady Cornwall concluded after a quick glance in the entry-way mirror. At that moment Harwood emerged from the blue salon, where he had been awaiting their return.

"Ah, I hope you will not. I see the mist renders your hair as vivacious as Sarah's." Tenderly the duke captured a long vining tendril of his daughter's curly hair around his forefinger. "What do you think, John? Do you not prefer this infinitely to a well-tamed chignon?"

The tall, craggy-faced man who had joined him in the doorway smiled noncommittally.

Sarah batted Harwood's hand away. "Papa! We look a fright, and you know it. I am certain Jennifer and Lady Cornwall do not wish to be brought to John's attention until we have had a chance to freshen up."

"Now, is that polite, to call your guests frights?"

"Ignore him," Sarah advised the other two, leading them up the stairs. "He thinks 'A sweet disorder in her dress' is some sort of biblical commandment women ought to follow."

Lady Cornwall glanced back, somewhat surprised at such an assertion, considering how impeccably turned out Harwood always was, but then she had a sudden vision of Eleanor, her hair standing out in a halo about her head. Deborah remembered well the day the duchess had, on an impulse, commanded a stylist to cut her hair to the newest fashion. They had been together on a shopping expedition at the time. The effect had been startling, for Eleanor's hair, freed of its weight, had rioted, rejecting any efforts to bring it to order.

Deborah had worried all afternoon and evening about

what the duke would do when he learned his wife had cut her beautiful hair and was left with such an untamed mop. She knew full well that had she done such a thing without her husband's permission, he would have beaten her.

But at the ball that night Eleanor had obviously been the object of the duke's adoration, her bright blond curls floating about her head completely unconfined except for a token ribbon pinned with a pearl brooch. Once or twice Deborah had seen him just barely brushing his hand over the soft curls in a gesture so tender it had brought tears to her eyes, tears of joy for her friend, and of sorrow for herself for having so intolerant a husband.

The duke lifted an eyebrow as he saw Lady Cornwall hesitate on the stairs, her eyes wide with some unknown emotion. She turned away then and dashed up without saying anything. One hand upon the newel post, he mused on her odd skittishness. "Hardly more settled than her green daughter," he muttered before turning back to follow John into the blue salon.

"What a pretty girl!"

The duke smiled at his young kinsman. "Yes, Sarah has turned out remarkably well."

"Her, too. Who *is* the brown-haired beauty?"

"Lady Cornwall."

John frowned and glanced away, not hiding his disappointment. "That is the new viscount's wife? Already married, then—and so young!"

"She's all of thirty-eight, as I recall. But cheer up, she's a widow. Dowager Viscountess Cornwall."

"Now, Justin, you know perfectly well . . ."

"Oh, perhaps you refer to her daughter. Jennifer is a child, not yet seventeen, even. But she has an enormous dowry—why, there's no pleasing you!" For John had begun to frown again, and shake his head.

"It just means there's no hope. Much too young, for one thing."

"Ah, yes. An old greybeard of eight and twenty would think so!"

John Warner was a very serious-minded man who was often baffled and frustrated by the duke's conversational gambits. He shook his head now, in irritation. "I was hoping to hear that she is an untitled girl of modest fortune."

"When I suggested you think of marrying, now you are a man of property, and a potential member of Parliament, I hadn't expected you to take the bit between your teeth quite so quickly or so eagerly."

"I hadn't seen those beautiful brown eyes then."

"Take heart, lad. Lady Cornwall seems to me to be the sort of mother who will place her child's happiness above fortune or title."

Indignantly, John demanded, "Then why has she brought her to market so very young? Surely, she is too young even to know where her happiness might lie? I would hesitate to court so young a miss, had I ten times more property and a title to boot."

The duke folded his length into a comfortable chair. "I've wondered why, myself, but the mother keeps her own counsel, at least so far. Ah, here is the curly-headed band."

Sarah bounced across the room and into her second cousin's arms. "John, you are back! And looking fit! Did you manage any trout fishing?"

"My land grows only sheep and trout, and I assure you I had my fill of both." John reminded Sarah of her manners with a meaningful glance toward Lady Cornwall and Jennifer, who stood self-consciously nearby.

"Oh! Yes, excuse me. Lady Cornwall, Jennifer, I wish you to know my cousin, well, actually my second cousin, John Augustus MacTavish Warner. John is my father's indispensable secretary."

Lady Cornwall, her face closed, offered her hand, a tight smile reflecting her alarm, for John Warner's glance had already strayed to Jennifer three times; it was clear he was smitten. As for Jennifer, instead of pinking up and retreating into her shell, she surprised her mother by offering her hand to John quite as if she'd known him all of her life.

"Where have you only sheep and trout?" she asked.

"John recently inherited his family's estate in Scotland," Harwood said.

"Yes, a mere thousand acres, most of it straight up." John shrugged his shoulders, disdaining to represent his property as a prosperous one.

"But some of the finest trout streams in Britain," the duke interposed. "However, I daresay you do not care to fish?"

"But we do, Your Grace! My mother learned from her father, and taught me. It is the best of all pastimes."

John quickly abandoned his defensiveness, enchanted by Jennifer's obvious delight. Since Sarah and her father also enjoyed the sport, conversation was on fish stories for a few moments. They were interrupted by a gentle clearing of Timmons's throat as the butler motioned a footman to set the massive tea service down where Sarah could preside.

"In addition, Timmons, please serve us champagne. We have something to celebrate." The duke winked at John, but shook his head when Sarah attempted to question him. "All in good time. How was your ride?"

Sarah told him of meeting Lord Alexander Meade and Henry Fortesque, and the duke was interested to see how animated her features became as she described the encounter. *One of those young men has caught her eye*, he thought, pleased. He glanced at Lady Cornwall and Jennifer. The latter had returned to her conversation with John, apparently not interested in the events in the park. Lady Cornwall wore a serious, almost grim expression that Harwood was coming to recognize. Something was not right there.

Timmons entered with the champagne, and when all the others had been served, the duke proposed a toast to John as the new member of the House of Commons from Little Twinnings. Sarah gave a pleased yelp. "Mr. Tarbridge came to resign, then? Oh, John! And you have agreed? That is of all things wonderful."

"Not only did Tarbridge resign, he brought what he hoped was his replacement, a disgusting toady who promised to do his best to reverse the House's support of the chimney sweep reforms. I think I can be a good king's man without insisting on the rights of tiny children to so lucrative and pleasant a form of employment."

"Congratulations, Mr. Warner," Lady Cornwall said. "I trust your sentiments are aligned with the duke's on this issue?"

"On that and many more, which is as well since he and three elderly retired farmers make up my entire constituency! Little Twinnings is one of those infamous pocket boroughs." John acknowledged her congratulations with a lift of his glass.

After they had drunk to his new position, Jennifer coughed a little. "Excuse me." She put one hand to her mouth. "I've never . . . that is, it is wonderful, but . . ."

"Much more potent than ratafia, is it not?" From her lofty experience Sarah was properly blasé. "But so much more delicious."

Smiling covertly at the two young women, John put his glass down. "Actually, this is an odd sort of celebration, since I made it clear to the duke that one of my absolute conditions in accepting the seat is that I be permitted to vote myself out of office at the first opportunity."

Jennifer turned adoring eyes on him. "Then you disapprove of holding parliamentary seats as property?"

John quickly agreed, hiding his surprise at finding her *au fait* with the situation. "Yes. I am not one of your reforming zealots, like Lord Langley and his ilk, but I do think voting rights should be extended to more property-owning Englishmen. Perhaps our agreement on this point is why Justin was so generous as to make me a gift of this seat."

For the first time Lady Cornwall's expression as she addressed John was one of real warmth. "I congratulate you both for your forward-looking position. And once you have extended the right to vote to more Englishmen, perhaps you will consider granting it to Englishwomen."

A silence fell. The duke lifted both eyebrows. John's

mouth dropped slightly open. After a moment Jennifer whispered, horrified, "M-o-o-t-h-e-r-r."

"Forgive me, gentlemen. I hope you will not reveal to the *ton* at large that I am such a radical. But so many of the indignities and mistreatment that women experience . . ." Suddenly she stood. "It is time and past that we were going, Jennifer. We must get back before it is dark."

"I am sorry that you must rush off without exploring this fascinating subject any further, Lady Cornwall." John stood, too, followed by the duke. "You might be surprised at how liberal some of our views are." He glanced for confirmation at Harwood, who only smiled enigmatically.

"Actually, I was more interested in storing up gossip I could retail to the *ton*," the duke murmured.

"Forgive me, sir, I didn't mean to imply . . ."

"No, I don't think I shall, unless you agree to permit me to escort you and Jennifer to Monsieur Pacquin's concert and recital this Friday. Sarah is one of his pupils."

Aware that she had as good as called the duke a gossip, Deborah was eager to mend her fences. "That would be delightful."

"Mother, are you forgetting that you were going to invite Sarah to spend the night tonight?"

"Perhaps the duke would prefer . . ."

Sarah confidently slid her arm around her father's waist. Resting her head against his chest, she looked up at him. "You'll be glad to be rid of me for the evening, won't you, Father? Indeed, so glad I daresay you'll summon the carriage so we don't have to ride in this mist."

He traced her small nose with one long forefinger. "How did you guess, mousekin?"

"See! I'll go and get my things. Come with me, Jennifer!" Catching her new friend by the hand, Sarah pulled her from the room.

"A deplorable lack of decorum." The duke motioned for Lady Cornwall to be seated while waiting. "Are you sure you want that hoyden?"

Deborah smiled. "Sarah is a darling girl, and so wonder-

ful for my Jennifer. I can't begin to say how relieved I am
that she's found a friend so soon."

"No more so than I, dear lady, as you well know. Now
tell me more of your revolutionary plans for the English
electorate."

Chapter 5

Appalled by the situation her runaway tongue had gotten her into, Deborah cast around frantically for some other topic of conversation. Suddenly she remembered the invitation they had received.

"Lord Alexander and Mr. Fortesque invited us to attend a military review tomorrow afternoon. Do I have your permission to take Sarah? I had the impression she was keen to go. Both of them were, in fact."

"Naturally. What young girl wouldn't wish to regard several hundred handsome young men in military regalia? But I don't believe I will allow you to take Sarah."

Deborah's glance flew to Harwood's face. "Have I quite sunk myself in your eyes, then?"

"Far from it. I wish for more of your company. I shall give myself the pleasure of escorting you. That is, if you are willing?"

Deborah looked at Harwood warily. Was he flirting with her? She mustn't encourage that! But on the other hand, she could hardly refuse his escort. She did not wish to do anything to prevent Jennifer's friendship with Sarah from ripening.

She looked at John for distraction, but he was blissfully unaware of Harwood's flirtation or her uneasiness. Once Jennifer had left the room, he had lost interest in the conversation in favor of the delicious cakes and sweet biscuits on the tea tray. He was making serious inroads upon the heaped bounty. Deborah decided to defuse the situation by bringing more people into it.

"Of course. And you will attend with us, too, Mr. Warner?"

John stopped with his fork in midair. The last thing he was expecting from the Dowager Viscountess Cornwall was a social invitation. She had looked daggers at him for admiring her daughter. He hastily replaced his fork and set down his plate.

"I beg your pardon, my lady. I wasn't paying attention."

"Lady Cornwall says that she and the girls were invited to a military review tomorrow. Naturally, you'll want to accompany us." Harwood chuckled at John's astonishment.

"Of course, my lady. I'd be pleased to be one of the party. I expect my old regiment will make up part of the review."

"Best get out your old uniform, John, or you'll be quite cast into the shade by all of these sunshine soldiers," the duke advised.

John grinned. "My uniform still has the hole it acquired at Waterloo. And from what I hear, these sunshine soldiers are seeing quite a bit of combat, right here in the streets of London."

"Is putting down the riots so very dangerous, then?" Sarah's alarmed question alerted them to the return of the young girls.

John could not resist teasing Sarah, with whom he had a brotherly relationship. "I think I'd rather face Napoleon's legions again than an angry London mob. And only think of the shame if one failed—imagine having lost a battle to a ragtag gang of civilians armed mostly with staves and rocks. Ugh!"

"That is horrible. Why would the king's troops have to do battle with the people of London?" Sarah's knitted brow and fretful tone caused her father's eyes to narrow with concern as he studied her face.

It was Jennifer who responded first. "The mob is hungry, and angry at the profligacy of the Regent. Only think how many could be fed on his extravagant architectural projects."

"Very true, Jennifer." The duke gave her an approving nod before turning to reassure his daughter. "I seriously doubt His Majesty's troops could be overcome by such a mob. And I expect these reviews do much to remind the mob not to make the attempt. Doubtless that is their purpose, at least as much as to drill the troops, wouldn't you say, John?"

Seeing that his little cousin was genuinely distressed, John hastened to reassure her. But after the ladies had departed, he turned, perplexed, to the duke.

"What was that all about? Thought Sarah was still wearing the willow for Allensby, yet here she is acting as if her true love were serving in the guards?"

"I don't know, but I mean to find out," the duke replied. "They were invited by a young man she met last year and his friend. Do you remember Lord Alexander Meade?"

John nodded. "Indeed I do, an attractive and personable young man."

The perplexed duke mused, "I had no idea that anyone had made the least impression on her last year. Perhaps it is the other one. But she could hardly have formed a *tendre* for him in one meeting, could she have?"

"I wish I could relieve your mind and say no, Justin, but I believe I have contrived to do just that for Miss Silverton. Did you see how quickly she comprehended the significance of my political position? And how aware she is of the things going on here in the city? Beauty allied to intelligence. I confess I have always found it an enticing combination, perhaps because so rarely found."

"I am beginning to think that tumbling head over heels in love at first sight runs in this family's blood." Harwood shook his head ruefully. "It is a dangerous business. Check on Lord Alexander Meade for me, will you? And the other one. I forget his name, but you'll meet him tomorrow."

"Absolutely." John stood and stretched, a wistful smile twisting his lips. "I expect that by tomorrow Lady Cornwall will have asked the very same thing about me of whomever she trusts with her affairs."

Deborah had no one to whom she could entrust her affairs but herself. She lay awake long into the night, pondering the events of the day, worrying over the three young men Jennifer had just met. She almost wished Sarah hadn't spent the night, so that she could have spoken with her daughter about them right away.

She feared that each of the three in his own way was ineligible, and Jennifer must be warned. If only she could find a man like the Duke of Harwood for her daughter!

She curbed her impatience to confer with Jennifer, however. How could she regret Sarah's visit, when the pert blonde was filling Jenny with practical information about dealing with the *ton*. Also, she was building Jenny's self-confidence almost every second the two were together. No, she could be private with her daughter tomorrow.

Let the girls giggle together all night. Deborah smiled to herself, remembering the long, long ago days when she had been that carefree.

When the duke and his secretary arrived at the Cornwall town house the next day, the footman who answered the door, and the butler who sauntered out to see who had called, both struck him as unkempt and rather surly—that is, until his rank dawned on them when he offered his card.

"Lady Cornwall is expecting us, though we are early."

"Of course, Your Grace. I'll announce you, Your Grace. I'm sure she'll be down right away, Your Grace." The obsequious butler escorted Harwood and John into a small front parlor overstuffed with furniture. Before he could quite succeed in closing the door on them, though, a shrill bark announced a furry intruder.

"Mittens! Stop!" Jennifer followed hard on the heels of her dog. Sarah, hair tumbled and eyes laughing, was right behind her. Lady Cornwall, looking decidedly embarrassed, brought up the rear.

"Well! What a welcoming committee!" The duke smiled at the little King Charles spaniel who was suspiciously sniffing his boots. He bent over, meaning to bestow a pat on the black-and-white head, but Mittens decided this tall man was a most alarming creature. She sprang back with a low growl and then, front feet down, rear up, began to bark loudly at him.

"Such a ferocious beast," John observed, laughing.

Lady Cornwall moved past the girls. "Quiet, Mittens. Down!" The little dog instantly dropped to the floor and even dropped her head between her front paws.

"I am astonished! An obedient lapdog. I would have told anyone who asked that the term was an oxymoron." The duke looked admiringly from Mittens to Deborah and back again.

"I am so embarrassed. She usually doesn't bark at our guests."

"It was my fault, looming over her like that." Showing that he knew something of canine behavior, the duke dropped down onto his haunches and held out his long fingers for the little dog to sniff. Her black button nose wiggled eagerly as she took advantage of this opportunity, and her tail, which had dropped like a sail in a calm sea, came up wagging.

Carefully, the duke slid his hand under her chin and stroked it, then patted her head. Ecstatic, Mittens turned over on her back and, paws waving, offered her tummy for a scratching. The duke obliged her, looking up at the surrounding people as he did so.

"She likes you, sir!" Jennifer's eyes sparkled.

"Dogs always love my father," Sarah bragged. "Isn't she darling, Papa? Lady Cornwall raises them. I want one."

John laughed. "Now you're in for it, Justin!"

"Don't you like dogs, Mr. Warner?" Jennifer turned anxious eyes on the young man.

"Of course not! That's why he is forever bringing home strays that I must find a place for on the estate! Cats, dogs, parrots, even a monkey have thus found a new home." The

duke stood, and Mittens jumped up, eager for more attention. She quickly dropped back down at Deborah's command, to prance gaily at the duke's feet.

"It is true that I am fond of animals of all sorts, Miss Silverton." It was John's turn to offer Mittens a petting, which
she eagerly accepted. "But the duke has an odd prejudice
against keeping them in town."

"I wouldn't mind a dog as well behaved as this, but in
general, yes, I do feel that animals are a great deal too
much trouble in the city. They are also safer and happier in
the country."

Deborah bent down and picked up the little dog. "We left
our other three with a servant, but Mittens is Jennifer's special pet, and she just couldn't bear to be parted from her."

"I quite understand." The duke reached out to stroke the
silky fur flowing over Deborah's arm. This simple caress
communicated itself to the woman, too, and had a strange
effect on her. She turned wide, startled eyes on him for a
moment, then pulled away. "Jennifer, take Mittens to the
kitchen now. The duke is obviously ready to go."

"Yes, I thought we stood a better chance of getting our
carriage in a good position to see the review if we arrived
early." He looked the three women over. "You appear to be
ready, and a more charming trio cannot be imagined."

Just as the two girls disappeared out the salon door on
the way to deposit Mittens in the kitchen, the knocker
sounded. A few seconds later, without even attempting to
determine if she was at home to them, the butler showed
Lord Morton and his two sons into the room.

"Oh, admirable servant," the duke muttered.

Lady Cornwall was trapped. Awkward introductions
were made all around, after which Morton, with a curt nod,
marched past the duke and John, who were still standing,
and took a seat in a sturdy armchair. His two sons followed
his example. "Where is that pretty daughter, Deborah? As
soon as I described her to my boys, nothing would do but
they must meet her."

The last thing Deborah wanted was for her daughter to

become involved with one of Morton's sons, but she could hardly say so. "She and Lady Sarah have gone to take her dog to the kitchen."

"Not bringing one of those wretched little toy dogs to town, are you, Deborah? Thought Seymour had broken you from such sentimental mush. Only thing a dog is good for is to hunt or herd sheep, or fight other dogs." Morton frowned. Now Seymour was gone, someone must take his wife in hand.

Fighting down an angry retort, Deborah sat near the duke and looked up at him helplessly. He sat beside her, and John reluctantly took a seat also.

Morton was just warming to his topic, the complete folly of keeping dogs for pets, when the two young girls returned. Deborah most reluctantly introduced them. Both girls were visibly impressed with Morton's handsome sons, in spite of the warning Deborah had given Jennifer after the ball. They took their seats nearby, exchanging smiles and exhibiting a tendency to giggle.

"Well, now, this is something like. A beauty for each of my boys. I've an idea! Why don't you two take these pretty young things for a drive, eh? Lady Cornwall and I can have a comfortable coze about old times." Morton gave the duke and John a dismissive look, sure their time for an afternoon call was about up.

"Afraid that won't be possible. We've already bespoken all three ladies. We were on our way out the door when you came in." Harwood stood and offered his arm to Deborah. John, taking his cue from the duke, offered his arm to the nearer of the two girls, Jennifer. She took the hint immediately; Sarah lingered a little before slowly rising to her feet over the protests of Morton and his two sons.

Embarrassed over the lack of manners this abrupt departure entailed, Deborah was nevertheless more than happy to permit the duke to extricate her from the situation. She was unable to prevent Morton from attempting to arrange for Harvey and Newton to take the girls for a drive the next day. Once again the duke intervened.

"I am sorry to disappoint you, Morton, but Sarah is spoken for tomorrow, and if I do not mistake the matter, Miss Silverton is included in the invitation."

Sarah studied her parent in some surprise, but did not contradict him. Jennifer, now fully aware of her mother's tension, agreed that their calendar was in fact quite full for, oh, weeks! Deborah gave Lord Morton a sickly smile and watched him, angry and insulted, stalk down the steps, closely followed by the two annoyed young men.

"I hope you do not mind my routing that brute, but for the second time I have gained the definite impression that you do not care for his company."

Deborah turned grateful eyes on the duke. "Indeed, I do not mind! In fact, I thank you. I did not know how to stop him, yet he is odious and I am sure his sons are no better. Not at all what I would want for my daughter."

What I want for her is a man like you, Deborah thought wistfully, looking up appreciatively at the duke. It was almost a pity Harwood and Jennifer were so far apart in age.

Jennifer and Sarah exchanged puzzled glances, but accepted John's escort, and, one on each arm, moved off down the stairs to the waiting barouche.

"You and I have more in common than marriageable daughters we must safely shepherd through a season." Encouraged by her warm look, Harwood winked at Deborah as he offered her his arm.

"I cannot think what you mean, sir," she answered, suddenly very cool. Harwood realized she meant to freeze him out of any flirtatious notions.

"I refer to the fact that we seem to be having to spend as much time fending off unsuitable partners for ourselves as we spend finding suitable ones for our daughters."

Deborah grimaced. "It is an unlooked-for and *most* unwelcome complication."

"You must not hesitate to call on me should Morton or any other aspirant to your hand prove to be importunate." The duke patted her gloved hand tenderly. "I shall stand your friend."

Deborah suddenly could not speak, for a flood of contradictory emotions threatened to overwhelm her: gratitude for his friendship; alarm at the heat that his large hand seemed to communicate when he touched her, even though they both wore gloves; an absurd pleasure at his tender treatment; and an inexplicable sense of regret. But no, it couldn't be regret. Regret for what? She certainly didn't want anything more from him than friendship.

Blushing as she had not since the age of eighteen, Deborah bit her lower lip and looked away.

Harwood studied her averted profile in some puzzlement. Deborah Cornwall was a complicated woman. Her behavior toward him was erratic—sometimes confiding and sometimes cold and stilted—though he had done his best to put her at her ease. She seemed terrified of Morton, too. One would have thought a mature woman with so much natural presence could have easily put that toad in his place.

The young people had thoughtfully left for them the seat facing forward, and had already fallen into an animated conversation as the duke helped Deborah into the coach. He gave his coachman permission to start, then turned to study the woman at his side.

It would take a while to know and understand her, but looking at her profile, and the sad, rather haunted eyes she briefly flicked up to his face and then away again, Harwood decided that she was well worth the time and effort. He crossed one leg over the other and set himself to diverting her with comments upon the passing scene.

Chapter 6

The pageantry of the military review was very much to Sarah's and Jennifer's taste. They exclaimed in awe at the precision movements of the mounted troops. Even a stray dog that took it upon himself to rout this herd of quadrupeds could not break the ranks of steaming horses.

Sarah was as enthralled as Jennifer. Last season her aunt, who inclined to the bluestocking, had taken her to innumerable lectures and concerts, but not to any of the military reviews. Both girls were flushed with pleasure by the fascinating sights and sounds around them. As the troops fanned out to join their friends and relatives after the parade, Sarah half stood in her eagerness to see whether Lord Alexander would ride over to speak to them.

"Do try for a little more conduct, Daughter," Harwood warned, though the warmth of his tone belied his words. "If you pitch out of the carriage and get trampled, your young man will hardly find you an attractive sight."

Sarah sat back down suddenly. "My young man! I don't know what you mean. I only . . . Oh! Hello, Lord Alexander. That was thrilling!"

Jennifer leaned over John. "Yes, it was, and Mr. Fortesque acquitted himself very well without Demon to contend with." Her eyes scanned the melee of prancing horses around them.

"I thank you, Miss Silverton." Fortesque appeared suddenly on the other side. Introductions quickly followed. The duke noticed that Fortesque's response was decidedly unenthusiastic upon being presented to John, and that his kinsman in turn looked very grim as he acknowledged the introduction with a curt "We've met!"

Lord Alexander curbed his overheated mount only long enough to ascertain Sarah's plans for the next two evenings. Then, expressing all that was proper, he excused himself, as his horse needed cooling down. Henry had, perforce, to excuse himself also, leaving two excited girls, two worried parents, and one agitated young man in his wake.

"Where had you met Fortesque?" Harwood asked him.

"He was in my regiment."

Harwood raised an interrogative eyebrow. Jennifer was waiting for more, too. When none was forthcoming in spite of John's obviously carefully reined emotion, she pressed him. "Was he a not good soldier, sir?"

John looked at her regretfully. "Yes, indeed, one of the best. Quite without fear."

"But?"

"Jennifer," Lady Cornwall cautioned, "do not badger Mr. Warner."

But Sarah joined forces with her friend. She had seen the tension between the two young men as well. "Yes, John," she urged. "You may as well say it, for we will only be imagining much worse than it is, you know."

"I expect it was just because of the anxiety that precedes battle, but he was inclined toward gaming beyond his means," John slowly admitted, not liking the role of talebearer. "Doubtless he has mended his ways now."

"And do you know anything against Lord Alexander?" Sarah held her breath.

"No. He is a bit younger. He didn't take up his colors until after Boney was defeated." Taking pity on Sarah's anxious look, John added, "Certainly he was very competent in his duties as the Regent's equerry last year when we were planning your ball."

Sarah's smile was radiant. "Yes, he was, and so kind when I felt intimidated by it all. And doesn't he look splendid in his uniform? And Mr. Fortesque, too."

Jennifer and her mother quickly agreed, while John and

the duke exchanged amused glances. "Ready to have that uniform mended now?" Harwood asked sotto voce, for his secretary's ears only. "Polish up your medals?"

John nodded solemnly. "Perhaps instead of standing for Parliament I should buy back my commission."

Jennifer startled them both by abandoning the distaff side of the conversation to put her slender gloved hand on John's arm. "Oh, please do not, Mr. Warner," she begged, raising adoring brown eyes to his. "You have been wounded in the service of your country. That is quite enough military glory, and now Britain needs your abilities in the government."

"I am very flattered," John responded promptly, "and will do exactly as you bid me."

Jennifer, as if suddenly aware of her boldness, blushed and looked down shyly, but her mouth curved into a pleased smile. Since she did not glance at her mother then, she did not see, as Sarah and her father did, that Lady Cornwall was looking decidedly alarmed at this exchange.

Hoping to distract her, Sarah coughed and waved her handkerchief about. "Such dust! And the heat is excessive. I am perishing of thirst."

"I have heard it said that only ices at Gunter's will overcome parade dust." Winking at his daughter, Harwood gave the coachman his orders.

Much later that evening, the day's dramas continued to have their effect on the various participants. In the Harwood mansion, Sarah and her father and John dined *en famille*, and Sarah ingeniously observed that she had changed her mind about purchasing new gowns. Only a few days earlier, she had refused her father's urgings to outfit herself in the newest fashions, remarking dispiritedly that her wardrobe from last season would be more than sufficient for her role in helping her father seek a wife.

But this evening she informed him that she had underestimated the number of gowns she would need, and as well, the extent of the changes in fashions. "It would not do your consequence any good, would it, Father, to appear the dowd? Indeed, it might discourage a very fashionable woman from marrying you."

Harwood quickly agreed. Delighted to see the sparkle back in his daughter's eyes, he offered to accompany her on a shopping expedition on the morrow. Silently, he prayed that John's investigations of Meade and Fortesque, to commence tomorrow, would unearth nothing to the detriment of either. Whichever of the young men had caught Sarah's eye, likely Meade, the duke would be grateful to him, provided he did not turn out to be an unprincipled bounder.

John smiled to himself as he listened to Sarah and her father make their plans. Harwood had always been an indulgent husband and father. He hoped his investigations would allow the duke to indulge Sarah in her choice of husband. Thank goodness it wasn't Henry Fortesque who had caught Sarah's eye. John had not told all that he knew about Baron Egerton's son. Fort had always taken full advantage of the devastating effect his looks had on the female sex. In short, the man was a womanizer as well as a gamester.

It looked as if Fort had his eyes on Jennifer. John's mouth turned down. From the second he had seen Miss Silverton, he had been a lost man. From the second he had learned who she was, he had realized his suit would probably be hopeless. His own prospects had taken a major leap forward with Harwood's gift of a seat in the House of Commons, but still, he had little enough to offer a beautiful, titled young heiress. And then to have Henry Fortesque come into the picture!

Fort would make a very serious rival, with looks that no woman could resist, and a title and prosperous estates to look forward to some day when Egerton died. John heaved a sigh and turned his attention to the syllabub.

While Harwood and Sarah were contemplating a new wardrobe, and John his dim prospects for marrying the lovely Miss Silverton, that young woman was listening to her mother's earnestly voiced concerns.

"I could tell that you were impressed by Lord Morton's two handsome sons, Jennifer," she began.

Jenny laughed. "They look like an artist had designed them, so beautiful they almost don't seem real. But I could tell you did not like them."

"I know their father. He was a crony of your father, a gamester and neglectful husband. I seriously doubt that his sons have had a chance to develop a more elevated character."

"Probably not, though you hustled me away before they could reveal anything of themselves."

"Forgive me, dear. I despise Morton, so any connection with him seems undesirable. Perhaps I'm being unfair . . ."

"Perhaps, Mother, but be assured I will not give either of them any encouragement."

"Can you make me the same assurance about Mr. Warner and Mr. Fortesque?"

Jennifer flinched a little. "Must I, Mother?"

Deborah sighed. "I am afraid so. Mr. Fortesque has an explosive temper, as well as being at the least a gamester. Mr. Warner did not, I think, tell all he knew."

"He is so terribly handsome, it would be wonderful, I suppose, if he did not capture female attention at every turn."

Nodding at her perceptive daughter's insight, Deborah smiled. "Just so. You are very quick. Just do not let such a man capture *your* attention, for heartbreak is sure to follow."

"Yes, Mother." Jennifer folded her hands in her lap. "But surely you don't think Mr. Warner is cut of the same cloth as Mr. Fortesque?"

Deborah sighed. "No, dear, of course I . . ."

"I mean, he is well-enough looking, but not dangerously handsome . . ."

Deborah suppressed a laugh. John Warner was tall and solidly built, but he had a plain face and nondescript hair and eyes. If her daughter was drawn to the man, it certainly wasn't for his looks.

". . . and he is so comfortable to be around, one cannot help but feel he would be kind, like the duke."

A pregnant silence followed as mother and daughter contemplated the blissful thought of a kind husband. At last Deborah had to intrude some reality into their wishful thinking. "If Mr. Warner were heir to Harwood's title and riches, I would positively throw you at his head, but—"

"Perhaps he *is* the duke's heir. Perhaps that is why the duke is grooming him for a career in politics?"

"Far from it. The duke has a younger brother, who has two sons."

"*I* don't care," Jennifer whispered mournfully.

"Nor do I, as you well know. A modest establishment for you, if it included a kind husband, is worth far more to me than three fortunes would be. But you also know that your Uncle Vincent would never consider as a suitor for you a man who lacked both fortune *and* title. So it would be kindest to treat Mr. Warner, who clearly admires you, with politeness but nothing more.

"Come, do not look so down-pin. As the season progresses, you will meet many other young men of the *ton*. What about that young Lord Threlbourne?"

While these conversations were going on in the Harwood and Cornwall households, Henry Fortesque was shuffling a number of tradesmen's bills and recording them on a much abused sheet of paper. Alexander Meade was vigorously polishing his boots. An open bottle of brandy stood at Henry's elbow.

"Heard that Brummel used champagne for that. Shall I purchase some champagne, Alex?"

"With what, Fort? Thought it was bellows to mend with you." Alex didn't look up, intent upon his task. "Besides, probably all a hum. I think the secret is in the buffing."

"Keep practicing. You'll make a damn fine valet one

day. Think I may take you on once I'm safely wed to the pretty beanpole."

"Sure of yourself, aren't you?"

"Very! But I must get my hands on some funds to launch a campaign. Blast!" Fort threw the much-mended pen across the table.

"Watch it! Don't splatter ink on my uniform. I hope to sell it for a good price."

"Sell?" Fort turned around in his chair, brandy glass halfway to his lips.

"Selling out. Told you so, but you've been too busy ciphering to listen. I'm sick of dancing attendance on the Prince Regent—that gross, self-indulgent old man! Sick of town life in general. I'm either going to marry well enough to retire to the life of a country gentleman, or go to India and try if I can't shake a few rubies out of a maharaja."

"Or perhaps a maharani? Isn't that what they call the lady nabobs?" Henry perked up. "An excellent idea. I shall do the same."

"You? Go to India? I was only jesting about the rubies, Fort. Those who go to India have to be willing to learn trade and be skillful at it. The days of looting the country are behind us."

"Trade!" Henry visibly shuddered. "Pah! Never. But perhaps I will sell out, too. Doubtless get enough from selling my commission, my kit, and my string of horses, to mount a credible assault on Lady Jennifer."

"Assault! Poor child."

"Don't mean anything by the military metaphor, as you well know. Only that mother isn't going to give her child to a bankrupt. Must outrun the bailiffs until after the wedding. Or be able to finance an elopement."

Alexander looked up sharply from his boots. "I hope you are jesting!"

"Not at all. I'll do whatever it takes to avoid Newgate. She won't suffer by it. I'll be an indulgent husband, you'll see."

Alex rubbed his forehead with the back of his hand. "Self-indulgent is more like it."

Suddenly Henry was serious. "Don't you put a spoke in my wheel, Alex, or I'll contrive to return the favor. The little blond Venus might look at you with stars in her eyes, but her father is awake to all suits. Staunch Tory that he is, he mightn't like a future son-in-law who admires William Cobbet, thinks William Godwin is a great philosopher, and regularly attends Lord Langley's salon."

Alexander frowned and stood up. "I don't mean to deliberately sabotage your courtship, Fort. You'd make no worse husband than many another. But I won't stand idly by and allow you to hurt Jennifer or any other young lady of the *ton,* as an elopement surely would do. Nor is there any need to do so. You've a title and a tidy fortune to inherit. I don't doubt you'll find matchmaking mamas swarming all over you once it is seen that you mean to take a wife. As for my politics, Harwood hasn't taken his seat in Lords in years—doubt he cares a fig for politics."

Fort stood, too, a little unsteadily, and forced a conciliating grin. "Then let us drink to one another's success, my friend, and no more strife."

Alex poured a small splash of brandy into a glass and touched it to Henry's in agreement, though not without some misgivings.

A very different sort of conference was taking place between Lord Morton and his two sons. Harvey and Newton had been ordered by their sire to present themselves in the family town house no later than midnight to discuss the morning's snub by the duke and Lady Cornwall.

Now he surveyed them in disgust. Harvey's coat looked as if it had been made by a tailor's apprentice, and his boots were dull and scuffed. Newton was attired like a coachman, for he had just returned from an invigorating spin as the driver of a fast flyer, a treat that he had obtained by a generous tip to the man hired to do the job.

He was still excited by his adventure. His eyes flashed

gleefully, and he was grinning from ear to ear, showing the pointed teeth he had had filed in imitation of the coachmen he admired.

It was not in Lord Morton's nature to see any flaws in himself, so he seized upon his sons' appearance as the explanation for the morning's humiliation.

"Look at you! The pair of you. No wonder a duke's daughter and a viscount's daughter are seen to be above your touch!"

"A duke's daughter *is* above my touch, sir," Harvey responded in the patient tone of one long inured to dealing with a dull-witted child.

Newton grinned even wider. "They both looked quite smitten with us, Pater. If you hadn't somehow queered it with their parents—"

"It is those young chits you have to attach. Never mind about their parents. Such pathetic grooming will never do the trick. From now until the end of the season, you two are going to be bang up to the mark, do you hear me! Go upstairs and inventory your wardrobe. Tomorrow you must go shopping. To marry a rich woman, one must look prosperous. More than one heiress will wed a handsome bankrupt this season. You must prepare yourself to be the lucky husbands."

" 'Tis hardly fair to the tradesmen, Father, nor honest neither." Harvey's upper lip curled with disdain.

"Got no wish to be leg-shackled," Newton complained.

"You'll do as you're told," Dolphus roared, "or I'll cut off your allowances!"

Sullenly, reluctantly, the two young men agreed, escaping their father's presence as soon as they could.

After his sons' departure, Morton brooded late over his brandy, his sense of injury increasing with each refilled glass. He'd received Turkish treatment from the Duke of Harwood and the Dowager Viscountess Cornwall, and it rankled.

He still desired Deborah, more than ever, but it appeared that she had her cap set for the duke. *I can scarcely com-*

pete with him. Not only is he rich as Croesus, he can offer her marriage and a lofty title.

But no! The duke surely would not marry her, for he still had no heir of his body. No one could convince Dolphus Heywood that any man would be content to have his title pass to his brother's sons if he had any chance of producing an heir of his own.

Morton considered the implications. Harwood would take Deborah as his mistress. Eventually, of course, he would tire of her, and Morton would have another chance. Still, the thought of further delay frustrated him.

It had not escaped the baron's notice that Deborah seemed to loathe him. Why, he couldn't imagine. Perhaps she thought he'd be a tame, tiresomely romantic lover, in spite of the hint he'd given her that he knew her preferences. Still, if he could somehow find a way to bring her within his power, the game would be all the more exciting for both of them.

Pity I have to dance attendance on the ton, Morton thought. *I could just abduct her and keep her until I'd had my fill of her. It's not as if Vincent would bother coming to cuffs with me to protect her.* Morton knew Deborah would never protest. She wouldn't want to face the scandal. *But I must marry, well and soon, and Lady Cornwall hasn't a groat.*

That was when the brilliant idea came to him. Lady Cornwall hadn't a groat, but her daughter did! Why should he let his sons court the chit, and probably bungle the job? He could go directly to his old friend's brother and offer for the girl. He had a title, which would weigh with Vincent. Doubtless Seymour's brother was heartily tired of the responsibility and bother of supervising his niece, and would be impatient to be rid of her.

Vincent's impatience might be augmented by alarm if Dolphus could convince him that the child was in danger of forming a *tendre* for someone who was entirely ineligible—someone like Harwood's private secretary, John Warner. *What business has that penniless Scotsman to be keeping her company?* As Morton thought of Warner escorting Jennifer out of the room under the very noses of his own highly eligible sons, his anger grew. Surely Vincent, so concerned with his newly acquired dignities, would feel the same.

But would mere dislike of a connection with John Warner be enough to convince Vincent to bestow his niece on Dolphus?

If only I had some way to bribe him, Dolphus thought. He knew that Vincent had been left badly purse-pinched by his brother. Then another flash of inspiration struck: He could promise Vincent something out of the marriage settlements! As Jennifer's husband, he could easily pay Vincent ten thousand pounds and never miss it.

Yes! If the matter was presented convincingly to Lord Cornwall, Dolphus would have his wealthy bride, and with her in his control, virtually unlimited power over her mother! *Deborah will leave Harwood at the mere crook of my finger, once I have her daughter in hand,* he thought gleefully.

Adding a piquant pleasure to the whole scheme was the thought of how vexed the haughty Duke of Harwood would be to have his mistress snatched from him.

I will start for Woodcrest tomorrow, Lord Morton decided, rousing himself to climb the stairs to bed.

Chapter 7

Sarah emerged from the ducal mansion the next day to greet a brilliantly sunny morning. She paused for a moment to admire the spring green on the trees on Grosvenor Square. Then, with her maid and a footman trailing behind, she walked as rapidly as her fettering skirts would allow, enjoying the exercise as she made her way the few blocks to the Cornwall town house on South Audley Street.

It was her intention to invite Jennifer and her mother to accompany her father and herself on their shopping expedition. Not only would she welcome the female companionship, but she was beginning to harbor certain notions about her father and Lady Cornwall. She had noticed that her father's eyes softened when he looked at Jennifer's mother, and suspected he was developing a *tendre* for the dowager.

Sarah thought it a delightful match, especially desirable because it would secure her a sister as well as a compatible stepmother. She had therefore decided to do whatever she could to bring the two together.

As these cheerful thoughts occupied her, a high-perch phaeton appeared at the end of the street. As Sarah watched, a handsome pair of matched greys drew the sporty vehicle abreast. Her heart gave an excited lurch at the sight of the handsome blond man driving the maroon carriage.

"Lord Alexander. How delightful to see you here." She smiled up at him as he halted his team beside her. "What magnificent greys."

"Yes, Ariel and Puck are fine beasts."

Sarah pulled off her gloves and stroked one of the vel-

vety muzzles. "Wish I had a carrot or sugar lump, you darlings."

Alexander dismounted and, stripping off his gloves in
turn, removed a folded napkin from the pocket of his
jacket. "Here. I came prepared."

Sarah took two sugar lumps from him, as willing as he to
make the opportunity to allow their hands to touch without
the intervening gloves. How warm his hand seemed, and
strong. She fought the urge to place her hand fully in his, to
explore the differences in size and texture between them.
Blushing at her wanton thoughts, she turned back to the
greys and let each one delicately lip a sugar lump from her
hand. Shivering a little at the sensation of their muzzles
grazing her sensitive palm, she smiled up at Alexander.

"They're both very well-behaved."

"That they are. Fort has schooled them well." Alexander
held out a handkerchief for her to brush off her hand.

"Fort? Oh, I see. You have borrowed them."

"Not exactly. I am trying them out. I may recommend
them to my father for my sister Hannah to drive. She as-
pires to be a whip."

"He's selling them?"

"He's selling out. Actually, we both are."

"You, too?" Sarah lifted startled eyes to his.

At the dismay on Sarah's face, Alexander wondered for
the first time about the wisdom of his decision. Perhaps
he'd be at an even greater disadvantage than he already
was, without his military employment, his impressive uniform, his connections with the Prince Regent. Would Lady
Sarah prefer a husband who would live in town and be involved in the active social life of the highest level of the
ton?

"What will you do?" The anxious look on Sarah's face
indicated that the answer was important to her.

He drew a deep breath. He'd decided from the first not to
present himself in any sense as richer or with better
prospects than he really had. Now he added to that a determination that Sarah must accept the kind of life he wanted

to live if he was to court her. "I am thinking of either becoming a gentleman farmer or going to India."

The smile faded from Sarah's face, and she stepped back a little from him. "India!" She turned and began to walk away from him, slowly, her head down.

"Wait, Lady Sarah! May I escort you?" Alexander passed the team's reins to her footman and fell into step beside her, leaving the servants to follow them with the horses and carriage.

"My India scheme doesn't meet with your approval?"

"I had hoped . . ." Sarah cast him a quick, distressed look before returning to her scrutiny of the cobbled walkway. She had begun looking forward to the season because of the many opportunities she expected to have to spend time with Alexander, but they were so little acquainted, it would be intolerably bold to tell him that.

At the word "hoped," Alexander's own hopes soared. "Of course, I would prefer to remain here."

"You would?" This time the grey eyes met Alexander's blue ones for a longer period of time.

"Yes, if I thought . . . I say, Lady Sarah, I simply must ask. Last year I was told you had an understanding with that young man you danced with twice at your ball. Do you, that is, are you . . ." Alexander winced. He was behaving as ineptly as a stripling.

Sarah, however, was not bothered by his stammering. Eyes shining with the knowledge that his interest in her must be serious, she lifted her face to his. "No, my understanding with Mr. Allensby is at an end."

"Ah!" Alexander nodded, the bright blue eyes suddenly caressing. "In that case, I believe I will stay in England."

"Lord Alexander!" But the reproof was too faint, her pleasure in his reply too palpable, to make the young man feel ashamed of his boldness.

He decided to dare even further. With a quick glance back at the footman and maid who trailed them, and who seemed to be deep in a conversation of their own, Alexander quickly confided, "I am no recluse, but my preference is for a life spent predominantly in country pursuits, not drifting from party to party in town."

"I am entirely of your opinion," Sarah assured him eagerly. "While I do enjoy the cultural opportunities London provides, I tire quickly of the social rounds."

Greatly relieved, Alexander relaxed and allowed himself to savor the picture Sarah made in her walking costume of Dresden blue. She had an attractive Ionian-cork bonnet on, but the early morning sun slanted its way beneath the brim to caress her skin. Obviously, she took care to protect herself from the sun, for she was all that fashion demanded in the way of fairness, yet she glowed with health.

Three dimples emphasized her smile, one at each corner of her cupid's-bow lips, and a third that appeared in her cheek on the right side when she smiled widely. Her warm grey eyes were huge in her round face.

She had lost a bit of weight since last year, but was still pleasantly rounded, just as Alexander would wish her to be. He offered her his arm, pleased at her petite stature.

Taking his arm, Sarah had a sudden sense of coming home. *It is happening too soon*, part of her mind cautioned her. *I hardly know him!* Yet the certainty that this man was everything she could wish for in a husband suddenly engulfed her in a warm, joyous glow.

He was handsome, perfectly proportioned from his broad shoulders to his muscular legs and long, slender feet. Though not so tall as her father, he was above average in height. Sarah did not mind that she had to tilt her head up to talk to him, to look into those brilliant blue eyes. He made her feel very feminine and protected, with his solid masculine height and bulk.

They talked of everything and nothing, and were well on their way to Hyde Park before the voice of her maid called Sarah back to herself. "Lady Sarah, Lady Sarah! You've passed Miss Silverton's house."

"Oh! So I have." Sarah's cheeks pinked.

Alexander laughed in delight at her embarrassment.

"Perhaps you might walk in the park with me for a few moments?"

"No, I mustn't. I am to invite them to go shopping, and Papa will be here soon with the carriage to pick us up. He'd be quite alarmed if I had never even arrived."

Mention of the duke lowered Alexander's euphoria. Sarah's father! He certainly did not want to do anything to antagonize that stern-looking gentleman. To convince the duke to allow him to court Lady Sarah would be difficult enough as it was, with his small fortune and limited expectations. "Very well, then. I plan to attend the musicale you told me you would perform in tonight. I suppose I can wait until then to bask in your beauty."

"Don't!" Sarah raised her hand almost to his lips. "There is no need to offer me Spanish coin, sir. I know I am no beauty, nor do I aspire to be."

Alexander was astonished, and his expression showed it. "Of course you are. As near the ideal as woman can approach."

"I am too short, and far too plump for that. And my nose turns up!" She wiggled the offending appendage disdainfully.

Alexander's blue eyes darkened as he told her firmly, "My ideal woman *is* petite and pleasingly rounded, with dimples just so." He very nearly touched her cheek, where the three dimples would be, were she not looking serious just now. "And her nose must turn up! I care not what any other man may prefer."

Sarah was all smiles again. It was not his words that pleased her, for they were hardly inspired. It was the utter sincerity of his tone and expression. What a balm for her wounded soul, after her rejection by Gregory. She took his other arm as they turned around to retrace their steps.

"Then I shall permit you to bask in said beauty tonight. Perhaps you might induce Henry to attend? Jennifer is going to be there."

Alex chuckled. "I doubt if I can. Though he is quite

taken with Miss Silverton, he abhors musicales, being not in the least musical himself."

"Do you like music? For I wouldn't want you to spend a miserable evening on my account."

"I deny that any evening spent in your company could be miserable, but your conscience may rest easy, as I am fond of music. Though I proved a sad disappointment to my music master in regards to any instrument, I have been told I have a credible voice. I have even been known to sing in public on occasion."

"I should like very much to hear you sing."

"Then you shall. A love song." He smiled tenderly at her blushes.

"You go too fast, Lord Alexander." Sarah turned her head away, unable to look as repressively at him as she should.

"I apologize, Lady Sarah. I shall not embarrass you again." Lord Alexander's solemn expression and hand placed over his heart both touched and amused her. She laughed and walked on with him without the least objection from her conscience.

He bowed over her hand and departed from her when they reached the steps to Jennifer's home. She looked back to see him reclaim the greys, looking the very epitome of the English gentleman as he watched to see her safely into the house. For the first time she was gloriously glad that she was free of Gregory Allensby.

"I've been shopping all day and haven't a thing to wear," Sarah wailed to her maid as she contemplated the contents of her wardrobe. "I need my new clothes *now*!"

"Tch! Lady Sarah, you know it will take quite a while to make all of those garments up. Here, why not try this peach muslin with the little flowers woven in. Such a clever design." Mary Robert's hands caressed the delicate fabric. "It brings out your coloring perfectly."

Sarah eyed the dress unenthusiastically. "It is so sadly

out of fashion now. The padding at the back of the neck, you know, is larger this year."

"Humph! Those silly bustles make you look like a snail. I'll never understand this fashion madness!" At Sarah's mutinous expression, Mary sighed. "Lady Sarah, you are only going to the Pacquins' musicale. You know they are not *haute ton*." She shook out the dress she had selected for Sarah.

"This needs only a little pressing. And those pink roses Lord Alexander sent you will be lovely in your hair." This idea appealed to Sarah, and she accepted the proffered gown from the maid.

It was true that the Pacquins were not *haute ton*. They were friends of her Aunt Alicia, Lady D'Alatri. Monsieur Pacquin, an elderly French émigré, was a violinist in the Philharmonic Society and gave violin lessons to support his family. Sarah had begun studying with him at her aunt's urging during the last season.

Though like most émigrés they boasted aristocratic connections to the ancien régime, the Pacquins showed no eagerness to return to their native land. In fact, they had even declined to visit when Aunt Alicia had kindly invited them to accompany her on her current trip to Paris.

However, the problem was not impressing the Pacquins, but pleasing the eye of Lord Alexander. Sarah held the dress up to her, then laid one of the roses against her curls to test the effect.

"Yes, that will do. Thank you for the suggestion, Mary."

As soon as her maid had departed to press her dress, Sarah started worrying about having invited Lord Alexander to such a decidedly unfashionable affair. Sarah had met people from various walks of life through her bluestocking aunt last year, and had frankly found many of them more interesting than the dandies, fops, and pretty fashion mannequins who seemed to people the *haute ton*. But Lord Alexander moved in rarefied circles. Perhaps he would be appalled to find himself in such unfashionable company.

She tossed her head to dismiss this notion. *If he is a*

snob, best to know now and be done with him, she thought. Sarah's closest friend had been of much lower social standing than she. The sight of others snubbing Davida while kowtowing to her had always filled Sarah with disgust.

Downstairs, her father was conferring with John, absorbing the details that his secretary had been able to obtain about Henry Fortesque and Alexander Meade.

"As you know, Henry is the only son and heir of Lord Egerton. They don't deal well together. Apparently, the father was furious when Henry purchased a commission with a small inheritance from his grandmother. He did not want his only heir fighting Boney. Until recently Henry has been involved in deep play, and had an enormous number of debts, but he seems to have paid most of them within the last month."

"Win at cards or faro, did he?"

"Doubtful. He has not been seen gaming in some time—some sort of rapprochement with his father. He has indicated that he plans to marry, which naturally would help appease the baron."

"Ah, yes, the succession."

"Just so. As for womanizing . . ." John frowned at his sheet of paper, reluctant almost to impart the surprising information he had obtained.

"Yes. Don't tell me—three high-flyers in his keeping?" Harwood studied John's expression, sure it meant bad news.

It was bad news to John, who had hoped to find that Henry Fortesque was quite ineligible, but he cleared his throat and continued. "Not at all. Fort has never had to pay for his pleasure. Women generally throw themselves at him, and he has only to choose. But for the last several months he has not, from what I could learn, had a mistress. He has announced his intention of changing his profligate ways. That he means to marry, and marry well, cannot be doubted."

"No harm in that, per se, if there is genuine feeling on both sides."

"True." John sat back in the chair, chagrined to see that the duke had so quickly reached the same conclusion as he had: Though his past made one a little uneasy, Henry Fortesque was an eligible *parti*.

"Were you able to find out as much about the other young man?"

John did not find it nearly as difficult to report that Lord Alexander was eminently eligible, given that the duke would not insist on a wealthy suitor. He doubted that Jennifer had the least interest in Meade, which meant he was not a potential rival.

Confidently, almost happily, he produced his second report. "He is the third son of the Marquess of Hanley and possessor of a small estate in Gloucester. He manages the income from it and his army salary so as to always be before-hand with the world. No debts to speak of, does not game. He is on excellent terms with his family, which is very close. It is not a wealthy family, and there are no less than six daughters, which makes it unlikely that Meade can have any large expectations from his father."

"And how many high-flyers does *he* have in keeping?" The duke tensed as he asked; he abhorred the notion of an unfaithful husband for his daughter, both for the heartache, and also for the health risks such behavior would bring her.

John smiled. "He seems as pure as the driven snow; at least, I could find no whispers of amours."

"Not ever?" As John shook his head, the duke grew even more tense. Ironically, this was not good news.

"I could not say that, but he at least does not have to pay for his mistresses, for his never having a member of the muslin company in keeping has caused comment more than once."

"Not one of the devotees of Greek love, I hope?"

Startled, John stared at him. "I hadn't thought of that."

"Could you find out if he was?"

"As it is a hanging offense, people are understandably discreet." Both men silently contemplated the serious consequences of such behavior. Knowledge of such activities, after all, were widely whispered to be the hold Lady Byron had over her husband, which had caused him to give her custody of his daughter and quit his country.

At last John said, "I know some men who are the right age to have been classmates of Meade's at Harrow and Cambridge. If any such tendency exists, it would certainly have shown itself in school."

"That it would. It has never ceased to amaze me that what will lead to a death sentence in a man is treated as a mere childish *jeu d'esprit* in boys. No one seems to take seriously Wordsworth's observation that the child is father to the man."

"Then I will pursue my investigation." John stood. No time like the present for this unpleasant chore. Probably one or more of the young men he needed to see would be hanging about one of the clubs.

"Oh, and John?"

"Sir?"

"I want you to send in a notice to the papers, to fill your position. It won't do for the upcoming MP from Little Twinnings to still be my private secretary."

John grinned widely. "I'll do it tomorrow." He had taken one more step up in the world. While the duke had never made him feel any less than a full equal, indeed a confidant and friend, society looked upon the position of secretary, even to a very great man, as a lowly one. The sooner he could shed that skin in favor of John Warner, Esquire, Member of Parliament, the better!

The duke's answering smile faded as he watched John stride jauntily from the room. What a paradox. He hadn't wanted to hear that Meade was a womanizer. Now he was worried because the man had too little contact with women.

He didn't agree with his country's savage treatment of homosexuals. Yet it would be a cruel fate, he knew, to allow a loving woman like his Sarah to tie herself to a man, however decent in every other way, who could not love her in return. *I must keep him well at arms' length until this question is settled,* the duke vowed to himself grimly.

Chapter 8

The discordant hum of musical instruments being tuned greeted Alexander as he entered the modest home in Paddington. He was a little surprised by the humble address, but it was clear from the sounds that he had come to the right place.

He gave his hat into the keeping of a servant as a flustered elderly woman, quite grey and in a grey silk dress, rushed up to him, exclaiming with a heavy French accent, "So 'appy to 'ave you, monsieur. Do come into our 'umble abode and make yourself comfortable."

Alexander thanked her and made his way into an already crowded drawing room. Chairs had been arranged around a dais, on which sat a new pianoforte, easily the best piece of furniture in the room. Just in front of it he spotted Sarah's bright head, bent over her violin, listening as she tuned it.

His glance swept the room twice before spotting Lady Cornwall and her daughter seated with the duke near the middle of the seating area. Beside the duke was an empty chair.

He hesitated, not sure where to sit. The chair was obviously for Sarah when she had completed her pieces. He saw no chairs available near them.

"Lord Meade? Alexander, here?"

He turned toward the voice and faced a buxom red-haired matron. "I am no less amazed to find you here, Mrs. Smithfield." He acknowledged her greeting solemnly, formally, bowing stiffly over her hand. The voluptuous woman's reputation made him wary of her.

"Oh, I adore music, especially the violin. Monsieur Pacquin taught the daughter of my good friend, the Duke of Harwood. I am quite sure he will be here tonight."

Alexander's eyebrows rose at her claiming the duke for a friend. "In point of fact he is."

"Where? Oh, I see. And he has saved me a seat!" Lydia charged forward, and Alexander watched, fascinated, to see what sort of reception she would receive. The duke was facing away from the empty seat, talking quietly with Lady Cornwall. Lydia had already glided into the chair before he realized she was coming. Alex could not be sure at such a distance, but he thought the duke looked startled. Certainly he did not welcome her effusively. After the briefest of greetings, he turned his shoulder on her and once again engaged Lady Cornwall and her daughter in conversation.

Alexander suddenly saw how this turn of events could be used to his advantage. He walked down as near to the front as he could locate empty seats. Sarah, her tuning completed, was looking around. She brightened when she saw him. He smiled at her, then very deliberately seated himself next to an unoccupied chair. He watched as her eyes moved to where her father sat, and then quickly, with comprehension in them, back to him, a smile dimpling her cheeks.

At that moment a hush settled over the room as Monsieur Pacquin moved to the center of the dais. Alex glanced at the program he had been given. Lady Sarah was to play early in the evening. He listened impatiently to several performances of widely ranging ability. Sarah, to his relief, was quite a competent player who acquitted herself well.

His patience was doubly rewarded when, after taking her bow, she joined him rather than return to her seat among the performers in the front row. She gave a little wave to her father and friends as she did so. Alex resisted the urge to turn and see what the duke's reaction was.

"Magnificent," he whispered as she settled beside him. He could see a fine sheen of perspiration on her forehead, and her hair was frizzing about her face in a manner he found charming.

"No Spanish coin, remember," she warned him, waggling a finger in admonition.

"I remember and I obey." He placed his hand on his heart.

Sarah stifled a giggle and shushed him, as the next performer was tuning up.

Vividly aware of one another, the two young people sat through the subsequent performances as though in a dream. The only reality for Alexander was the golden hair, the soft curves, the delicate rose scent of the girl next to him. For Sarah, it was as if Alexander gave off a furnace's heat, so warm did she feel sitting this close to him. When the audience's applause announced the end of the program, she was startled, and stared around in a daze.

A deep masculine voice murmured in her ear, under cover of the applause, "As far as I am concerned, they could have just begun and ended the program with you."

She tipped her head up as they both rose to their feet. "Nonsense. Monsieur Pacquin is a virtuoso."

"But . . ." Alexander looked embarrassed. "Did he play?"

"Didn't he? I mean, he was planning to."

Their eyes met and each realized the other hadn't been listening. Giggling and blushing rosily behind her quickly deployed fan, Sarah turned. "I must find Father and . . . oh! Who is that hanging on his arm?"

"That is Mrs. Smithfield. She claimed to be a good friend of his, for whom he had saved a seat."

Sarah smiled, then lowered her eyes. "The seat was for me, but I'm glad she took it."

"As am I. But we had best join them, else your father may think I mean to abduct you."

"Silly! Father will be delighted to see you."

Alexander could be excused for doubting such a thing, because as they joined the Harwood party, the duke's cool grey eyes surveyed Sarah's hand linked around Alexander's arm with a decidedly frosty air.

"There the dear girl is. And the picture of her mother.

My darling child, how beautifully you played," Lydia gushed.

Harwood cleared his throat. He was forced to do the pretty, introducing his daughter to Mrs. Smithfield.

Sarah gave the older woman a polite curtsey, trying her best to keep her dislike of this effusive, blowsy creature from showing. "May I present Alexander Meade, Mrs. Smithfield?"

"But of course. Lord Alexander and I are dear friends. In a manner of speaking, he was my escort tonight." Oblivious to Alexander's startled look or Sarah's stifled gasp, Lydia rattled on. "I am perishing of thirst after watching all of you performers work so hard." She attempted to angle the duke toward the back of the room. Most of the audience had left in search of the refreshments by now.

"I would not wish to deprive your escort of your company, I am sure." The duke smoothly detached Lydia's arm. "And I am fortunate enough to have a plethora of lovely ladies to escort."

Without quite knowing how it had happened, Sarah found herself on her father's arm. Alexander's strongly ingrained sense of good manners made him offer one arm to Lydia, the other to Jennifer, as the duke gave his other arm to Lady Cornwall.

Wishing to make it entirely clear that he had not escorted Lydia to the affair, Alexander excused himself as soon as he decently could, and left. Lydia, busy interrogating Jennifer as to the changes her uncle had made at Woodcrest, scarcely looked up. Sarah, seeing this, excused herself just as Alexander was disappearing into the foyer.

"I must be sure my music doesn't end up in someone else's portfolio," was her less than convincing excuse. Her father frowned at her, but for once she ignored his wishes. Hastily, she quitted the room and found that luck was with her. Lord Alexander had stopped to speak with some acquaintances who were also leaving.

She caught his eye as she walked across the room and

was not surprised when he appeared at her side in the Pacquins' drawing room minutes later.

"I am trying to find my music. I forgot to put it in my violin case." Sarah pretended to sort through the sheet music
stacked on top of the piano. They had an audience, as several people had carried their plates in from the crowded
dining room.

"Let me help. What is it?"

"Never mind. I just wanted you to know that I see what
kind of woman she is. I know you didn't escort her here."

Alexander's eyes widened with pleasure. "I only hope
your father comes to the same conclusion."

"He will. Papa is always very fair. You'll see."

Alexander tried not to look dubious. It was clear that
Sarah adored her father. "Will you be riding tomorrow
morning?"

"Will you?"

They grinned at one another. He took her hand and be-
stowed a quick kiss on it. "*À demain.*"

While Sarah was agreeing to meet Alexander, the duke
was faced with a direct frontal assault by Lydia Smithfield.
"I am having a small dinner party next week, Justin. You
will have your invitations tomorrow. I have just the most
divine young man for your pretty daughter. He is musical,
too. They can entertain us afterward."

"That depends upon what evening it is. I have a very
busy schedule next week."

"What evening have you free? I haven't sent the cards
yet."

The duke glanced up to see Lady Cornwall studying him
gravely. He sent her what he could only hope was a plead-
ing look, though he wasn't sure how she could help.

"I believe the duke was bemoaning the fact that he had
something scheduled every evening next week." Deborah
met Lydia's furious glare steadily. "Being a peer, he has
political matters to attend to as well as the usual social
events, you know."

"Then perhaps the week after," Lydia persisted, unwilling to loose her quarry.

"Perhaps. I will check with my secretary when I receive your card."

Jennifer appeared to have caught a crumb of prune cake in her windpipe, for she began to cough vigorously.

Lydia Smithfield stood abruptly. She might ignore any number of snubs if it suited her to do so, but it wasn't because she failed to recognize them for what they were. She decided to leave while she still had her temper under control. "Well, then, I can only live in hope. It's been a delightful evening. I had hoped to congratulate Lady Sarah once more on her playing, but I see she has disappeared."

At this reminder of his daughter's defection, Harwood's eyes narrowed, but he wouldn't give Lydia the satisfaction of seeing that he had any concern. He half stood to acknowledge her departure, then reseated himself beside Lady Cornwall.

"Now 'tis I who am in *your* debt."

Deborah fluttered her fan nervously. The duke was an imposing figure of a man. Sitting so close to her, he made her feel like a green girl. "Nonsense; I was returning the favor for rescuing us from Morton the other day."

"As I said, we are in the same boat." Harwood chuckled, the laughter softening his face in such an appealing way that Deborah felt her heart give a most unexpected little jump.

Jennifer came from behind her napkin, eyes dancing. "You'll check with Mr. Warner when you get her card, so you can be sure to be busy that evening!"

"Jennifer!" Deborah frowned repressively.

"No, don't scold her. That is exactly what I shall do. Except it won't be Mr. Warner who'll be assisting me in evading her invitation, I expect."

"Why not?"

"He is far too dignified a being now to act as my secretary. He will be needing to begin his preparation for a political career. Though in actuality I've been grooming him for that for some time."

Jennifer tried to keep the disappointment from her voice. "Then I expect he won't be living with you anymore?"

"Oh, I hope he will, whenever he is in town. John will always be welcomed—no, expected—to make his home with us whenever he is in London. Sarah would be quite indignant if he were to do otherwise, for he is a great favorite, almost a brother to her."

Deborah noticed that Jennifer looked relieved by this news. *And in spite of my warnings!* Vexed, Deborah regretted giving Jennifer permission to spend the night with Sarah. The less time she spent near John Warner, the better.

In spite of her mother's misgivings, however, Jennifer did spend the night with Sarah, though she was disappointed not to catch so much as a glimpse of John. By midnight she was sharing confidences with her new friend. They were lying across Sarah's enormous bed, under a magnificent canopy strewn with embroidered golden daffodils. It was a beautiful room that had been lovingly decorated with a young girl in mind. Jennifer could not help contrasting it in her mind with her own dark, barren room on the nursery floor at Woodcrest. Her father had thought money spent on a daughter was money thrown away.

As they lay there baring their souls to one another in the way of young girls, Sarah learned of the previous Lord Cornwall's brutality to his wife and daughter, and Jennifer learned that it was really the duke who was interested in the marriage mart, not Sarah.

"We are both agreed in preferring not to marry, then," Jennifer observed, one finger tracing the elaborate daffodil pattern carved on the dark wood of the headboard.

Sarah murmured her assent. "Though not because I fear marriage, as you do. It is just that I don't want my heart broken again."

"I had thought perhaps you regarded Lord Alexander in

the light of a suitor?" Jennifer's wide brown eyes assessed Sarah's expression.

"I didn't intend to, but . . . he is so very handsome, and so very . . ." Sarah stopped and flopped over on her back. "Words can't quite express how I feel about him. When I am with him, I just feel so safe, so secure, so . . . at *home*. And when he smiles and looks at me a certain way, I get this funny, bubbly feeling all over. But surely I can't already have fallen in love with him? If so, then I was never in love with Gregory, for *he* never made me feel this way."

"Never having been the least in love, I cannot say." Jennifer sighed.

"Did your mother love your father once?"

Jennifer shook her head vehemently. "She admired him, for he was handsome and witty. But her parents had arranged the marriage before she had time to know him well. Almost as soon as she was pledged to him, he began to say cruel things to her. After they were wed, he made her feel that she was the worst wife in the world. It wasn't until after I was born, and it was clear there would be no heir, that he began to beat her."

"Beat her!" Sarah sat up straight. "Truly? What did her parents do? I cannot imagine my father letting anyone beat me."

Her friend sat up, too. "My grandfather cared a great deal for what people would think. When Father began to beat me, too, mother took me and ran away to her father for protection, but he only scolded Father and let him take us back. Grandmother wanted my mother to ask for a legal separation, but she, like my grandfather, has so much distaste for the least hint of scandal, she refused."

Tears came to Sarah's eyes as she heard this recital. "How did you stand it? I am sure I couldn't have. My father has never laid a hand on me in anger."

"Most of the time Father lived in the city. It was only in the fall when he brought his hunting cronies to Woodcrest that he stayed with us. We used to dread the end of summer so." Jennifer closed her eyes in pain. "I am ashamed to admit it, but I was glad when he died."

"Oh, Jennifer!" Sarah leaned forward and put her arms around her friend, patting her back. "I cannot imagine anything so terrible. My father's greatest pleasure has always been making Mother and me happy. No wonder you don't want to marry."

"But I must," Jennifer sobbed. "My Uncle Vincent is my guardian, and he says I must choose a husband this season or he will choose one for me. He is tired of being my guardian, he says. It takes up his time, and by the terms of my grandmother's trust, pays him nothing."

"But you may find someone good and kind, like my father, to marry." Sarah smiled encouragingly at her friend.

Jennifer looked dubious. "It will be difficult to be sure, though. What if I make a mistake? There is so little time in which to choose."

"I know!" Sarah brightened. "Your mother can marry my father, and you can live with us. He can be your guardian."

"I am afraid not, Sarah. My mother will never, never remarry. The very suggestion is enough to give her the spasms."

"Oh, dear." Sarah began to worry her lower lip. "And I had hoped my father was beginning to develop a *tendre* for her."

Jennifer shook her head dolorously. "You had better hope he does not, for he would be doomed to disappointment."

Chapter 9

While Sarah and Jennifer took chocolate and toast in Sarah's sitting room the next morning, the duke and his cousin were discussing what John had learned the night before.

"Hampton remembered him well, though they weren't close friends. He told me Meade was an unusually studious young man, who rarely participated in the usual youthful follies. I didn't dare ask a direct question, you understand . . ."

"Of course not."

"So I did not get a definitive answer. However, Hampton is the sort who would certainly pass on such scandalous information if he knew it."

"So my concerns are likely unfounded." Harwood drew a deep breath of relief.

"Probably," John replied. "But I learned something you may not be pleased to hear."

Harwood folded his arms. "Yes?"

"Meade's friends tended to be Whiggish, even radical types. Benthamites, that sort of thing. He was considered a potential revolutionary by many of his fellow students. Hampton said there was considerable grumbling when he was appointed to the Prince's staff, by those pretending to fear he might leak state secrets."

"Many a young cub espouses radical politics when he is in school," Harwood mused.

"I know that, sir. But Hampton says he continues his radical associations to this day. He visits and contributes to the support of Godwin, and is a regular member of Lord Langley's salon."

The duke considered this thoughtfully. "I am not as alarmed about that association as Hampton perhaps is. Langley has mellowed somewhat since his marriage, you know. And Godwin, after all, has taken a government sinecure."

"And then there is Shelley, whose disgraceful behavior in eloping with Godwin's daughters is still causing tongues to wag."

"Shelley?"

"Yes. Hampton says Meade was an intimate of his, who now openly admires and champions Shelley's poetry. Hampton claims Meade continued the association after the elopement, defended them when the 'League of Incest' was on everyone's lips. He was a frequent visitor when they returned to England, even before Shelley married the older daughter. Not a very comfortable association for Sal's potential marriage partner."

Harwood groaned. "The infamous 'League of Incest!' I'll not have my daughter dragged into such an association."

He paced the room in agitated thought. "Still, it doesn't necessarily mean he shares Shelley's loose morals. Isn't Meade about the same age as Lord Pelham?"

John ruffled through his notes. "Twenty-six. Yes. They should have been at Cambridge at the same time."

"Pelham is the scion of an old Whig family, though not at all a radical. Perhaps they knew one another?"

"Should you like to ask Pelham, though?"

"I don't like doing any of this, but if I must explore such unpleasant subjects, Davida's husband is an honest young man upon whose discretion I can rely."

John nodded his head. His kinsman had never been very forthcoming on the subject of Davida Gresham's flight from London to Harwood Court, so he had no idea to what extent the duke's heart had been at risk in the whole escapade. "Do you want me to ride up there and talk to him?"

"I will ask Sarah if they are planning to come to London for the season. No need in making that long trip if they are on their way here."

Just then they heard the girls' voices echoing in the entryway. Harwood jumped up and went out to see them crossing to the door, dressed for riding.

"What ho? Fox hunting in April?"

"Papa!" Sarah gave a guilty little start. Her giggle lacked spontaneity. "No, of course not, but it is the perfect morning for an invigorating ride."

"And so thought I." Harwood gestured to indicate that he, too, was dressed for riding. "I have had Tuppence saddled; I thought I'd act as your escort." Harwood took a closer look at his daughter's flushed countenance. "That is, if you don't mind?"

"Why, no, of course not, Papa. I . . . we'd be pleased to have you join us. We are going to collect Lady Cornwall, too."

"Have you heard from Davida lately, Sal?" John asked from the door to the library.

"No, I haven't, but I'm glad you asked that. I've written her a note this morning, Papa. Would you frank it for me?" Sarah skipped over to the basket that collected their outgoing mail. Her father willingly scrawled his name across the sealed missive.

"Then you don't know if they are planning on coming to London any time soon?" John persisted.

"No, I don't. I've begged her to join us, though."

John looked questioningly at the duke, who shook his head, indicating that he did not feel sufficiently alarmed about Meade to want him to saddle up immediately and ride to Yorkshire to interview Pelham.

John toyed with the idea of joining the three on their morning ride. Daring a glance at Jennifer in hopes of an encouraging smile, he was disappointed to see that she was regarding the tile on the entryway floor as if her life depended upon memorizing the pattern. He watched pen-

sively as the three departed, never regretting his lack of a
title or fortune more than at that moment.

Lady Cornwall was nowhere in evidence, nor was her
horse awaiting her when the three arrived in South Audley
Street. Harwood dismounted and gave Tuppence's reins
into Sarah's hands. He took the steps two at a time and
rapped loudly on the knocker. Receiving no immediate response, he started back down the steps, unwilling to leave
Sarah in such a vulnerable position for long.

The door opened just as he reached the bottom step.
"Harwood! I am so sorry." It was Deborah. He turned, astonished to see her answering her own door.

"What is wrong, Lady Cornwall? Is there some problem?"
He retraced his steps and was at her side almost in an instant.

"No. That is, yes, there is an aggravation, at least. My
butler seems to be ill. All of the servants are at sixes and
sevens. I sent a footman to the mews for my mare quite an
hour ago, but as you see, she still hasn't appeared. I expect
you must go on without me."

Harwood turned to study his restive mount and the two
young girls perched on their eager animals. "I expect so,
but shall we go by the mews and see what is the matter?
We could bring your mount to you."

Deborah wrinkled her nose. "No, I think with the staff so
disordered I had best remain, or who knows what will happen. I may need to send for a doctor."

Regretfully, Harwood parted from her, promising to stop
in after their ride to see how things stood.

As they clattered away toward Hyde Park, Harwood gently questioned Jennifer, who seemed very worried. "Does
your mother have many such problems with her servants?"

Suddenly defensive, Jennifer lifted her chin. "It is not
Mama's fault. They do not consider that they work for her,
and so they are intolerably lazy and insolent."

"Hmmmm." Harwood said nothing. He led the way to
the park, thinking his own thoughts while the two young
women talked. Once they had crossed into the park and the

horses were safely on Rotten Row, they moved up alongside him, and the three began a sedate canter.

"There is more traffic than the other day," Jennifer observed.

"Doubtless because of the gorgeous weather," Sarah responded. The duke noted that her eyes were unusually busy studying the other riders on the path. He began searching for a familiar face himself, and was not much surprised to see Lord Alexander and Mr. Fortesque placidly walking their mounts ahead. *That explains her guilty look.* The duke's suspicions were confirmed. *She has arranged to meet him here.*

"Oh, do look, Jennifer." Sarah unthinkingly let her mare break from the canter into a brisk trot, dangerously close to being beyond what was acceptable speed in the park. Jennifer looked questioningly at the duke, and held her horse steady when she saw the disapproval on his face.

"Sarah!" He growled a warning that reminded his daughter of her whereabouts. Pink-cheeked, she slowed Lorelei.

By this time the two young men, obviously on the alert for them, had stopped and were awaiting their approach. Henry Fortesque was beaming, but Lord Alexander looked a little guilty upon sighting Sarah's father. The duke smiled with grim satisfaction. *At least he has some shred of conscience.*

He acknowledged the two young men coolly, before reining up to let the girls pair off with them. He rode alone at the rear, studying the quartet. Sarah, her embarrassment quickly conquered, was conversing animatedly with Meade, while Jennifer seemed surprisingly reluctant to respond to Fortesque's gallantries, as if perhaps she had been warned off.

The duke decided he would share the information he had on Egerton's heir with Lady Cornwall. Perhaps it would put her mind at ease. Nothing was going to put his mind at ease until he knew more about Alexander Meade.

The duke escorted the two girls back to Jennifer's mother. On reaching the Cornwall town house, they found an under-footman in charge of the door. Jennifer and Sarah scampered away in search of Mittens, while the duke asked to be shown to the viscountess.

"The viscountess is not in residence. I suppose you mean the dowager viscountess." The young man sneered with more punctilio than wisdom.

"I mean your mistress and employer, and I'll thank you to keep your insolent tongue between your teeth." The duke's eyes were grey flint. He took a menacing step toward the footman, who suddenly remembered his manners.

"Yes, sir, right away, sir. I mean Your Grace, sir."

"Poorly trained as well as totally devoid of manners and polish. How on earth did you get a position in a noble household?"

"I, er . . . Mr. Rayburn, the butler, is my uncle, sir. I mean Your Grace."

"Why am I not surprised? Conduct me to the viscountess without further delay!" The duke gave a dismissive wave, and the footman scurried ahead of him into a small study near the back of the building.

"My lady, the Duke of Harwood."

Deborah looked up, amazed by the footman's awed tone. "Yes, Thomas, show him in."

"I see your butler is still not at his post. Nothing serious, I hope?" The duke took the chair she indicated, noting briefly the shabby nature of this cubbyhole, which Deborah seemed to be using as an office.

"It is the most vexing thing. He tried to convince me he had contracted an influenza, but I suspect he has a hangover, and I believe the other servants must have been carousing with him, for they are all down-pin this morning from the footmen to the tweeny. My message probably never so much as reached the mews, though I wonder if my grooms are also nursing hangovers."

"I think you should send the lot of them packing."

"I can't, though, and they know it. 'Tis why they dare behave so. They aren't my servants. They're Vincent's, and . . ."

"Surely he would not wish to see you so poorly served?"

Deborah sighed. "If he were here, they'd all be performing with military precision. He would think me a hysterical female for complaining."

The duke looked at her closely. She seemed near tears. "Shall I put a flea in their ears?"

"Oh, no, sir. Goodness. You have far too much to do without taking on my domestic problems."

Harwood crossed one booted foot onto the other knee. He was surprised to find in himself a deep-seated need to ease her burdens. "Perhaps you can help me with a problem in return."

"Gladly, if I am able."

"I would like to enlist your help in curtailing my daughter's time spent in the company of Lord Alexander Meade. She had arranged to meet him in the park today, the minx."

"Why, is he not eligible?"

"I am having his background investigated and would prefer to know a little more about him before I let him court Sarah. She seems alarmingly willing to receive his attentions. Odd, isn't it. A week ago I would have been in alt to see her eyes sparkling again when she looked at a man."

Deborah nodded. "I felt quite the same way. But now I am hard put to explain to Jennifer why she cannot follow her inclinations."

"If it is Mr. Fortesque you are worrying about, my investigation indicates he is quite eligible."

Surprised, Deborah exclaimed, "But he is a gamester."

"Apparently he has conquered that tendency. He has not played heavily in several months. He is Lord Egerton's son and heir, you know. He will be a man of wealth and property someday, and titled, too."

"No, I didn't know."

"Yes. They had been estranged, but recently Fortesque has paid all of his debts and mended his ways, which indicates a reconciliation with his parent, who would be delighted to see him set up his nursery."

"I see." Deborah studied the duke thoughtfully. His

words in no way convinced her of Henry Fortesque's eligibility, for she believed from bitter experience that once a man was a gamester, he was always a gamester. Still, it was kind of Harwood to share this information with her, when he was surely hoping his own daughter might catch Fortesque's eye. Would he be as forthcoming about his own kinsman?

"Actually, it was Mr. Warner whose effect on Jennifer I was concerned about."

"Ah ha!" The duke leaned back in his chair. "It must have been love at first sight for both of them, for I have never seen John so affected by a female before. He is ordinarily the most phlegmatic of men. Do you consider him entirely ineligible, then?" Harwood's voice was gentle, without condemnation.

"That depends upon his prospects. Actually, it is not that I myself am so concerned. Character is much more important to me than wealth, but I know that my brother-in-law will be, and he must approve her husband, 'ere she can come into her fortune. My mother, you see, thought a great deal of Vincent's judgement, so she gave him enormous power over Jennifer's future."

Harwood templed his hands and gazed steadily at Deborah over his fingers. "That is, if she and her husband-to-be should insist on possession of her fortune."

"Quite." Deborah's mouth firmed. "Is Mr. Warner to be independently wealthy, then?"

The long fingers tapped against one another in a pregnant silence.

"I thought not."

"He *will* have a competence, and there will doubtless be governmental sinecures to come his way. And I will make a settlement on him if need be."

"As I said, sir, Vincent will decide, but I feel sure he will expect her to marry a titled lord, or a great fortune, or both."

The duke sighed. "Then we will have to help one another

watch to see these girls do not select ineligible mates, won't we."

Relieved at his acceptance of the situation, Deborah nodded. "That would be best." She had not told the duke just how truly unpleasant Vincent might be if Jennifer were to attempt to defy him. While not cruel for the joy of it, Seymour's younger brother could be quite as ruthless as her deceased husband in the pursuit of his own will.

When they returned home, the duke requested that Sarah join him half an hour early for dinner, which was to include some friends of his who could be helpful to John in his political career. "I have a small matter to discuss with you, Sarah."

Guilty awareness of her father's probable topic made Sarah duck her head. "Yes, Papa."

At the agreed upon time she presented herself, prettily gowned in one of her new dresses, in the gold salon. Her father was alone, staring into the empty fireplace, a brandy in his hand.

"You wanted to speak to me, Papa?"

"Yes. Sit here with me, child."

After a long silence while Sarah studied her father's profile in increasing anxiety, the duke slid his arm around her and tucked her against him.

"Sal, I have rarely denied you anything you wanted."

"No, Papa."

"Nor do I mean to begin now, unless absolutely necessary."

"No, Papa."

"So I do not want you to misinterpret what I am going to say."

"No, Papa."

"I wish you to be a little less encouraging to Lord Alexander for the next week or so."

A little sob escaped Sarah's lips. "I knew you were going to say that. Why? Why don't you like him? He said that you didn't, but I couldn't believe it, for I can't see why not . . ."

"It is not that I don't like him, though I admit I cannot feel comfortable with his making assignations with you—"

"It was my fault. I told him I was riding in the park!"

"Yes, well." He studied her distressed face, tilted up so her eyes could search his. "It is just that I asked John to check on him, and . . ."

"He found out that Alexander isn't going to be wealthy. Well, why does that matter? Alexander wants to be a gentleman farmer, and he already owns an estate the size of Gregory's farm, so why should you object to him when you didn't object to Gregory."

The duke removed his arm and looked ahead. "In point of fact, I did object to Gregory, though not because of his lack of fortune. But we had known the lad all of his life. While I did not think he would be the best choice for you, I was sure that some of the worst effects of a bad marriage would never befall you at his hands."

"If it is not fortune, then what? Alexander is kind, and gentle, and intelligent, and *au fait* with the *ton,* without being in the least shallow. I should have thought he would be just what you hoped I'd find last year when you made me come to London before I married Gregory."

"I may yet conclude that he is. But my investigation is not complete, and until it is, I must insist that you treat him politely but distantly. Give him no special encouragement. Do you understand?" The duke gave his daughter a direct look she could not mistake.

"If I only knew why. What do you suspect? Do you think he would beat me?"

"It is something I can't discuss with you. For once, I shall have to insist on blind obedience, daughter."

Astonished and distressed, Sarah pulled herself away from her father. There was no question of disobeying him, but she did not like it. Stiffly, she got up.

"Very well, Father. It will be awkward, for we have become very good friends, very quickly. Alexander is sure to notice something different. May I be excused tonight? It is going to be a political evening, and I haven't Jennifer's interest in the subject. I would prefer to take a tray in my room." She looked close to tears.

The duke rose, kissed his daughter on her forehead, and uneasily watched her walk from the room, her very posture and way of moving speaking eloquently of her unhappy state of mind. *Alexander, is it? Very good friends, hmmm?* By the time John had joined him, fifteen minutes later, his mind was made up.

"That trip to Yorkshire, John, to speak to Lord Pelham—I believe it will be necessary to make it after all, as swiftly as you can."

John accepted this dictum calmly. A trip out of town might be helpful to him, too. Away from the sweet, hopeless temptation of Jennifer Silverton.

"I will leave at first light, sir."

Chapter 10

There was a great hubbub in the streets as they drew near the Royal Opera House the next evening. The new opera by Rossini, *The Barber of Seville,* was being performed, and it seemed the entire fashionable world had turned out to see it.

By the time the duke had successfully shepherded Sarah, Jennifer, and Lady Cornwall to his box, he was beginning to yearn for the peace and quiet of the country. He knew Lord Alexander would be in the pit, for Sarah had confessed as much on the way over. After all, she hadn't known he would ask her to avoid the young man when she had seen him that morning. It was painful for Harwood to see her downcast expression as she fretted over how she would conduct herself toward Alexander, and what his response would be.

When she saw Meade in the milling throng below her, looking eagerly up at her, Sarah gave him the briefest of smiles, before turning to stare blankly ahead of her. Harwood's heart clenched at the sight of unshed tears in her eyes.

Lady Cornwall looked from father to daughter sympathetically, and then tried to distract Sarah by asking her to identify the occupants of the various boxes. Jennifer entered eagerly into the activity, even inquiring in all innocence as to the names of the beautiful Cyprians who occupied one particularly scandalous box.

"I never saw them before," Sarah admitted, "but I feel they must be some of the *nouveau riche,* who simply don't know how to go on. Wouldn't you say so, Father?"

The duke eyed the indicated box judiciously, allowing himself a moment's enjoyment of the charms so bounteously displayed there. "I don't know them either. You probably have the right of it, Sal," he drawled. At that moment he caught Deborah's eye and winked at her.

"What is it, Mother?" Jennifer asked solicitously as her mother seemed to collapse in a fit of coughing into her handkerchief.

Deborah, eyes flashing, turned her back on the duke in pretended annoyance, but he noticed that her shoulders shook with suppressed laughter.

In her survey of the boxes, Sarah caught the eyes of several young people whom she had known last year. "Oh, look, there's Gilbert, Lord Threlbourne; you remember him, Jenny. And Harrison Curzon has returned to town at last. I told you how he frightened Davida. And there are Lord Whitham and his new wife, Elspeth. And Arnold Lanscombe—oh, bother—he's seen me!"

Sarah nodded her head in polite acknowledgment when London's biggest gossip stood in his box to bow to her. Thus far she had avoided Lanscombe and others of his ilk. She dreaded the encounter she knew must come eventually, for he would surely seek her out and pry into her lack of fiancé or husband.

When the intermission arrived, the Duke of Harwood's box was quickly filled by young people. Sarah introduced Jennifer to those who hadn't made her acquaintance yet, and chatted casually with her friends and admirers, keeping one eye on the entrance to the box. In equal parts she dreaded and looked forward to Alexander's visit. She wanted to see him desperately, but hated the fact that she must treat him just as she did all of the other beaux who crowded the box.

But before Alexander arrived, Arnold sauntered in. He had come determined for answers and quickly insinuated himself into the semicircle around Sarah and Jennifer. The duke, who was propping up the wall at the back of the box while observing the scene, saw his daughter's unease and moved nearer.

"But Lady Sarah, what is this? You are standing here entertaining beaux quite as if you had no young farmer waiting for you to marry him."

Arnold looked around in exaggerated mystification. "Where is your rustic lover? I declare he made such an impression on me, I have been quite breathless to learn of your engagement. Each day I have searched the papers in vain."

Sarah lifted her small chin. "There is no engagement. Mr. Allensby and I decided we wouldn't suit." All of her attention was now concentrated on Arnold. She didn't notice that Alexander had slipped into the box.

"But you seemed so hopelessly besotted last season! Did you tire of his countryfied ways so soon, or did he find another sweetheart during your absence?" Lanscombe's eyes glittered with malicious curiosity. It seemed to Sarah that the other visitors to their box had all stopped their conversations to listen intently for her response.

Sarah opened and then closed her mouth, a blush of embarrassment staining her cheeks. She was drawing breath to confess once and for all that she had been jilted, that Gregory had preferred someone else, when the duke stepped forward. He couldn't protect his daughter from every heartache, but he certainly would not permit this jumped-up dandy to torment her.

"With your obviously high powers of discernment, Mr. Lanscombe, surely you didn't think a mere farmer suitable for the daughter of the Duke of Harwood? I will protect my daughter from *any* and *all* who would take advantage of her good nature." Harwood looked down his nose at Arnold, his steely eyes conveying a message that the dandy interpreted without delay: There had better not be any wicked limericks at *his* daughter's expense!

"Very natural, sir. I always said you were ill-matched there, Sarah." Suddenly eager to be elsewhere, Arnold bowed to her, then to the duke, and excused himself.

He followed closely on the heels of Lord Alexander Meade, who had overheard the duke's remarks. Alexander

had felt the blood mounting to his face just as if the duke
had been speaking in those disparaging tones of himself.
No wonder Sarah barely looked at me earlier, he thought.
*The duke obviously has put an end to all my hopes, for I'm
nothing but a farmer, at least in my prospects.*

Sarah breathed deeply for the first time since Arnold
Lanscombe had entered the box. The duke had played the
repressive father to save face for her. She flashed him a
smile of adoration before resuming her observation of the
door, expecting any moment to see Alexander. But soon the
orchestra was playing the overture for the second act, and
she had to face the fact that he was not coming.

The box quickly emptied. Sarah became aware that Harrison Curzon was frostily receiving a rejection from Jennifer, whom he had invited for a drive tomorrow afternoon.
It appeared that Jennifer had taken the story of Curzon's
rough treatment of Davida to heart and intended to have
nothing to do with the handsome, wealthy rake.

Sarah was surprised and disappointed that Alexander had
not come to see her. She wouldn't have been able to show
him any particular attention, but she at least would have
been able to see him and hear his voice for a few minutes.
She knew perhaps it was for the best. This way there was
no danger of his feeling snubbed by her. She could not help
searching the pit in vain for another sight of him, however,
and heard not a note of the remainder of the opera.

"And so he'll never let me marry her. I know that now."
Alexander, in a brocade dressing robe, was clutching a
nearly empty bottle of wine, the second one broached that
evening while retailing the events in the Harwoods' opera
box for Henry, who, true to his dislike of music, had not attended.

Henry shook his head sympathetically. He had played his
part in the killing of both wine bottles and was feeling quite
protective toward his friend. "He's a cold, calculating bas-
tard. You have only to look at him to know it."

"I actually don't blame him. In a worldly sense Sarah

can do much better than me. But I thought she might be able to convince him. Ah, the way she looked down on me in the pit tonight! So unhappy. Now I know why. Doubtless he'd forbidden her to encourage me."

"So steal her away. She's infatuated with you. She'll go willingly enough, and—"

"Absolutely not!"

"Such a lack of enterprise, of fortitude. You don't deserve her if you are unwilling to take risks for her." Having delivered himself of this wisdom, Henry held out his glass for another refill.

"Fort, you don't understand. Not having been close to your parents, I suppose you can't. Sarah adores her father. Even if I could persuade her to marry me against his wishes, an estrangement from him would make her miserable. And then, there is my family to consider. They would be extremely hurt were I to do something so unconscionable. They'd be delighted to add Sarah and her father to our family circle, but appalled to have the connection repudiated and despised by the duke."

"I see your point. All my father cares is that I marry a healthy girl to produce an heir for his precious title. He even said if I'd beget an heir before I left to join the army, he'd be glad of my going and purchase my commission himself. If marrying weren't the only way I can come about, I'd stay single as long as he lives, just to spite him!"

Appalled at such a lack of filial feeling, Alexander was silent as he divided the rest of the wine bottle between himself and his friend.

Henry tossed off the wine and stood up, swaying slightly. "Ugh. That wine on top of the several brandies I had after dinner has about finished me. I mean to call on the lovely Miss Jennifer Silverton tomorrow, so I think I'll turn in."

Alexander watched passively as Henry left the room. His mind was still occupied with Sarah. How should he act toward her? He'd moved too fast, courted her too aggressively, because she'd been so receptive. Now he felt responsible for her unhappiness. She'd begun to form a *tendre* for him, which he shouldn't have allowed to happen without being sure of her father's ultimate approval.

The thought that he must give Sarah up brought a wrenching pain to his chest. He tried to reason his way free of it. *You couldn't be in love with her so soon, Alexander,* he chided himself. *You've only spent a few hours in her company.*

The deep sadness permeating his being argued against his rational self, however. He decided that the best, the wisest course, would be to leave London as soon as he could wind up his affairs, and sail for India. In the meantime it would be best could he avoid *ton* events. Unfortunately, he wouldn't be able to do that without severely disappointing another young miss who was very dear to him.

Alexander rolled across the bed to pluck the letter he had received that day from his seventeen-year-old sister. He loved all of his sisters, but Hetty and he had always been especially close. She had written him all of the news at home, and concluded with a request.

> And so, Alex, Papa's gout keeps us all penned here at Colby Chase, all except Carlton, who is coming down on his own next week. But you know Carlton won't do the pretty for Anna, so promise me you will. She's a sweet girl, but terribly shy. She needs a nonesuch like you to take notice of her, if she is to attract any attention at all. Perhaps that rapscallion of a friend of yours, Mr. Fortesque, might be interested in her, for she has a tidy fortune, and is not so *very* plain, is she? Or perhaps you might consider her yourself, Alex. She would make you a perfect wife, for I know her heart, and she is as good-natured a creature as lives. At any rate, you will call on her, dance with her, squire her about a bit, until she begins to take, won't you, darling brother of mine?
>
> Hetty

Alexander lay on his back and tried to remember Anna-Marie Allistair. A nondescript girl with mousy brown hair and pale blue eyes, painfully thin and painfully shy. But by no means so plain as to be ineligible. Perhaps . . .

A pair of large grey eyes and three delightful dimples in an adorable round face suddenly drove out Anna-Marie's dim memory. Alexander groaned. *I could try to love her, Hetty,* he thought. *In fact, I will try. But I doubt if I'll succeed, for my heart has already felt cupid's arrow, I fear.*

After delivering Jennifer and Deborah to their home after the opera, the duke studied Sarah's face in the dim light of the carriage lamps. She looked miserable, as she had most of the evening. She made no attempt to engage him in conversation, whereas usually she would be bubbling over with comments on the performances or the members of the audience.

Harwood sighed and leaned forward in his seat, taking her hands in his and shaking them a little. "Sarah, please don't take it so hard. You barely know this young man and . . ."

"And now I never shall." She turned her head away, lower lip quivering.

"You make me feel a beast!"

"No, Papa, you're not a beast, but . . ."

"A monster, then."

"Not a monster, either, but . . ."

"I'm not sure I want to hear the rest of either of those sentences. Sarah, don't you see? I *would* be a beast, a monster, to carelessly let you develop a deep affection for someone when there was a good possibility you could never marry him."

"Yes, Papa." She sighed and turned back to meet his eyes. "I know. It hurts, but I know you are doing only what you think is best for me."

To distract her, Harwood observed, "Jennifer and Lady Cornwall certainly seemed to enjoy the opera, didn't they?"

"Jennifer is almost as enthralled by it as Davida was."

"Lady Cornwall, too. She has a magnificent voice, by the way. When your mother and I knew her, so long ago, she was begged to sing wherever she went."

Sarah looked speculatively at her father, who was smiling fondly now. "You like her very much, don't you, Papa?"

"I like them both. I am very glad you have found a new friend; I know you missed Davida sorely. It seems the connection comforts *both* of us for the loss of Davida."

He grinned almost boyishly at her reference to his growing fondness for Deborah. "I was wondering how long it would be before you noticed."

To his surprise, Sarah did not smile back, but instead began worrying her lower lip with her teeth. Before he could question her, the carriage came to a stop before their door. A footman handed Sarah down the steps. She waited for her father, taking his arm as they climbed the steps.

While they made their way into the house, Sarah's mind was racing. She had been sworn to secrecy. She couldn't tell him about Lady Cornwall's miserable marriage, and hence her very understandable determination never to marry again. And yet . . . her father had spoken truly. It would be wrong to let a loved one develop a deep affection for someone if there was no hope of a happy outcome.

Now it was her turn to perform the painful duty of warning him that pursuit of Jennifer's mother would likely be fruitless.

"What is it, daughter? Don't you like Lady Cornwall? I had thought . . ."

"I like her very well. In fact, I had begun to lay matchmaking schemes, did you not realize how perfect she was for you."

The duke studied her downcast, sorrowful countenance for a moment, and then led her into the silent library, waving off the servants. "We shall converse a while, Timmons. Go to bed. I'll see to matters down here when we are finished." Taking a taper from a wall sconce, he lit a few candles, bathing the book-lined room in a mellow light.

"Now, then," he continued once they were settled together on a sofa, "why so somber at the mention of Lady Cornwall?"

"I don't know how to tell you, for I was told in confidence. I don't want to break my word, but on the other hand . . ."

Sarah bent her head, thinking. Jennifer, knowing her mother felt a deep sense of shame, of responsibility almost, for the way her husband had treated them, had sworn Sarah to secrecy before describing their home life.

Choosing her words carefully, she tried to enlighten her father while adhering to her promise. "I can say, Father, only that Lady Cornwall was not a happy wife and has sworn never to marry again."

Harwood leaned back and stared at the ceiling, an old memory surfacing. Eleanor, nearly in tears, had asked to leave early after a dinner party one night. Her urgent request had come immediately after a tête-à-tête in the withdrawing room with her friend Deborah.

When he had tried to discover if they had quarreled, she had shaken her head. In almost identical words to their daughter's, so many years later, she had sobbed, "I can't tell you, for I gave my word. But, oh! Justin. She is so desperately unhappy. I wish there were some way to help her."

She had been unwilling to say more, and he had respected her determination to keep a confidence. Soon thereafter Deborah left London. She spent the remainder of her marriage a virtual recluse at her husband's principal seat, Woodcrest, though Seymour had preferred town.

Other memories surfaced, more recent ones—of Deborah stiffening when he offered her his arm, refusing to dance, rejecting his assistance with her servants, changing the subject whenever he tried to hint that they make any sort of plans together that did not involve their children.

Her father's bleak face almost undid Sarah. "Papa! Now I know how you must feel about me and Alexander, for I fear I may have destroyed your happiness." She threw herself into his arms.

The duke enfolded her in a firm hug. "It is a wretched position to be in, isn't it? Well, we both may yet come about. I may yet receive a good report on Lord Alexander, and who knows, Lady Cornwall could change her mind."

Head buried against his chest, Sarah shook her head. "It may already be too late. Did you notice he did not come to the box tonight? Alexander is proud. He may have felt that I cut him, in which case he won't be back. And I am sure Jennifer's mother will never change her mind."

"Ah, the much vaunted optimism of youth!" The duke gave her another quick hug and stood, half lifting her to her feet. "It is getting very late. You must have your beauty sleep."

"Aren't you coming up?" She looked back when she realized he wasn't following her.

"No, I believe I will sit here and think for a while. Always a painful endeavor, best conducted without an audience."

Sarah blew her father a kiss and slowly climbed the stairs, her mind once again drifting to the alarming nonappearance of Alexander Meade.

Her father's ruminations were no happier. The *ton* was surely the most effective gossip machine in the world. Yet he had heard nothing about Deborah's marriage that would explain such an aversion to remarrying. Why had she been unhappy? Was it because her husband philandered and gamed, and left her stuck in the country? Would a woman swear never to marry again for such a reason?

Or had Cornwall mistreated her? Harwood remembered how Eleanor had clung to him that long ago night after telling him how unhappy Deborah was. She had whispered over and over how fortunate she was to have a gentle, loving husband. He had been too wrapped up in soothing Eleanor to pay much attention to Deborah's problems back them.

And then there was Sarah's question yesterday—"Are you afraid he would beat me?" Had that been just a possibility she had plucked at random, or had a recent conversation with Jennifer put such husbandly behavior in her mind?

If that had been what was wrong with Deborah's marriage, no wonder Eleanor had been so upset! The duke's mind recoiled in horror at the thought of any man beating his wife. It seemed to him to be the ultimate betrayal. The very person a woman should be able to look to for protection in a cruel world should be her husband. Cruel, cruel irony, for that husband to be himself the one from whom she needed protection.

A deep melancholy settled on the duke as he pondered Deborah's past and its effect on his future. *I must be half in love with her already,* he thought, groaning in dismay at his hasty heart. He had not expected to love again, and it would perhaps have been better that way.

Harwood looked around the library, which oddly enough reminded him of his beloved Eleanor more than any room in the house, though it had been the one she had changed the least.

Once she had gained the confidence to follow her own taste, Eleanor had shown a decided flair for decorating, and he had given her free rein both at Harwood Court and here in town. But she hadn't done much to his library at either place, declaring them to be perfect masculine sanctuaries.

She had had decrepit chairs comfortably recovered, and in general cleaned and polished, but had left the dark, masculine color scheme, the hunting scenes on the wall, and the sturdy timeless furniture. Both libraries were his favorite rooms. But suddenly they seemed haunted—haunted by a laughing, loving presence that he could never enjoy anymore.

When the Duke of Harwood at last mounted the stairs to his own bed, he was feeling lonelier than he had done since coming to London and rediscovering Lady Cornwall.

Chapter 11

Both the duke and his daughter awoke the next morning in a much better frame of mind. Sarah, with the resiliency of youth, had decided that a fine man like Alexander would pass whatever investigation her father was conducting. Harwood, with the wisdom of age, had decided that patience might yet win him the affections of Lady Cornwall, if he could content himself with being her friend until she was quite comfortable with him.

Thus it was that father and daughter attended the ball of Constance Dalrimple in an optimistic frame of mind. There had never been any thought of crying off, for Lord Proctor was a friend of Justin's from his days at Oxford. Moreover, Sarah liked Connie, a bubbly, friendly girl who was another pupil of Monsieur Pacquin. Like Arnold Lanscombe she loved to know the latest *on dits,* though she was never malicious or spiteful.

The duke and Sarah were invited to dinner, while the viscountess and Jennifer were to arrive later for the ball. The duke watched for them, and felt a warm glow of satisfaction at observing how different mother and daughter appeared this night from the way they had looked at the first ball of the season.

Though Jennifer still looked a bit coltish and ridiculously young in her high-waisted white muslin dress, she had gained poise. With her courage restored, her natural beauty could shine through. Before the duke could even make his way to them, she was approached by several young men and calmly, graciously accepted several invitations to dance.

Her mother also was much improved from that first ball. Less anxious about her child, she also was in her best looks in a royal blue gown with an appealing though not unusually deep décolletage. She, too, had begun to make friends, and was engaging in a friendly conversation by the time the duke reached her.

The wary look she had given Harwood that first evening was replaced now by a welcoming smile that made the duke's hopes shine even brighter. *She is changing,* he thought. *As the season goes by, she will be able to put aside her previous experiences and see me for myself.*

Sarah's optimism was less justified by events. It was quite late into the ball before Alexander arrived. She had been surreptitiously observing the entrance to the ballroom all evening, scarcely able to believe he would not attend this ball. The entire *ton* was there.

At last, stirringly handsome in his elegant evening attire, Alexander appeared, escorting a young girl wreathed in white spider gauze in the latest kick of fashion. His manner toward her was protective, almost proprietary.

Sarah was standing with her partner at the top of a set, awaiting their turn to go down the dance. Just behind her stood Connie, who had left the receiving line long since. She satisfied Sarah's curiosity about Alexander's companion without her even having to ask.

"Oh, do look, Sarah," she whispered, leaning forward. "That is Anna-Marie Allistair with Lord Alexander. They say she has an enormous dowry. Such a quiet girl! She and her mother called on us yesterday, and she hadn't a word to say for herself."

Sarah studied the young girl with interest. She was very nearly plain, with a long face dominated by a long nose. Her expression, however, was sweet, and her slender figure was lithe and graceful. She was almost as tall as Jenny. Suddenly, Sarah hated being short!

Her partner whirled her into the patterns of the dance and Sarah executed the steps faultlessly, but her mind was elsewhere. When the dance was over, she could remember none of it. Only by the fact that she was overheated and thirsty could she be sure she had actually spent the last half hour in vigorous exercise.

She was relieved when she saw Alexander advancing on her, escorting Anna-Marie. Her fears were groundless! This was doubtless a family friend; his interest still lay with Sarah. Forgetting her father's strictures, she smiled warmly as the two approached her.

It was one thing to know the correct thing to do, and another to do it, Alexander found. His noble resolve to behave in such a way as to set Sarah entirely free wavered in the face of the rush of admiration he felt upon first laying eyes on her this evening. She was dressed in a shimmering yellow silk with sufficient décolletage to show her lovely shoulders to advantage. His breath caught in his throat as her movements in the dance whipped her dress around, outlining her perfect, curvaceous form.

Alexander had never been forced to hold a tighter rein on his emotions than when he led Anna-Marie up to Lady Sarah to introduce the two. He had decided that the correct path was to be punctiliously polite to Sarah, but without allowing himself the least sign of partiality. Soon she would cease to harbor notions of a deeper acquaintance, and would be free and heart-whole to marry where her father would approve.

His pain was intensified by her radiant smile. She was so adorable, so obviously uneasy about his failure to appear at her side last night at the opera, and at the same time so eager to welcome him tonight. He yearned to put her mind at ease with a warm smile, a quip, a request to dance. But he must do the right thing. And so he introduced Anna-Marie, chatted briefly about inconsequentials, and then led his sister's friend away for a dance.

As Sarah watched him go, her hopes plummeted. Surely that single indifferent greeting last night had not offended Alexander so much that he would turn to another woman?

But he seemed so distant to her, so concerned about Miss Allistair. And he hadn't even asked her for one dance!

Henry Fortesque watched this tableau from across the room. His own feelings were bruised tonight. Jennifer Silverton had treated him with cool indifference. She had refused his invitation to drive out with him this morning. This evening she had granted him a dance, but her demeanor was unencouraging.

The mother's doing, he thought, grinding his teeth. That the viscountess had disliked him from the first, he did not doubt. She had pokered up at his first reference to gaming, and no amount of exertion had succeeded in charming her.

Alexander and I would both seem to be without a prayer, he thought. Henry pitied his friend for having to exchange the adorable Lady Sarah for plain, shy Anna-Marie. *But lucky Alex has another heiress to fall back on,* he thought.

Henry watched Sarah's crestfallen countenance as Alexander walked away, and suddenly a brilliant notion struck him. *I have another heiress to fall back on, too! And mine is a lovely, likable pocket Venus!*

Sarah was surprised but not displeased to find Henry Fortesque asking for a place on her dance card. She hoped that this man, who shared quarters with Alexander, might drop some hint to let her know what was going on. She accepted a waltz with him immediately and found him such a good dancer and conversationalist that for a few moments she forgot her other troubles. A glimpse of Alexander waiting out the waltz with Anna-Marie brought her back to herself.

"Miss Allistair seems quite a sweet young lady," she observed, studying Henry's face.

Henry heard the question behind the comment. He wouldn't have betrayed Alexander's confidence in any case, but now his own interest lay in helping his friend disguise his true feelings for Sarah.

"Yes, I believe Alexander admires her very much. She is quiet, biddable—just the sort to make him a good wife. And the family approves of the match, you know."

"No, I . . . you mean they've already . . ."

"By no means. She is to have a season before a decision is made. A wise approach, don't you agree?"

"At least my father would agree with you," Sarah responded, not without some bitterness. The dance was ending. One final twirl placed Sarah so that she could see Alexander, and he seemed to be looking her way. Pride brought her chin up. She lifted sparkling eyes to Henry. "You dance exceptionally well, Mr. Fortesque."

"Aided by a delightful partner." He gave her his most charming grin and bowed. "May I escort you to supper?"

Only then did Sarah realize she had given Henry the supper dance, the one she had saved, hoping Alexander would claim it. With her audience firmly in mind, Sarah flashed Henry a brilliant smile of acceptance and left the dance floor on his arm, in animated conversation.

Jennifer did as her mother had bid her. She gave no one more than one dance to any suitor and studied each one carefully as they shared commonplaces, determined to keep her wits about her and encourage only those who might make good husbands. When the handsome Heywood brothers pressed her with their attentions, she was polite but cool, even though she thought the older one, Harvey, might actually be a worthwhile person to know.

Thus she felt she had been sufficiently virtuous to be entitled to accept the request of Mr. Warner for a dance, though she avoided looking at her mother as she allowed him to lead her out.

But once she had danced with John, her interest in her other partners diminished; it became much easier to see their defects, and impossible to see their virtues. Everyone she met seemed a useless fribble beside John, who did not talk down to her, but paid her the compliment of speaking to her as a thinking being. He even disagreed with her, which to Jennifer seemed a sure sign he respected her opinion.

Not only that, but the short periods when they were able to touch in the figures of the country dance were moments of pleasant discovery, not jarring distaste, as with some of her other partners.

Still, she knew her duty. After the dance, she thanked him with an air of finality that did not encourage him to request another.

Lord Threlbourne stood and talked with Jennifer, Deborah, and the duke during the supper dance, which he had asked to sit out with her, thus gaining the privilege of her company at supper. Gilbert, too, was able to hold a sensible conversation with a female, she noted approvingly. But when she saw John dancing with Connie, she suppressed a sigh, for the eminently eligible Lord Threlbourne did not appeal to her the way John Warner did.

Harwood and Lady Cornwall stayed together through most of the evening, sharing one another's pleasures and concerns over their offsprings' behavior, and fending off would-be partners. Harwood was well-satisfied with the results, for Deborah obviously was growing more trusting of him, and even dependent on him, by the hour. He could not despair of a happy outcome to his suit.

About Sarah, though, he was less sanguine. He saw and comprehended the sequence of events from the time Lord Alexander entered the ballroom. He felt a measure of relief that Meade was looking elsewhere. It appeared the man was a fortune hunter who had decided to pursue a more vulnerable prey.

But he also felt a pang of sympathy for his daughter. No matter how correct he had been to warn his daughter away from Meade, the knowledge must hurt her. He was grateful when Henry Fortesque stepped into the breach.

Deborah watched her daughter in animated conversation with John Warner while they waited their turn at the dance. There was too much ease in their manner with one another, too much obvious pleasure in one another's company, to suit her. Her concern was allayed somewhat when, after supper, Jennifer brought Lord Threlbourne to her and that fiery-haired young worthy told them of a projected picnicking expedition to Richmond Hill two weeks hence.

"Everyone is going, almost. It will be a jolly group, and Eberlin is spreading a feast for us near the Star and Garter Inn. I would like to escort Jennifer if I may?"

Deborah gave her permission with pleasure. How fortunate they would be if Jennifer could form an attachment with this kindly, intelligent young man. Seeing both his title and handsome fortune, Vincent would be pleased to give his assent to the match.

Later in the evening Lord Eberlin himself invited not only Jennifer but her mother and Harwood along on the trip to Richmond. "Additional chaperones might be useful, sir," he explained. "My mother and I shall be challenged with so many lively young people about." Eberlin was sponsoring his sister in her come-out and looked as concerned as any father as he monitored the girl's behavior while she danced.

"The occasion is growing like a snowball. Everyone seems in the mood for an outdoor entertainment. Hope the weather is clement." Eberlin glanced up at the ceiling as if it held some portent of the coming event.

The duke and viscountess both accepted readily. When Harwood rejoined his daughter late in the evening to depart for home, he learned that she had accepted the offer of Fortesque's escort, and felt a good deal of paternal self-satisfaction.

However, in the carriage on the way home, Sarah's mood grew progressively more pensive. When they had mounted the steps and entered the foyer, the duke asked her if she wanted to talk for a few minutes.

Abruptly, she whirled around. "I couldn't bear it!" Tears were starting in her eyes. "May I be excused, sir? Please?"

"Of course, Sal." Harwood kissed her forehead. "You're tired, and why not? It's been a long evening."

She nodded, biting her lower lip, before turning and dashing up the steps as if hoping to outrun a demon.

Hardly more satisfactory was the end of Deborah's evening. When she rhapsodized upon Lord Threlbourne as a suitor, Jennifer looked dubious.

"Yes, he is all you say, Mother, but I somehow don't feel that he is considering me for a wife."

Ignoring the uncharacteristically formal way Jennifer had addressed her, Deborah responded briskly, "What nonsense. He kept by your side during the waltz, for the privilege of taking you in to supper—"

"I know, but—"

"And asked to escort you on Lord Eberlin's picnic. What more would you require as an expression of interest—that would be decent, that is?"

Jennifer looked doubtfully at her mother. She knew how inexperienced she was. Her mother knew a great deal more about the world and the male of the species. Yet . . .

"Somehow there is nothing of the lover in his manner toward me."

"That is because he is a proper gentleman, not a loose fish like Mr. Fortesque, or a fortune hunter like—"

"Don't, Mother." For the first time in as long as Deborah could remember, her daughter was suddenly looking at her defiantly, her voice harsh with agitation. "Don't you dare say anything to Mr. Warner's detriment. He can't help it that he is poor, and he is quite the finest gentleman of my acquaintance."

Then Deborah, too, was treated to the sight of her daughter dashing up the stairs ahead of a bout of weeping.

Chapter 12

A loud knock followed by raised masculine voices awoke Deborah from a sound sleep the next morning. Groaning, she consulted the clock on her mantel. It was but nine, a most unfashionable hour for anyone to be calling during the season.

Her maid bustled into the room, alarm on her face. "That there Lord Morton be below, demanding to see you instantly. The old reprobate!"

"Let him demand. I do not owe him obedience." Deborah pulled the covers up to her chin, her defiance masking alarm.

"Nay, my lady." Her old retainer smiled sadly at her. "You must go down before he causes a scandal with his bellowing. He first demanded to see Miss Jennifer, calling her his bride-to-be. Then he asked for you."

"Wh-what?" Deborah sat upright, horror washing over her. She threw aside the covers, terror lending speed to her morning toilet, before hurrying down the stairs to enter the drawing room, where Morton paced in front of the fireplace.

"Lord Morton?"

Corsets creaking, Morton hastily approached her, trying to catch up her hands as he asked, "Dearest Deborah! Did you miss me? I returned as soon as I could."

Pulling away from him and primming her mouth, Deborah responded with asperity, "I had absolutely no idea that you were gone! I am extremely busy this morning, sir. Please state your business and then leave."

"Hoity-toity, madam. Once you hear what I have to say, you will not be so eager to send me away!" Morton drew himself up, savoring this moment of triumph. "Please be so good as to send for Miss Silverton. I wish to pay my addresses to her."

"Don't be ridiculous," Deborah retorted, trying to affect a laugh, though she was quaking inside.

"Nothing ridiculous about it! I've decided to make her my second wife. A charming stepmother she'll make to my sons, don't you think?" Morton grinned slyly at her.

Suddenly all of Deborah's innate caution was overwhelmed by fury at the sheer effrontery of this statement. "You are quite mad, sirrah, if you think I'd let my precious daughter marry an aging degenerate such as yourself."

"Mind your words, madam." Morton's face purpled, and he sprang toward her, fists upraised.

"Oh, yes. You would hit me, wouldn't you. You and Seymour, just alike, so brave in combat with females and servants. Get out! And never come here again!"

"But soon I shall have every right to run tame in this house, not that it signifies, for you both shall be living in mine." Reaching into his coat pocket, he withdrew a folded bit of parchment.

"I have Vincent's permission to pay my addresses to your daughter. As this letter makes clear, she has no choice but to accept my suit. Now be so good as to have her brought here immediately." He waved the note under Deborah's nose.

She snatched it from his hand with trembling fingers and smoothed it to read, in Vincent's unmistakable spidery hand:

My Dear Sister-in-law:
   I know I said you might select Jennifer's husband this season, but Lord Morton has made a most satisfactory offer in all respects, and I cannot think of any reason why I should not accept it. I have therefore given him leave to offer for her, and I give you notice that she must accept him

forthwith. As Lord Morton is an impatient bridegroom, I have given him permission to wed her by special license as soon as may be.

Sincerely, &c
Vincent

Deborah felt the room tilt. A sort of blackness veiled her vision. "This can't be. Why, you are three times her age, if nothing else. Why would Vincent . . ."

"True. She will be like a daughter to me in many ways. Including the fact that her mother and I shall be, ah, how shall I say it, *très intime*." Morton's fleshy features spread in an unmistakable leer.

Deborah drew back as if a snake had struck at her. "You vile, base creature . . ."

"Yes, rage at me, beauteous Deborah. It adds a piquant spice to the conquest." Morton closed the distance between them, his thick hands closing brutally over her shoulders. "You'll soon see that I know how to tame you, better than Seymour ever did."

Deborah twisted free of his painful grip and slapped him. Shaking in every limb with fury, she stormed at him. "Seymour was a monster and so are you. I'll ruin you in the *ton* if you ever so much as breathe on me or my daughter. Seymour was not above bragging about some of your disgusting orgies. I can make all of society turn its back on you."

Jowls shaking with fury, Morton hissed at her, "Listen to me, you bitch. I have permission from your brother-in-law to wed your daughter without delay, and wed her I shall, this very day. And then, Deborah—listen well!" He raised his voice when she began to speak. "The kind of treatment she shall have as a wife will depend very much on how you treat me." Morton's voice thundered with purpose. "Do I make myself clear?"

All color drained from Deborah's face. He meant it! This obscene old man meant to marry her daughter and force her into being his mistress. *This is a nightmare. I have to have some time to think.* Deborah took a deep breath, willing herself calm. With iron self-control, she replied, "Yes, very clear."

A wolfish smile lit Morton's features. "That's better. You are an intelligent female, who knows when she's been mastered. Come here, Deborah." He pointed to the floor directly in front of him.

Reluctantly, Deborah obeyed. He thrust a hurtful hand into her hair, holding her head steady for a crushing kiss. His other hand invaded the front of her dress, hard and cruel in its exploration of her soft curves.

After interminable minutes, Morton drew away, breathing heavily. "That's much better, my dear. Now send for Jennifer. I wish the two of you to accompany me as I go for a special license."

Deborah rearranged her clothes, willing herself not to throw up at his feet. "Yes, Lord Morton. She is still asleep. I must wake her, and we both must dress suitably for this auspicious occasion."

Morton grinned triumphantly. "I knew you would see reason, dearest Deborah. Do not take too long, though. I have an appointment with the archbishop."

Deborah forced herself to give him a respectful curtsy before quitting the room. As she climbed the steps, her racing mind in sharp contrast to her slow progress, she tried to decide what she must do.

Jennifer was deep in slumber, her soft mouth slightly open, her hair curling out of its braids. It seemed cruel to awaken her from such sound, innocent sleep for such a horrifying reason, but there was no time to waste. Deborah shook her daughter by the shoulder until her eyes fluttered open, then urged her up. Betty was already laying out a walking dress and matching pelisse.

"Make haste, Jennifer. We must leave immediately."

She quickly explained part of the situation to her daughter as she helped Betty to dress her. She did not tell Jennifer that Morton intended to force Deborah into his bed with threats to harm his young wife. It was terrible enough to Jennifer to hear that he expected to marry her.

When they were finished, Deborah turned to her servant. "You come with us, Betty."

Betty nodded. "I'll get me cloak, mum. And a change of clothes, shall I?"

"Yes, and get my jewel case."

"Where are we to go, Mother?" Still a little groggy with sleep, Jennifer's brown eyes were large with anxiety.

Deborah passed her hand over her brow. "I don't know. I can't think. I only know we mustn't stay here." She was throwing a change of clothes for Jennifer into a carpetbag as she talked.

"I know. We shall go to Sarah's."

Deborah stopped and straightened up. "I don't know. The duke is such a proper gentleman; I don't know if he would countenance a girl running from her guardian. I've avoided scandal all my life, but I can't avoid this one. Still, I hesitate to involve another family in it."

Jennifer shook her head. "Mother, I don't believe for a moment the duke would allow me to be forced to wed Lord Morton."

Deborah thought a moment, and then nodded. "He may not be best pleased to be placed in such a situation, but I think he will stand our friend. Perhaps he will help me sell my jewels, or . . . I suppose the first thing to do is talk to Vincent. We must go! Quickly, now." She helped Jennifer into a voluminous cloak.

The three women tiptoed down the servants' stairs, carpetbags in hand. A couple of servants looked at them curiously, but none attempted to stop them. Once outside, they hurried back through the mews rather than risk being spied by Lord Morton's tiger, sure to be walking his horses in the front of the house.

They traversed the few blocks to the duke's mansion so fast that Deborah got a stitch in her side and had to be assisted up the steps by her elderly maid, who was also breathing heavily.

Just as they reached the top, Jennifer turned back. "I forgot Mittens!"

Deborah took her firmly by the arms. "She'll be all right with Cook in the kitchen. You can't go back there, dearest. We'll retrieve her when all of this is settled."

Jennifer looked as if she would argue for a moment, then slumped against her mother. "Yes, Mother," she whispered, biting her lip to keep the tears at bay.

Timmons's expression carefully masked any surprise he may have felt at this early visit. "His Grace is not at home just now, my lady. Would you like to wait?"

Deborah allowed him to seat them in the blue salon and agreed gratefully to a tea tray.

"Is Lady Sarah awake, Timmons?" Jennifer asked.

"No, miss. Still abed. She came in quite late last night, you know." There was a very faint sound of reproach in Timmons's voice.

"So did I!" Suddenly, the alarums of the last thirty minutes caught up with Jennifer, and she burst into tears.

"When do you expect the duke to return, Timmons?" Deborah spoke to him as she cradled Jennifer against her shoulder.

"Not until around noon, my lady." Timmons bowed at her and then left the room.

Deborah comforted her daughter while she thought. *What am I to do? I must reason with Vincent, but what if I can't convince him? I must keep Jennifer away from him.*

Just then John Warner, only this day returned from his visit to the Pelhams to investigate Alexander Meade, strolled in. Timmons, worried by the obvious distress of the three women, had asked him to look into the matter. "May I be of service, Lady Cornwall?" he asked, his sympathetic glance traveling from Deborah's anxious countenance to Jennifer's tearstained face.

"Oh, J . . . Mr. Warner." Jennifer jumped up. "You must help us. Lord Morton intends to marry me. That odious man has gotten my uncle's permission, and . . ."

"Never!" Shock and determination were equally present in John's firm reply as he took Jennifer's outstretched hands in his.

A few minutes of conversation placed John in possession
of the facts and induced him to agree readily to Deborah's
hastily contrived plan. "I will leave Jennifer here. None
must know she is here, though. I will go to Woodcrest, try
to make Vincent see reason. If he won't . . ." Her voice
quavered.

"He will. And if you cannot, I am sure the duke can
make him understand just how odious such a match is."

Together they consulted the posting inn schedules in
John's possession. Woodcrest was not too far off the major
coaching routes, near the Welsh border. Finding that a fast
coach was leaving within the hour, Deborah determined to
be on it. "Do you think Harwood will be angry if I leave
my daughter here while I travel? I don't want to take the
chance that Vincent will physically remove Jennifer from
my custody."

John shook his head. "I know he would want her to stay
here, though I fear he will not like you to travel alone. If
you would delay your departure until this evening, perhaps
the duke or I can accompany you."

"I'd best go right away. It takes two days to reach Woodcrest, providing the roads are dry." It was perhaps cowardly, but Deborah liked the idea of leaving before the duke
had a chance to say no. "Morton had already begun the
process of obtaining a special license. There is no time to
lose."

John could only agree. He ordered a carriage around
from the mews to take Lady Cornwall to the posting inn.
"Do you require any funds?"

"No, I brought along my quarterly allowance." Deborah
lifted up a heavy reticule. "Indeed, I had best leave some of
this here, rather than tempt fate by traveling with my entire
fortune." She essayed a smile, but realized with a sense of
shame that Mr. Warner pitied her for having so few re-
sources.

"I'm coming with you," Betty announced as Deborah
rose to leave.

"No, you need to stay and look after Jennifer."

"I'm thinking that she'll not lack for those to look after her." Betty cast a meaningful look at John.

"She is right, Lady Cornwall. Between Sarah, Harwood, and myself, Miss Silverton will be well looked after. But you risk unwelcome consequences if you travel without a maid."

Deborah hesitated. Last night the idea of Jennifer being looked after by Mr. Warner would have been alarming to her. But today it seemed the lesser catastrophe.

"All right then. Jenny, stay indoors until I return. Do not give Morton a chance to snatch you away."

"No, Mama, I won't." Jennifer hugged her mother tearfully. "You be careful."

"Go upstairs now. Mr. Warner, would you have one of your maids prepare her a room? She got very little rest last night, and if she could sleep now, it would do her a world of good."

"Oh, Mama, I couldn't sleep now."

"I will see to it, Lady Cornwall," John reassured her.

Looking back doubtfully at the two before descending the steps, she saw them framed in the doorway, two solemn-faced young people standing a little too close to one another. A twinge of unease assailed her. But the coach was at the door, and time was passing. Abruptly turning, she ran down the steps, cloak flying behind her, and followed Betty into the carriage.

Chapter 13

When the Duke of Harwood returned from his meeting, it was nearly noon. His butler urgently directed him to the blue salon. Timmons's manner alerted Harwood that something unusual was in the offering, but he still was not prepared for the sight that greeted him. John Warner was seated on a sofa with his back to the duke, and the golden-brown hair fanned out over his shoulder suggested that he was not alone.

John turned his head. Seeing the duke, he raised a finger to his lips in warning. Harwood silently rounded the sofa and then stopped in astonishment. Jennifer Silverton, disheveled and with tear tracks on her cheeks, was curled in the crook of John's arm, fast asleep.

Carefully easing her away from him and then guiding her to a reclining position, John tucked a cushion under Jennifer's head before motioning the duke to follow him to the other end of the room. In a hoarse whisper he explained the events of the morning.

"And after her mother left, she succumbed to a fit of the vapors, and told me that she suspected something even worse, even more sinister afoot than her mother had been willing to tell us."

Harwood frowned, stroking his chin. "Did she have any idea . . ."

"No. She is too innocent, but my guess is that he plans to force Lady Cornwall into his bed once he has her daughter in his power."

"It sounds like some Gothic romance! Surely it is only

the child's money he covets." But the duke paused, remembering Morton's behavior toward Deborah and her obvious revulsion at his advances. *Perhaps it is possible. Such villainy, right here in London in modern times!*

"Well, he shan't get away with it," Harwood growled. "I wish Deborah had waited for me. I don't like to think of her traveling on a public conveyance, and I would have liked to accompany her to see Cornwall."

"You could catch her, I suppose. Even a fast flyer can't travel faster than a man on horseback."

Harwood nodded, frowning. "Or is my presence here more important? I must give this some thought. In the meantime, let us take the child upstairs and get her into a proper bed. She needs some coddling now."

John gently lifted Jennifer. He was surprised at how light she felt in his arms. Mounting the stairs with his precious burden, he felt his heart swell in his breast. He loved her! Unwise, ill-timed, impossible love!

Jennifer roused as he mounted the steps with her. She stiffened in surprise for a moment, then, relishing this closeness as much as John, she murmured and dropped her head against his chest again, feigning a return to sleep so she might continue in his arms a little while longer.

A maid was summoned to prepare a bed and assist Jennifer in undressing. John gently, reluctantly relinquished the half-awake girl and then stepped into the hall with Harwood, only to find him in whispered conversation with Sarah.

Sarah had been lying abed this morning. Aware that her father had an early meeting, she had slept late and then ordered a tray with chocolate and toast brought to her room. She had been unaware of the events below until she opened her door, fully dressed and determined to take a long walk to clear the cobwebs from her mind.

Her father quickly, quietly told her what he thought she needed to know, and then informed her of his intention to pursue Lady Cornwall. To his surprise his daughter objected.

"No, Papa, you haven't thought. If I cease going about in

society, Lord Morton may guess that she is here. And . . . oh! dear! Jennifer's first evening at Almack's is to be this Wednesday. Such talk if she misses it!"

Harwood scowled. His daughter had the right of it. It would be best for Jennifer's future if she could continue to follow her social calendar. A sudden absence would be noticed and lead to talk.

"That's true," he admitted. "I expect I had best escort you and Jennifer just as if nothing had happened."

John rang in with an objection. "Morton will know where she is, then."

A mirthless smile lifted one corner of Harwood's mouth. "Morton will catch cold trying to claim her now, whatever Vincent does. I'll settle him down, see if I don't. Actually, Lady Cornwall is making an unnecessary trip. I wish I had been here when she arrived. I could have reassured her of my intention to stand by her. Morton is brave enough when it comes to intimidating a pair of females, but let us see how willing he is to come to points with me!"

Sarah threw her arms around her father, hugging him wordlessly.

"What, minx. Tears? You aren't afraid for me, though?"

"Oh, no, Papa. I could almost pity Lord Morton! But you're just so wonderful!"

Harwood grimaced over his daughter's head as his eyes met John's. Very early this morning John had returned from his visit to Lord Pelham. Would his daughter think him so wonderful if she knew he had needlessly alienated her young suitor, Alexander, whom Pelham had pronounced an excellent suitor, sound in every way, though a bit staid and bookish for Pelham's tastes.

Pelham had laughed off any suggestion that Meade shared the lax views of Shelley on marriage. "He told me himself that he deplored the man's behavior, though he admired his poetry," Pelham had told John.

Jennifer was quite nervous about the duke's plans to go out after her mother warned her against it. But she wanted to accompany him and John to her home to pack her wardrobe and collect Mittens. They refused, however, insisting that she stay safely in Sarah's room until they had returned.

The Cornwall servants informed the duke that Lord Morton, purple with fury, had announced he would be back with the special license, and expected Jennifer and her mother to be there, ready for a wedding.

The duke told them to say nothing of Jennifer's whereabouts, though he confided to John on the way home that he had very little hope the servants would keep quiet.

"Even supposing Morton too cheap to bribe them, servants love to gossip quite as much as their betters," he observed ruefully, stroking the soft fur of the little dog curled in his lap, shedding merrily over his jacket and breeches.

In the evening Jennifer uneasily ventured forth at the duke and Sarah's urgings, to attend the Trentons' rout. There was such a crush that the duke led the way, opening a passage with his body. Sarah and Jennifer were sandwiched between the duke and John.

"This is disgusting," Sarah moaned. "Why do they invite more people than can possibly fit in the house?"

"Now, Sal, you know that the only way to measure the success of a rout is by how many people are crushed in the press of the crowd." Harwood braced himself in a doorway and motioned the girls under the space he created.

"This one seems a *succès fou,* then," Jennifer said, giggling a little at the phenomenon of so many elegantly-dressed people packed into so little space.

"I think it has passed the bounds of humor and become a dangerous situation," John muttered, bracing himself after a sharp elbow to the ribs almost toppled him against Jennifer.

"Agreed. Let us bid our hostess farewell and . . ."

Jennifer giggled again. "We only just bid her hello."

"That is really all that is expected of us. Sal, does this plan meet with your approval?"

Sarah nodded without enthusiasm. She had had little to say for herself this evening. Her father had explained to her that his inquiries about Lord Alexander had been satisfactorily answered. He had given her permission to further the acquaintance.

But her hopes that she would meet Alexander at the Trentons' rout had turned to ashes when she saw him three feet away, barely glimpsed through the crowd. A scowl on his face, Alexander stood trying to listen to someone who was red-faced with the exertion of making himself heard. Next to Alexander, with his arm curved around her protectively, stood Anna-Marie Allistair.

Too late, she thought. *Too late.* Yet she didn't blame her father. It had probably been too late all along. Doubtless Lord Alexander had been just toying with her until his soon-to-be fiancée came to town.

Sarah made no attempt to catch his eye or speak to him. She passively allowed herself to be led through the crowd. She was more than ready to go home.

Lord Morton climbed the steps of the Harwood Mansion the next morning earlier than most of the *ton* considered a decent hour. When he had returned to the Cornwalls', he waited for hours for the missing women to return, unable to believe they would have dared to defy him. Finally, he had bribed the butler to learn their whereabouts. He had gone to Harwood's, only to learn that they had gone out.

Morton's early arrival was to prevent the duke from claiming he or his guests weren't at home. He was nervous about facing the duke, but after all, he had right on his side. His Grace High and Mighty could not legally prevent him from wedding Jennifer.

"His Grace is not yet receiving callers," Timmons informed him firmly.

"He will see me, sirrah, never fear. Unless he wishes to send Lady Cornwall and Miss Silverton to me instantly, I demand to speak to him."

With a sigh Timmons acquiesced, showing Morton into the smallest receiving room in the mansion while he conveyed news of this unwelcome visitor to the duke.

In no hurry to accommodate Morton, Harwood first made a leisurely toilet, and then ate breakfast. It was almost an hour later that he sauntered into the room in which his secretary usually received tradesmen and petitioners, giving his visitor an unwelcoming stare before closing the door.

Morton's temper had not improved in the intervening hour. His face was mottled with anger.

"About time! If you think to put me off by rudeness—"

"Visitors at such an ungodly hour have no business to complain of delays," Harwood snapped. "I am very busy. State your business and be off."

Morton's face turned a deeper crimson. "My business is my bride-to-be, whom you are keeping from me in direct defiance of her guardian's orders. I have a special license in my pocket, and intend to be married before the morning is over. Send her down, and I will trouble you no more."

"Whomever can you be thinking of? The only person in this house other than myself and my daughter is a friend of hers, entirely too young to be your bride."

"Don't toy with me, Harwood. You know that Lord Cornwall has given me permission to wed Miss Silverton."

The duke raised a doubting eyebrow. "That cannot be. Vincent is not a fool."

Goaded, Morton pulled Vincent's letter from his pocket. "Here! Not that I doubt for a minute Lady Cornwall has told you of it, but read this."

Harwood perused the letter with great interest, then raised eyes that glittered like polished steel. "It appears that I was mistaken in Vincent's intelligence—and yours." He folded the letter and put it into his own pocket.

"Here, now. Give that back to me!"

"Sorry I cannot oblige you. This will be very important evidence in chancery court."

"Evidence? Ch-chancery?"

"Yes, it is chancery that protects orphans, after all."

"I know that, Harwood, but only when there is no suitable guardian. In this case—"

"Just so. By allowing such a match, Vincent clearly

proves himself unsuitable. They will have only to decide whether to assume guardianship themselves or to appoint another guardian to Miss Silverton. I, of course, shall apply."

"Chancery has no jurisdiction here! Vincent was appointed by the girl's father and approved by the court—"

"But he can, I assure you, be challenged and removed for just cause, of which such an infamous betrothal is surely an instance."

"Bah! *You* may not think so, but many would believe me an excellent catch for that chit, and Cornwall to be commended for landing me." Morton puffed out his chest and threw back his head, to better display the magnificent figure he was sure he must make to an unbiased judge.

"The court might think so. I have heard whispers that occasionally bribes are successful. But it would certainly take a substantial sum. In the meantime, the *ton* might be vastly entertained at the sight of a penniless, old, fat baron aspiring to the hand of a wealthy, beautiful young heiress who should still be in the schoolroom."

"Your impertinence will be punished, sir!"

Suddenly Harwood looked alert. He had been lounging carelessly against the mantel of the fireplace. Now he stood straight, the half-hooded lids flashing open eagerly. "Are you challenging me, then? I should be most appreciative of the opportunity to treat this as a matter of honor."

It was fascinating to the duke how quickly Morton's mottled purple visage drained of color. Pale as death, the baron shook his head. "No! No! I didn't mean that. I . . ."

"Oh! Well, then." Losing interest, Harwood drifted toward the door. "That at least would have been quick. Instead, it is to be a battle of the purses. It will take years, doubtless eat up Jennifer's inheritance in the process. Your lawyers and Cornwall's against mine—a slow, expensive business.

"But mind me!" Harwood turned suddenly back to the shaken baron. "If you win, there will still be a duel to be gotten through. Put quite simply, I had much rather kill you than let you have Jennifer Silverton to wife, or her mother to mistress."

"I can't believe she told you . . ." Morton had been counting on the dowager viscountess's dread of scandal to prevent her revealing the other half of his plans.

"Aha! I guessed right!" Harwood leapt across the room and grabbed Morton by his cravat, snubbing it up so that the shorter man could hardly breathe.

"I advise you to put all thoughts of Jennifer Silverton or her mother from your mind, else you are a dead man. Write Lord Cornwall today withdrawing your proposal. Do you hear me?" Harwood shook Morton like a rat.

Terrified, Morton choked out his agreement and suddenly found himself alone in the room, gasping for breath and wondering if a repairing lease in France might not be in order. Or perhaps he should look to that too-willing widow, Lydia Smithfield, for a rich wife.

The Duke of Harwood stormed out of the room and upstairs to his library. He could never remember having been so angry before. The violence of his feelings surprised him. He found himself regretting that Morton was such a cowardly worm, for his anger was so great he didn't see how it could be quenched short of spilling that despicable man's blood.

A shudder ran through him at the thought of those fleshy lips and sweaty, pudgy hands touching either Jennifer or Deborah. It was an obscenity. The duke paced to the window and watched as Morton's curricle moved rapidly up the avenue.

The duke decided two messages must be dispatched to Woodcrest instantly, one for Vincent, making crystal clear what Morton had in mind for Deborah and Jennifer. In plain terms he would set forth his objections to the match and his willingness to intervene. The other, to Deborah, would reassure her of his unequivocal support.

Within the half hour these messages had departed in the vest pocket of one of his best grooms, mounted on his fastest saddle horse, and with the purse to hire the best cattle along the route. With luck and hard riding he would arrive at Woodcrest not too long after Deborah. *I hope she does not resent my interference*, Harwood thought. *I want to make sure Cornwall knows Deborah isn't alone.*

Chapter 14

"I'll announce myself, Croyden." Deborah pushed past Vincent's surprised butler and hastened to the Egyptian drawing room, where she felt certain she would find her brother-in-law at this time of the evening, nursing a brandy while Winnifred pricked away at her embroidery.

She had not delayed a moment since entering Woodcrest's grounds, though she was exhausted after two days of travel. She didn't want to give Vincent any advance warning, for he might avoid her and make her cool her heels for an indefinite period of time.

Croyden stared after the unusually assertive dowager viscountess, scowling. Her coming very likely meant he had lost a bet with the housekeeper, who had insisted the dowager wouldn't allow Lord Morton to wed her daughter.

Rushing into the drawing room with a militant look on her face, Deborah was standing in front of Vincent before he could quite realize she was there. "Do you wish to discuss Lord Morton here or in your library, Vincent?"

Her brother-in-law motioned with his hand, and Winnie reluctantly withdrew. She had voiced some concerns over the Morton betrothal, and Vincent didn't want to have to battle with two irate females. Winnifred was concerned that Morton's rackety ways would reflect badly on her two girls, soon to make their curtsies, and perhaps eventually cast a pall on their social ambitions for their son Brompton, still in the nursery.

"Sit down, Deborah. You look a sight. What kind of start is this, showing up on my doorstep in the dead of night—"

"Spare me these empty protestations, Vincent. I have come to ask you to withdraw your approval—nay, your command—of a match between Lord Morton and Jennifer."

"What a surprise. Will you take some tea first?"

"Don't try to fob me off, Vincent. What can you have been thinking of, giving Jennifer to such a man?"

"He has a title and is a man of taste and discernment."

"He is almost three times her age, fat, immoral, and penniless. Far from being a man of taste and discernment, he is a crude buffoon. Moreover, he is barely received."

"Is he received more widely than John Warner, recently secretary to the Duke of Harwood, whom I understand is Jennifer's preferred suitor?"

Deborah drew in a composing breath. "So that's how he convinced you. I don't suppose it would have occurred to you that it is the duke and not his secretary who courts Jennifer?"

Deborah studied the effect of this bombshell with satisfaction. Vincent's mouth had dropped open; for a rare few moments he was utterly speechless.

She had decided on this ploy while pondering their situation during the long hours spent jostling along in the coaches. The notion had grown out of her lament that, if Jennifer must marry an older man, it couldn't be one such as the Duke of Harwood. Her desperate mind clutched at this notion. It *could* be Harwood, couldn't it? He was kind, gentle, attractive, and wealthy.

Harwood had expressed himself strongly on the notion of May-December marriages, which had discouraged any such ideas on her part. But since then, Jennifer had told her of Harwood's infatuation with Sarah's friend Davida, barely older than Sarah. If he had actually considered marrying another young girl, perhaps he could be convinced to marry Jennifer.

Of course, Jenny must make him see that she would welcome him as a husband. He had made all too clear his opinion of mothers who pushed their daughters into such marriages.

While Jennifer might be surprised at the notion, she certainly couldn't find it a disgusting one. The duke, for all he was more than twice her age, was a handsome and virile man. And Vincent could hardly prefer Morton to Harwood!

Vincent's stare was less one of delight, however, than consternation. Harwood! A stellar match, one he could hardly refuse. Yet the duke doubtless would not feel it necessary to offer Vincent ten thousand pounds out of Jennifer's fortune in gratitude, as Morton had. Vincent had the baron's handwritten promissory note locked in his desk, to be paid once Jennifer's dowry was released by her trustees.

"What trick is this, Deborah! I hardly think Harwood the sort to look to so young a bride. Indeed, it was my understanding that he pursued you, and for a less honorable position than wife."

"Harwood does not yet have an heir, so a young bride is just what he will seek. And as for dishonorable intentions, it is Morton who has them, not Harwood."

"Your fanciful imagination—"

"Don't you dare! Don't try it, Vincent. The day I left London, Morton told me as plain as can be that he intended to make me his mistress, and that any recalcitrance on my part, Jennifer would pay for!" Deborah's eyes blazed with fury and contempt.

"This is the 'gentleman' you have attempted to force Jennifer to marry. He is cut from Seymour's cloth. Or do you dare to claim it was my fanciful imagination that conjured up the way your brother treated me?"

Vincent stroked his chin thoughtfully. He would never claim that, for he had been not only a witness, on more than one occasion, of his brother's brutality. When he was a boy, he had been a victim as well.

"So the duke has offered . . ."

"Not yet, not in so many words. He may pick and choose, and take his time about it. But it is obvious that Jennifer has caught his attention."

"Or that you have. You could waste the whole season trying to snag that man and end up with no husband for her at all."

"You gave me the season. Keep your word."

"And if you fail, she shall have Morton."

"Never. Not if I have to kill the man to prevent it. If you end up arranging a husband for her, it must be someone who will treat her decently. And not expect me to be his whore! Really, Vincent, I had thought better of you."

Flushing angrily, Vincent stood, mustering enough indignation to give himself a good escape line. "I had no notion of such an intention on his part, nor am I sure I believe it even yet. You get above yourself, woman. I am Jennifer's guardian, and I will decide what to do with her." He stalked to the door and jerked it open. "Go to bed, Deborah. Croyden, have a room prepared for Lady Cornwall."

"I must have an answer . . ."

"Tomorrow morning, if you have gotten yourself under better control, we will talk again. Good night, sister." Vincent gave her a curt nod and removed himself from her sight.

Fighting tears, Deborah informed Croyden that she would not be spending the night at Woodcrest. "I kept the hackney I hired. It waits outside to take me to the dower house. Betty is there, readying a room."

Croyden barely sketched a bow, still put out by losing his bet. "As you wish, madam."

Vincent spent a nearly sleepless night. When he arrived upstairs, his wife immediately began prying, and when she learned that Deborah expected an offer for Jennifer from the duke, her voice became shrill with determination.

"You mustn't stand in her way. Think how advantageous it would be to our girls, to be related to Harwood. The parties we would go to . . ."

Repressively, Vincent reminded her of the lack of affection between Deborah, Jennifer, and his family. "Your fault, you know. You haven't exactly cultivated her."

June Calvin

"Then it is time to begin. We will go to London for her ball. It is in three weeks, I believe. Perhaps he will offer by then, and you will have the opportunity to announce it at the ball. He can't cut you when he has to petition you for her hand. Don't lose any time, Vincent. Establish your position with him before the betrothal; then he will be hard put to deny us after."

When Vincent promised to take the matter under advisement, Winnie then began on the numerous disadvantages of the match with Morton. Finally, head ringing, he gruffly ordered her to shut up and retire to her room. Treated to a bout of tears as her parting shot, he then climbed into bed and found all of these arguments vying with his desire for that ten thousand pounds.

When morning came, he avoided Deborah's presence at breakfast by having a tray sent to his room. His sister-in-law had, his valet informed him, arrived at the crack of dawn, determined to see him as soon as he arose.

Vincent still didn't know what to do. Just as he was finishing his coffee, a footman scratched at the door.

"There's a messenger here, my lord." The footman, obviously impressed, held out a folded, sealed piece of heavy cream-colored writing paper. "Says he's from the Duke of Harwood."

Hastily, Vincent perused the duke's firm representations of Lord Morton's villainy. His Grace's scorn was so deep it almost scorched the pages as he denounced the betrothal of Jennifer to Morton and urged Vincent to cancel it. There was no word of a partiality to Jennifer, but reading between the lines, Vincent decided that perhaps Deborah was right. Surely, no one would take that much umbrage at the betrothal if he were not himself affected by it.

Even if Harwood wasn't considering Jennifer for a bride, it was clear that the duke meant to make trouble. A long, drawn-out legal battle would make unacceptable demands on his purse. And even if he prevailed in the end, the duke could ruin his daughters' chances of a good match.

Cringing at the thought of his wife's sharp tongue if he

did anything to harm her darlings' chances, Vincent gave up the game. Somehow he would just have to try to extort the ten thousand from Harwood, though the duke certainly had no need to pay to gain a bride. Any parents in the country would fall all over themselves to offer their daughter and a handsome dowry besides, to see her become a duchess.

His mind made up, Vincent dressed in a leisurely fashion and sauntered downstairs, pondering how to extract maximum advantage from Deborah in exchange for his capitulation.

As Deborah laid her weary head on her pillow at the dower house Wednesday evening, her daughter was making her first appearance at Almack's. The worry over Deborah's confrontation with Vincent had been kept at bay by a constant round of activity, but for Harwood and his young charges there was little pleasure in the experience. Deborah's absence had been noted, and the white lies that had to be told to halt gossip had not come easily to Jennifer or Sarah.

Jennifer was truly in fidgets by Wednesday. At dinner that evening she wished aloud that John could accompany them, for she always felt at ease in his company.

"Now, Jenny, he is not invited to Almack's, you know." Sarah regretfully reminded her friend of the exclusivity of the *ton's* premier marriage mart.

"Of course not." John laughed. "I am just such a one as Almack's was formed to keep out—a penniless nobody with some pretensions to gentility but none to nobility. Heavens, the *ton* cannot allow such as me too near innocent young maidens."

"I feel sure that I frightened Lord Morton out of his matrimonial ambitions," Harwood said, hoping to reassure Jennifer. "But even if he were brave enough to still pursue you, I have no doubts that Lord Morton will avoid any hint of scandal in the vicinity of Almack's."

Jennifer flounced in her chair. "Well, I think it is a shame that such rackety people as Lord Morton and Mr.

Fortesque can go there, and John cannot. I, for one, would much rather go with you to the ambassador's reception."

John's eyes glimmered with appreciation. "Would that I could take you, but I fear you would quickly be bored to tears with a bunch of old men gabbling in French all evening, pretending they know how to solve the problems of the world."

"You are not old. And I would love to hear what they have to say about the new Bavarian Constitution."

"Not really, Jenny!" Sarah looked perplexed at her friend's strange enthusiasm.

An hour after arriving at Almack's, Sarah was feeling that an evening at the Russian ambassador's would have been preferable to the torture of seeing Alexander tenderly introducing Anna-Marie about, securing dances for her and leading her out himself for the first dance.

Once again she found herself turning to Henry Fortesque to cover her own sense of abandonment. And once again he managed to be amusing enough that she could forget Alexander, at least during the time of their dance.

She studied her father as she returned to him from the dance floor. He was talking without much enthusiasm to a hopeful young woman whose beaming mother stood nearby. Anyone who did not know him well would suppose he was his usual dignified, self-composed self. But Sarah saw the signs of strain about his mouth, the shadows in his eyes.

Her eyes turned to Jennifer, just then being returned to the duke's side by Lord Threlbourne. Her friend also looked unhappy and wasn't bothering to hide it very well. To top matters off, gossip was growing hard to ignore or refute.

We are doing ourselves no good here tonight, Sarah thought. Thanking her partner for his escort, she stepped up to her father and whispered in his ear. Looking at Jennifer's face, and then Sarah's, the duke nodded his head. Immediately, Sarah informed the swains gathered around that she had the headache and must leave.

Sarah managed to convince her father that her headache would suffice for excuse enough for them to spend the next evening or two at home. The duke decided perhaps this was wiser than taking the youngsters about when they were obviously miserable. He certainly had little desire for the frivolous activities of the *ton* while he did not know how Deborah was faring.

So the next two evenings they stayed at home. John was commandeered for a fourth at whist, they took turns providing musical entertainment, and the duke even managed to get both girls to sit still for some chess lessons. But mostly they read or talked quietly. John and Jennifer carried the conversation a good deal of the time.

It was increasingly obvious that John and Jennifer had a great deal in common, not just in their interests, but in their serious turn of mind. Sarah took up embroidery, which she usually detested, and listened to them debating issues of the day, with her father throwing in a comment here and there.

They belong together, she thought. *They have that natural sympathy that I believed Alexander and I had.* A tear dropped on her stitches, and she wiped surreptitiously at her eyes. It would not do to let her father see her so moped. He had already offered to go to Alexander and speak to him on her behalf. Sarah had angrily refused.

"He is as good as promised to another, Papa. Do not blame yourself. Any attention he paid to me was doubtless merely to amuse himself until Anna-Marie Allistair joined him for the season," she had insisted. "I am well rid of him. I don't care so much as I thought I would, anyway." She had given a prideful toss of her head. "Mr. Fortesque is very amusing. Perhaps we shall suit."

Sarah had a feeling she hadn't convinced her father. It certainly wouldn't do to let him see her crying. She couldn't bear the humiliation of pursuing Alexander, even by proxy.

Thus they passed the anxious two days until Harwood's

messenger returned bearing a missive from Jennifer's mother.

"I told you to stay and escort her back," Harwood growled as the man appeared before him, exhausted and travel-stained.

"Yes, Your Grace, but the lady insisted I bring this message to you as fast as might be, and Lord Cornwall also sent one."

Taking the two letters from the exhausted footman, Harwood relented. "Good work, Samuel. You will be well rewarded. Now go and get some food and a good night's rest, man. You look to need it."

"Aye, that I do, Your Grace." Samuel tugged his forelock and then winked at Sarah, who was standing in the door to the blue salon, watching curiously. Jennifer and John stood right behind her.

Glancing at them as he broke the seal, Harwood disappointed the three by turning into his library to read the letters. But a few minutes later he came hurrying back into the drawing room, looking ten years younger, and swept the two young girls into an exuberant hug.

"She's done it! Vincent has withdrawn the permission."

"What does he say, Papa?"

"All that is proper." Harwood's mouth quirked ironically. "That he had no idea of Lord Morton's character, that he looks forward to making my acquaintance and so forth. He says he plans to come to your ball, Jennifer. Don't tell me he had not intended to do so?"

"No, sir, nor would he have been missed, but for this he may come, and be welcome."

There was something in the fawning, insinuating tone of Vincent's letter that set Harwood's back up, but like Jennifer he was sufficiently relieved to overlook it.

"Your mother is going to rest a day before returning. She plans to be here in good time for Eberlin's picnic. Here, you'll want to read this."

Harwood relinquished the letter to Jennifer and hugged his daughter against his left side as he extended his right hand to John. "Crisis over! We can get back to normal now."

"Yes," John sighed, his eyes following Jennifer's lithe figure as she danced about the room with her mother's letter held on high.

Chapter 15

After a tearful, joyful reunion with her daughter, Deborah urged her to get ready to leave. Eager to impart her plan to Jennifer, she declined an invitation to dine with the Harwoods, firmly asserting that it was time to take themselves off.

Jennifer and Sarah scampered away to find Mittens, leaving Deborah to sincerely thank the duke for taking care of her child.

"You owe equal thanks to John, who guarded her like a miser's gold."

This was troubling news. Deborah frowned anxiously. "I am grateful for his help, but I hope they've formed no greater attachment than friendship would allow. Morton had told Vincent that I was permitting Mr. Warner to court her. That was one reason he gave his permission for that vile betrothal. He made it very clear to me—"

"Pax, Deborah. I understand." The duke's smile was regretful, but not condemning. He took her hand and patted it. "I only hope these two young people can."

"The duke? You must be bamming me, Mother!"

"Please do not use such improper terms, Jennifer. Cant sounds so unattractive on a young lady's lips."

Jennifer dropped her head. "Sorry, but . . ."

Deborah launched into an explanation of the reasons that Jennifer should set her cap for the duke. Her daughter listened quietly, the large brown eyes serious, as befit such a serious subject.

A deep sigh signaled Jennifer's capitulation. "Very well, Mother. I don't think it will serve, but I will try. But I am quite sure the duke has a *tendre* for you—"

"You know I will not—"

"And I can't imagine a dignified, intelligent man like the Duke of Harwood being caught by a green girl like me."

"I am not suggesting 'catching' him; I am suggesting engaging his affections."

"He is like a father to me—like what I would have wished my father to be. And I am sure his feelings for me are strictly paternal."

"I don't doubt that they are, now. But you are a very attractive young woman. It is up to you to change his mind."

"But what of Lord Threlbourne? Lord Eberlin? Or even Mr. Fortesque?" Jennifer's heart was crying out, *What of John*, but she knew better than to give voice to this sentiment.

"I haven't changed my opinion of Mr. Fortesque. Yes, you should continue to encourage Lord Threlbourne. Eberlin does not seem to be on the hunt for a wife, but perhaps I am wrong. If it becomes clear that you will fail with the duke, either of them would be acceptable to Vincent."

Deborah tipped her child's head up by gently grasping her chin and looked directly into the sad brown eyes, as if she had heard the silent cry of Jennifer's heart. "Acceptable to Vincent, do you understand? He made it very clear that Mr. John Warner was not in the least eligible."

"How did he know . . . ?"

"It seems Lord Morton told Vincent of John's attentiveness. It is a man's world, alas. We cannot direct our own affairs; all we can do is to try to modify the terms of our slavery."

A mulish look chased the sadness from Jennifer's face. "With John Warner I would not be a slave."

"No, with him you would be a pauper."

"I don't care. It isn't true, anyway. We would live modestly, but better than most people on the earth, you know. I would live in a hut and eat gruel rather than—"

"Jennifer! I must know if you are going to try an elopement."

Jennifer looked away, hands fidgeting with the fringe on a sofa cushion. "Nothing has been said. But I would gladly . . ."

"My poor child. You must realize that a runaway marriage would doom Mr. Warner's career in politics. That would be a great shame, wouldn't it?"

Jennifer whirled around. "Oh, no! I hadn't thought. But it would, wouldn't it. The scandal . . ."

"Precisely."

"But England needs moderate reformers like John."

"Then you must act the unselfish part and choose another husband. If you cannot do this, then I must tell you that I think it is time to sell my jewelry and go to America."

"America!"

Deborah stood and strode agitatedly about the room. "Yes. I have thought of it a great deal. Rather than let you marry Morton, I would kill him, if I could. But then I would go to prison, perhaps die, and Vincent would be left with absolute power to choose another husband as bad as he or worse. Do you understand, daughter? This is a very dangerous situation."

"Lord Morton wants more than just me, doesn't he?"

A deep flush stained Deborah's cheeks. "My poor child. I wouldn't have had you know that for the world. But can you think of the horror for both of us, each the hostage of the other's misery."

"Oh, Mama! That odious, odious man!" Jennifer launched herself into her mother's arms. "I shall do as you say. I promise that either Lord Threlbourne or His Grace, the Duke of Harwood, shall be my husband."

Jennifer had an opportunity to test her power over the Duke of Harwood the very next evening, when he escorted the three women to *The Merchant of Venice* at the Theatre Royal in Drury Lane. Jennifer subtly maneuvered, with her mother's help, so that she sat next to the duke. During the entr'acte, she asked him careful questions about the play and his evaluation of the acting of Edmund Kean.

Somewhat startled by this sudden show of interest by Sarah's young friend, Harwood tried to catch Deborah's eye, but she avoided looking directly at him, instead employing her opera glasses to carefully study the boxes across the way and comment upon them to Sarah, who sat next to her.

During the supper that followed, Jennifer continued to engage the duke in conversation as often as she could. Sarah was beginning to notice something different, too. Perplexed, she stared at her friend, who had hitherto reacted to the duke just as she ought to a dignified older man. She was actually batting her eyes at him!

Why, she's acting as if he were a man! Sarah hadn't questioned the likes of Lydia Smithfield trying to entice her father; after all, he was rich and unmarried, and she was old, too. But Jennifer? The notion of her friend seeking to attach her father seemed most odd.

There was no opportunity to discover her intentions, though, because when she arose and suggested Jennifer accompany her to the withdrawing room, Lady Cornwall quickly stood, too, and joined them. She kept them busy with mild gossip until they rejoined the duke.

At home Harwood asked his daughter if she had noticed Jennifer's behavior.

"Yes, and I thought it quite odd at first. But I have been thinking. I believe she is grateful to you for helping her. Her new interest in you doubtless is the result of that gratitude."

Harwood grinned ruefully. "Of course. You don't suspect me of believing she feels any sort of attraction for me, do you?"

Sarah put her arms around her father, hugging him tightly. "You are a devastatingly handsome man, Father, for a man of your age. Any older woman would be mad for you."

"Thank you, sweetheart." The duke grinned. "You are so very good for my *amour propre,* my love."

Seeing no irony in this statement, Sarah returned his smile.

The duke sadly watched his daughter mount the stairs. Smiles had been few and halfhearted for her most of the evening, for once again she had been forced to observe Lord Alexander Meade courting Anna-Marie Allistair. Once again she had turned to the eager attentions of Mr. Henry Fortesque, who probably didn't guess what her father clearly saw—that she feigned most of those brilliant smiles at his witty repartee.

Still, he thought as he loosened his cravat before repairing to his library for a brandy, she hadn't withdrawn into herself the way she had this summer, and he had Mr. Fortesque to thank for it. *Must see about inviting that young man for dinner soon,* he thought.

The next evening was a ball at the home of the Penton-Smythes. Again the Harwoods were invited to dinner and the Cornwalls were not. The ball was already under way when Deborah and her daughter arrived. To the duke's great surprise Deborah accepted an invitation to dance after Jennifer left her side, partnered by Lord Threlbourne.

Harwood did not like the shaft of jealousy that pierced him. He hadn't the right to feel it, nor was it wise considering how carefully the dowager viscountess kept him at arm's length.

When the set ended, Sarah was returned to him, and to his relief Jennifer's escort delivered her to him also. That meant Deborah would soon join him.

"I am so glad Mama decided to dance, are you not, sir? I think she deserves some pleasure. It must get very tedious for you, too, standing about all evening, watching Sarah."

"It hasn't seemed so, actually. I've had your mother to visit with, you know, until this evening." The duke tried to keep reproach from his tone, not entirely succeeding.

"Oh, but then you must dance, too. It is as I told

Mama—I am not a green girl, anymore, that she must watch my every move, and I am quite sure Sarah knows how to conduct herself, don't you think?"

"Of course, but—"

"That's settled, then. Will you dance this minuet with me? Most of my friends don't like it. They think it terribly old-fashioned, but I like its elegance."

"Oh, do dance, Papa. You know you want to. I'll be quite all right. Gilbert and I are going to find the punch bowl."

"That is, if you don't mind, sir." Threlbourne waited for the duke's permission, but he was obviously eager to be off. "Truth to tell, I'm one of the ones who avoids the minuet. I always feel like a crane stalking through a marsh instead of a dancer."

Chuckling, Harwood glanced from his three young tempters to Deborah, who was standing several feet away, looking up into the kindly, wrinkle-lined face of Sir Horace Darby. She clearly intended to allow the old knight to lead her out for the next dance.

"I would be honored," he said, offering Jennifer his arm with a smile.

Jennifer returned the smile eagerly, and they joined another couple as the music began.

Jennifer danced well and looked exceptionally lovely this evening. Harwood felt a glow of pride in her, once again pleased and impressed with how far she had progressed since the first ball of the season. Lady Penton-Smythe would not find any reason for criticism now.

He enjoyed the dance and told her so quite sincerely afterward. But he managed to guide their steps so that they would be standing near her mother when the dance was ended.

"Well, it seems we have decided to dance."

Deborah looked a little self-conscious as she turned to face the duke. "I am glad Jennifer talked me into it. You surely have been holding back out of kindness to me, and . . ."

"Nonsense. I had far rather visit with you among the chaperones than dance with anyone else on the floor."

Deborah stiffened and looked serious. "You must not say so, sir!"

Harwood contented himself with a raised eyebrow. "The next dance is a waltz. Will you stand up with me?"

"Oh, I, uh, that is, I was hoping . . ." She glanced helplessly at her daughter, who was standing nearby with several young people. At just that moment Jennifer moved a bit closer to the duke.

"Thank you, Mr. Lanscombe, but you know I do not yet waltz. The patronesses of Almack's have not approved me to do so yet. I have already agreed to promenade with the duke." She put her hand lightly on Harwood's arm and looked up appealingly into his face.

The duke could but agree and lead her away, grinding his jaw a little at seeing from the corner of his eye that Deborah was standing up with Lord Eberlin. Jennifer's manner during this promenade was blatantly flirtatious. The duke felt a prickle at the back of his neck, almost like a warning of danger. And indeed, any man might feel himself in danger when a lovely young woman like Jennifer brought all her newly-learned sophistication to bear on him. He frowned at the tall, slender girl at his side.

"What May game are you up to, Jennifer?"

"I . . . What do you mean, sir?"

"Dear child, do you not know that you are doing an excellent imitation of a young miss setting her cap for an old man?"

Jennifer flushed to the roots of her hair, but defended herself. "You are not an old man; you are a highly eligible *parti* and I am a grown woman. Why should I not let you know that I enjoy your company."

"Why not, indeed?" The duke looked thoughtfully down into the limpid brown eyes. "If this is somehow the result of my championing your cause . . ."

"You were magnificent. I can never thank you enough."

"I do not require your thanks, only the satisfaction of knowing that you are happy."

"There! Who could not be all admiration for someone so kind and selfless," Jennifer said with enthusiasm.

"I do not doubt the sincerity of this sentiment, but I have no wish to take advantage of your gratitude." The duke patted her hand where it rested on his arm. "You save those fluttering eyelashes and flashing dimples for young Threlbourne or some other young blade, my dear." The duke decided it was time to end the conversation, for Jennifer was beginning to look upset.

"Here is another dance, and a young swain approaching with a mission in mind."

Reluctantly, Jennifer joined her partner for the next dance, looking back soulfully at the duke as she was led away.

The duke rubbed his chin thoughtfully, his eyes turning to Deborah. She was standing with Sarah, looking most uncomfortable as Sir Alfred Morley, a man with a rakish reputation, appeared to be attempting to engage her for the next dance.

"Excuse me, Sir Alfred, but I believe this was the dance I had reserved. Or was I mistaken in the matter, Lady Cornwall?"

Deborah accepted the invitation gratefully, though it seemed to him she looked rather torn by the necessity. It was a country dance, never one of the duke's favorites, but worth it to aid Deborah. He turned to check on Sarah and found her accepting Henry Fortesque's invitation to dance with apparent pleasure, which relieved him greatly, for Alexander was nowhere in sight. Perhaps this might indicate she was starting to truly enjoy Fortesque's company.

Beginning to dance opened a Pandora's box for both Harwood and Lady Cornwall, for women of all ages began making a bid to dance with him, and without being absolutely insulting, he found he must offer to lead several young and not-so-young ladies onto the floor. It was much the same for Deborah, and he was not surprised to see her plead the headache and take a seat after supper.

He did not join her, however. He had not liked the reluctance she had shown to dance with him, nor the stiffness of her behavior during the country dance. He would not foist his company on an unwilling woman!

Instead, the duke, after telling Sarah where he would be, took a turn in the card room, reappearing only when he judged his daughter would be ready to return home.

He found Jennifer with her. The two girls were laying plans to ride in the park the next morning. "Will you give us your escort, sir," Jennifer asked, looking at him hopefully.

"Of course, Jennifer. You will join us, Deborah?"

"No, I thank you, Harwood. I have a great deal of work to do toward Jennifer's ball. Vincent sent a letter with me that I hope has awakened the servants to their duty. I must get the house turned out, and invitations addressed, and—"

"I understand." The duke's mouth curled at one corner. *And I do,* he thought, secretly planning to call on Lady Cornwall very soon. It was clear that her daughter had somehow decided she must have the duke for a husband, and Deborah was trying to help her.

There was such a thing as carrying doting motherhood and complacent friendship too far, though. He would nip such thoughts in the bud the very next day.

Chapter 16

The duke bounded up the steps to the Dowager Viscountess of Cornwall's doors, mischievously aware that the lady probably did not want to see him. She had proclaimed the necessity of remaining home to work on Jennifer's ball, however, so she would hardly be able to tell her servants to say she was not at home to him.

A footman answered the door punctiliously, and the butler announced him properly before escorting him into Deborah's presence. Apparently, Vincent's admonition to the servants had borne fruit.

"Harwood. Is anything wrong? Where are the girls?" Deborah stood, scanning his features anxiously.

"Nothing at all, my dear. I left the two of them at home with their heads together over Ackerman's latest drawings. I needed to speak with you privately, you see."

Relieved, yet suddenly wary, Deborah came from behind her desk. "Let us go into the drawing room. This room is too cramped for entertaining visitors."

She slipped past him and led the way.

"Now," the duke began after refusing refreshments. "No more stalling, Deborah! I have something to say to you about Jennifer."

A worry line appeared between Deborah's eyes. "You said there was nothing wrong—"

"She has apparently taken it into her head to enthrone me as a knight in shining armor, to whom she must perforce offer herself, because of the role I played with Lord Morton."

"That's only partially true. She has come to admire you very much."

"I can hardly believe you seem so complacent about this. Shouldn't you be alarmed to find your daughter throwing herself at a man over twice her age?"

"You are hardly an elderly man! Your age is not an impediment." Embarrassed and distressed at this plain speaking, Deborah nevertheless persisted. "You would make Jennifer an excellent husband. So as her mother I can but hope she has not given you a disgust of her, by her obvious bid for your attention."

"Not that, of course, but . . ."

"And she would make you an excellent wife, Harwood, could you but see it. She is well-mannered and biddable, and knows how to manage a great house—"

"Acquit me of such folly as taking a sixteen-year-old girl to wife!" The duke was suddenly angry that Deborah could be so obtuse.

"B-but you very nearly married a girl scarcely older than Jennifer last year." Deborah bit her lower lip to still its trembling. Harwood had never been angry with her before. Old fears and new sensibilities combined to make her extremely uneasy at his scowl and sharp tone.

"I suppose I have Sarah to thank for passing on that evidence of my loss of sanity. Well, I did contemplate it all of ten minutes, but I thank God I was saved from having to live with the consequences of my temporary madness. No, Deborah. I have another candidate for wife in my eye, one much more suitable to a man of my age and very much to my taste besides." With a swift movement the duke possessed himself of Deborah's hand. He carried it to his lips before she had a chance to adjust to this sudden change in mood.

On a gasp she pulled away and stood, pacing the length of the room in agitation before turning to him. "I assumed Jennifer had confided in Sarah, and that you had some inkling of what my marriage was like. I have no intention of ever marrying again."

"Odd. You consider me entirely ineligible as a husband for yourself, yet wish me to wed your daughter."

"Jennifer must wed and soon, by her guardian's decree, or I would have her remain single."

Deborah raised her chin and stared at him down her patrician nose.

"I see." Harwood stood and walked slowly toward Deborah. She stood her ground until the last minute, then attempted to turn, but his hands on her forearms gently restrained her.

"Tell me about your marriage, Deborah."

She averted her face. "I can't. I couldn't bear it."

"Did he beat you?"

"I don't wish to discuss it."

Seeing how distressed she was, the duke let her pull away. He sighed deeply. "Well, I am sorry, but I cannot marry your daughter, for even if I were so foolish as to marry a chit just out of the schoolroom, I certainly wouldn't marry the daughter of the woman I love."

Deborah faced him suddenly. "You mustn't say that!"

"No, mustn't I?" He smiled tenderly. "Well, then I won't. Your wish is my command. May we remain friends, at least?"

To his surprise Deborah put her hands to her face in horror and exclaimed, "Oh, my God! What shall I do?"

"What is it, my dear?"

"It's Vincent. Oh, can't you just at least try to care for Jennifer?"

"I already care for her, as a daughter. Has Vincent ordered her to attach me?"

The duke had to lean forward, for Deborah whispered her admission. "I convinced him that you were courting her. That is why he agreed to cancel the betrothal to Lord Morton. If he sees that you are not, and if there is no other titled suitor in sight, he will force her to wed Dolphus."

"No, he will not, for I made Morton see that pursuing that marriage would be a death-defying act. In short, I promised to challenge him if he persisted. He has escorted Lydia Smithfield to France."

"He has?" For an instant Deborah looked relieved, but then her brow creased again. "Vincent will just find another such."

She walked back to the sofa and sank down. "It is as I feared. We shall have to go to America. I shall have to sell my jewelry and . . ."

The duke joined her. "America! Don't be ridiculous."

She rounded on him, furious. "I'm not being ridiculous. He told me so himself. He said, 'I know at least five titled lords who would wed Jennifer in an instant and pay me every cent as much as Morton was to do, for the privilege.' "

The duke's grey eyes took on the steely glitter that had made Morton shudder. "Payment! Is that what made him agree to such a match?"

"Yes. Ten thousand pounds is the price for which he is willing to sell my daughter." Deborah did not tell him that Vincent had ordered her to obtain such a sum from Harwood, an order which she had firmly refused.

Suddenly, the hopelessness of the situation overwhelmed Deborah, and she began to weep copious, hopeless tears. Harwood could not resist comforting her. He pulled her into his arms and stroked her hair until she had calmed down.

Tear still drenched the brown eyes she at last lifted to meet his. "Will you help me sell my jewelry? I fear I will be taken advantage of."

"You're that afraid of Vincent's machinations?"

"Yes, oh yes! With his permission and a special license, she could be spirited away and irrevocably wed within a half hour's time. If he comes up to London for her ball and does not find you dancing attendance on her, or another *parti* as eligible as you, he will certainly approach one of his candidates for her hånd the next day!"

Harwood sighed. "Then it looks as if I had better be very attentive to little Miss Silverton, doesn't it? But sooner or later Vincent will realize the truth, for I won't marry her. It would be a disastrous mistake to do so, for all three of us." *And for a fourth,* the duke added to himself, thinking of John.

"Lord Threlbourne has been paying her a great deal of attention. He may yet come up to scratch, if we can only gain some time." Deborah searched the duke's face anxiously.

"Ah." Harwood leaned back. "Yes, I have seen him with her several times." The duke considered Deborah as she sat there, despair and hope warring on her face. She was desperate. The last thing he wanted to do was let her get away to America. If he could keep her nearby, his own hopes that he could bring her to love him were still very much alive. But let her set sail . . . no! So he would have to appear to court her daughter for a while.

Wincing at the thought of John's reaction, the duke slowly stood up and looked down into the anxious brown eyes. "Very well, Deborah. I will spend sufficient time with your daughter to at least justify the suspicion that I am courting her. We can begin this very night at the Vauxhall party if you wish."

"Oh, yes, I do! I had been about to cry off, for both of us, as I am so busy. Would you escort Jennifer?"

"Yes. And if need be, I will have a very serious talk with Vincent."

Deborah shook her head. "Vincent would not take meekly to being menaced the way Morton did. I fear you'd have a duel on your hands if you tried such a thing." She stood and dabbed at her eyes with a handkerchief.

"That might not be an entirely bad idea, sweet watering pot." Harwood's long, slender fingers closed over the scrap of lacy cloth as he took it from her and applied it where it would do the most good. Then he cupped her chin. "Be brave, Deborah. You are not alone. I will stand your friend."

"Thank you, Harwood." She offered him her hand. Instead of shaking it as she had intended, he once again car-

ried it to his lips. Surprised at the pleasant shiver this brief
contact with his lips caused, she stood rooted to the spot as
he strode from her drawing room, a slight smile on his face.

Vauxhall was a squeeze. It seemed as if the entire *ton*
had turned out, and every mushroom and Cit, too. The duke
saw that he would have his hands full, watching after the
safety of both young women. Thus it was that he gladly
turned Sarah over to Henry Fortesque soon after they arrived, only warning the young man in cordial but firm tones
not to decide to take her away from the lighted area for a
stroll along any of the dark walks.

Jennifer startled her friends by refusing to join the
younger set. Her mother had explained that the duke would
pretend to court her. She told her daughter, "What I hope is
that he will find himself enamoured of you as he gets to
know you. The pretense must become reality."

After the concert, the duke rose to dance with Jennifer.
From behind them, a hearty masculine voice boomed out.

"Harwood, as I live and breathe. You sly dog." It was
Roger Vine, a crony of his from Eton and Oxford. Looking
Jennifer up and down in a most improper fashion, the stout
squire demanded, "Introduce me to the fair incognita."

"Roger!" The duke shook his old friend's hand, but
hastily disabused him of any mistaken notions as to Jennifer's class. "This is Jennifer Silverton, daughter of the
late Viscount Cornwall."

"Ah, yes." Roger lifted a quizzing glass ostentatiously.
"Heard she was a beauty, like her mother. Never thought to
hear of you robbing the cradle, but looking at her, I can see
why you couldn't resist."

Jennifer gave Vine a graceful curtsy and looked at Harwood for direction.

The duke was embarrassed by the man's lascivious look.
Denial was on the tip of his tongue, but he had promised
Deborah. And besides, Roger was just the sort of gossip
who would see that news was put about that he was courting Jennifer.

So instead, the duke patted Jennifer's hand, tucked it under his arm, and with a curt "Quite so," excused themselves, as the dance was about to begin.

"Going to marry a breeder after all, Justin? Young Andrew not shaping up as you would like? Well, can't blame you. A man likes to sire his own heir, especially with such a delicious young morsel for a dam, eh?"

Wondering why he had ever made friends with such a crude man, the duke whisked Jennifer out of earshot of Roger's suggestive speculations.

Jennifer reported the entire evening in detail to her mother, including the duke's embarrassment and her own sense of unease at putting him in such a position. Deborah was distressed to find she had caused Harwood to become the object of jests and sly innuendoes.

The day of the planned trip to Richmond dawned fair and warm, but blustery. As a result, plans to drive out in the young men's curricles were put aside in favor of closed carriages. There was some obvious tension between Justin and Deborah in the Duke of Harwood's carriage, but Jennifer and Sarah's lively spirits soon dispelled it.

"I have the perfect idea. Let us play Twenty Questions," Sarah suggested. "And let the object be something we can typically see from our carriage window."

"Let me be first," Jennifer begged, giving an eager little bounce on the carriage seat. "I already have something in mind!" They quickly drew the two adults into the game, which kept them all well occupied until they arrived at their rendezvous at the Star and Garter.

There they found that Lord Eberlin had modified their plans a little because of the wind, which continued to erupt in strong gusts.

"No pleasure in fighting tablecloths or eating dirt," he asserted. "I've taken a large dining room. The innkeeper and my servants are setting it up now."

Once they were all assembled, about twenty guests were found to have accepted Lord Eberlin's hospitality. The indoor picnic featuring a wide array of delicacies took the better part of two hours to consume, and by the time they were finished, all the guests were in agreement that some exercise was just what was required to aid the digestion.

The hilly promenades around the Star and Garter challenged several of the young couples to try to climb higher, the better to admire the picture the Thames made coiling through the valley below.

The duke offered his arm to Deborah as their children, accompanied by their escorts Henry Fortesque and Gilbert, Lord Threlbourne, joined a noisy coterie in making the climb. Alexander and Anna-Marie were in this group, but Sarah appeared to take no notice of them. She seemed to be entirely absorbed in conversation with Henry.

The knot of young people drifted ahead of their chaperones, chattering gaily about the day and quizzing each other as they climbed a steep path to the next rise.

Justin and Deborah walked in silence. Justin was grateful that Jennifer already had an escort today, so that he wasn't required to spend his time with her. Even silent and embarrassed, Deborah's company was what he craved.

The two were startled when the front ranks of the young people ahead of them suddenly broke and milled about for a few seconds, peculiar exclamations hinting at something extraordinary on the rise above. Then they beat a hasty retreat back along the path.

"What's wrong?" Deborah asked, noting her daughter's abashed countenance.

Gilbert, his face as red as his hair, stammered out, "Someone's up there, ma am, ah . . . two someones, having a picnic on the height."

The duke raised a curious eyebrow.

"A *private* picnic, sir," Henry clarified with a knowing smile.

Alexander gave his friend an indignant look, his own expression clearly saying this was not a subject for levity. "Best not to take Lady Cornwall up there, sir."

"Ah! I see. Yes, well, doubtless as fine a view can be obtained elsewhere." The duke waited until the youngsters had all passed them in pursuit of an alternate destination before turning back to Deborah.

"I'm grateful Sarah and Jennifer were not at the very front. From the look on all their faces that must be a rather scandalous assignation taking place up there." With his chin Harwood indicated the rise a few feet above them.

A little embarrassed herself, Deborah turned and took his offered arm. "The wind is picking up again," she remarked, changing the subject.

A strong sudden gust could be seen twisting tree branches, bending grass, and blowing up skirts as it swooped up the hill. Squeals of laughter from the young women below accompanied the blast as it whipped up a little whirlwind of dust along the footpath.

Deborah let go of the duke's arm to grasp her hat with one hand and her skirts with the other.

"Look out!" The duke tried to turn her facing away from the dust cloud, but too late.

"Oh! My eyes!" Deborah let her skirt and hat go to shield herself. "I've gotten sand . . . oh!" She felt as if she'd had a fist full of dirt thrown in her face. Blinking rapidly, she instinctively started to rub her eyes.

"Here, don't, let me see." One strong hand detained her own as the duke tilted her chin up with the other. She couldn't hold her eyes open for him to examine. They were fluttering of their own will, and she trembled with pain. Again she tried to wipe away the torturing dirt.

"Dee, wait. Don't!" Once again Harwood grabbed both hands. "You'll scratch your eyes and cause a serious problem. You need some water."

"Yes, yes! Please get some from the inn," she almost sobbed.

"Too far. Sit down." The duke pushed her onto the grass beside the path. "Wait here," he commanded urgently, "and whatever you do, don't scratch your eyes."

Biting her lip, Deborah nodded, folding her hands in her

lap and twining her fingers together to keep from tearing at the maddening sensation.

Harwood vaulted up the path in three giant strides and topped the crest, where he surprised a couple in a passionate embrace beneath a tree. What few clothes the lovely Cyprian in Harrison Curzon's arms was wearing had been considerably disarranged, and Curzon groaned as he levered himself away from her.

"Not again . . . can't you young cubs . . . Duke!"

"I need water immediately." Harwood had already scanned the picnic cloth beside the pair.

" 'Fraid all we have is wine, but . . . "

Seizing the bucket of ice and melted water, Harwood tossed the wine bottle down beside Curzon. "Excuse me, no time to explain," drifted back to them as the duke disappeared down the hill.

"Here, Dee." Suddenly, Deborah felt strong arms gather her as Harwood, dropping down beside her, sat the bucket in front of her. "It'll be cold, but . . ."

Between blinks Deborah saw the water in the ice bucket and eagerly began dipping it out, splashing it in her eyes. After several minutes she stopped, shuddering with cold, and blinked experimentally.

"Better?"

"Much, but it still feels like I've got a rock in my right eye."

"Let me see." The duke tilted her chin up and gently lifted the twitching lid. "Ah, I see it, in the upper right corner. More like a log, actually." He gave her an encouraging smile. "I'll get it."

Before she knew what was happening, she found herself lifted onto his lap and laid back across his arm.

"What?" She tried to sit up.

Removing a snowy handkerchief from his pocket, the duke gave her a little shake, settling her back against his arm, as he murmured in a soothing voice, "Be still. I am going to do delicate surgery here. Open your eye wide."

She obeyed, resisting the violent urge to continue blinking her eyelid. Holding his kerchief so that the very tip of one corner barely extended from his thumb and index finger, the duke gently, delicately probed and stroked the bit of matter.

"Such a tiny bit of chaff, yet I know it feels like an entire haystack in your eye. You're a brave one. Just hold still a moment longer, I've almost . . . ah!"

"Is . . . is it gone?"

"I think so. Open your eye as wide as you can. Look up. Look down." As he examined her eye carefully, Deborah could feel his warm breath on her face, which was chilled by the cold water she had splashed over it.

"Looks good. Let's rinse it a bit more. No, don't move. I want to direct some water right on that area."

So saying, he cupped his big hand in the ice bucket and carefully dribbled the water over her eye.

She jerked as the cold water splashed her eye and ran down her face. He shifted so that she was more firmly in his arms and talked to her soothingly as he continued laving the eye. At last, satisfied, he cupped her head tenderly in his hand.

"How does it feel when you blink now?"

She tried one or two deliberate blinks, which quickly degenerated into distressed flutterings again. "It hurts," she moaned, "though not as much."

"I think it is scratched. I don't see any more matter to be washed out. Just lie still a few moments. Let your tears soothe it."

Deborah closed her eyes, permitting them to blink at will. Gradually, the pain lessened and the tension left her body. She became aware of being cold, as the breeze whipped through her wet clothing. A shiver caused the duke to wrap his arms about her, sheltering and warming her. With a sigh she relaxed against him.

In the quiet that settled over them, the duke heard a slight sound from above. Harrison Curzon was standing not far away, observing. Harwood shook his head, then glanced at the bucket with a wordless command.

Grinning, Curzon silently stepped forward and picked it up, then as silently disappeared back toward the curious woman peeping over the rise.

Giggles and shouts from below penetrated Deborah's reverie, and she opened bloodshot eyes.

"The children," she gasped.

"The children are fine. I can see them clearly. They're in the trees just below, cavorting like puppies."

"I . . . should get up." Awareness of her position had Deborah's face turning to match her eyes, yet she was curiously reluctant to escape.

"Not just yet. Relax." Harwood gently combed her hair from her face. "You've had a painful experience. Let yourself recover."

His hand was so soothing as it brushed her hair and smoothed her brow. Deborah let her eyes drift closed. It registered on her that his hand was sinking oh, so gently into her hair, his fingers curling around and behind her head, his thumb stroking her neck and ear.

It was a caress, she realized, and she knew she ought to stop it, but it felt so good. She could never recall such a warm feeling from any other human touch. Certainly Seymour had never . . .

At the thought of Seymour, Deborah's eyes flew open and surprised such a look of tenderness on Harwood's face that she was stunned.

"Dee," he breathed, moving his thumb forward to feather a caress across her lips. "Dearest Dee."

"Justin." Deborah lifted her hand, brushing the silver streak at his temple in an unconscious imitation of his movements. His hair was silky beneath her fingers. She stroked her trembling hand over his hair, savoring its smooth texture.

For a long, trembling moment they looked at each other, and then Harwood began to lower his head.

Chapter 17

*H*e's going to kiss me, Deborah realized, wondering at herself for lying there so passively. Part of her wanted to push him away; part of her wanted to urge him closer. As his lips settled softly on hers, Deborah moaned, half in desire, half in alarm.

His lips seemed so warm on hers, and their pressure, at once firm and gentle, led her to slip her hand behind his neck and cling to him for a few sizzling seconds.

Then, recollecting herself, Deborah pulled away, shaking her head. Instantly he released her. Still regarding her tenderly, Harwood nevertheless respected her obvious wish to rise. He helped her to stand, rose himself, and found her hat. He stood patiently while she brushed herself free of as much dirt and grass as she could, averting her face from him all the while.

His eyes on her were unnerving. What was he thinking? That she was a wanton, doubtless, on whom he could press his attentions at the earliest opportunity. She felt a bit of a wanton right now! Her body seemed to glow with pleasure from their kiss.

"Thank you so much for helping me with my eye, Justin," she murmured, embarrassed. How could she have let such a thing happen?

Showing no similar embarrassment, the duke shrugged. "We were fortunate indeed that Mr. Curzon was picknicking so close by."

"It was Mr. Curzon at the top of the hill, who threw the young people in such panic?"

"They don't call him 'The Golden Rake' for nothing."

"I am thankful, then, that Jennifer discouraged his attentions." Deborah primmed her mouth and started briskly down the path, this time sheltering her eyes against the wind.

"So the children are in plain sight right below," she snapped, stopping abruptly as she realized the view was devoid of humanity.

Harwood stepped up beside her, chagrin in his voice. "I guess while my attention was focused, ah, elsewhere, they moved on. Come. Let me get you in out of this wind and then I will find them."

A general movement back to the Star and Garter had left Sarah and her escort behind, for Henry had used the brief absence of chaperonage to maneuver Sarah a little away from the group. He quickly took advantage of the tête-à-tête to declare his love for her.

"Mr. Fortesque," Sarah responded, alarmed by his proximity and their isolation. "You should not be speaking to me so before receiving my father's permission. And I am sure this is not the place . . ."

"Forgive me, Sarah. You look so fetching today, and I am growing desperate for some sign of hope. I do not wish to offer for you unless I know you would like it." He took her hand and peeled back her glove to expose the slender white wrist, which he pressed to his lips while watching her expression carefully.

Sarah's nostrils flared at the touch of flesh against flesh. It was unexpectedly pleasant. Her eyes met his, surprise clear in her expression.

"I think you are not indifferent to me." Henry slid his arm around her waist and drew her close.

"N-no, but this is not proper, and . . ."

"Sarah, do you have another suitor whom you prefer? Is it still Alexander?"

Drawing back as far as his restraining arm would allow,

THE DUKE'S DESIRE 171

she gave a rueful smile. "I am sorry, Fort. I do like you, very much. But at one time I had hoped, had believed . . ."

"I understand. You were disappointed by his engagement to Anna-Marie." Henry dropped his arm and stood back.

"Then he *is* engaged to her?"

"Not yet. He appears to be hovering between that and going to India."

Sarah looked at the ground, moving her toe back and forth despondently. "Oh! I see."

Henry took her hand and tucked it under his arm, patting her hand gently. "At least tell me whether I have reason to hope?"

He was being very sweet and understanding, Sarah thought. And indeed, why should she not encourage him? Her father seemed pleased by her friendship with him. He was very likeable and devastatingly attractive. She was no longer sure she felt equal to choosing spinsterhood; if for no other reason, pride dictated that she not wear the willow permanently for Alexander Meade. She could do much worse than Henry Fortesque.

Eyes demurely averted, she told Henry, "We should become better acquainted, to see if we shall suit."

"Say no more. I am content. And now I had better get you back to our friends before your father finds us alone together and calls me out." He led her briskly to rejoin the knot of young people from one direction just as the Duke of Harwood strolled up from the other. Sarah and Henry exchanged conspiratorial grins as they melted into the crowd before the duke spotted them.

Jennifer was sweetly sympathetic to Deborah's need to leave the picnic early. Once their maid had undressed the viscountess and put her to bed, Jenny treated Deborah's eyes with warm salt water and then sat with her in the darkened room.

"Did you have a good time today, dear? I hope Lord Threlbourne wasn't provoked that we had to leave early."

There was a long, pregnant silence.

"Jennifer?"

"Oh, Mama, I hate to distress you when you are not feeling well."

Deborah sat up, dislodging the cloth over her eyes. "What is it, sweetheart?"

"Nothing so terrible, Mama. But . . . but I do believe I had better concentrate on winning the duke's affections."

Deborah collapsed against the pillows. "Why do you say that? Has Lord Threlbourne behaved badly?"

"Oh, no, Mama. Never that. It is just that Gilbert spent most of our time together talking about his cousin. He thought she would make her come-out this year, and then they would be married, but she declared herself unwilling and her parents kept her home to punish her.

"He is distressed about it, thinks this is the wrong way to deal with her. It is very clear to me from the way he worries over her that he loves her."

"Oh, my. That doesn't sound promising, does it?" Deborah put the cloth back over her eyes.

"So you see, it will just have to be the duke." Jennifer's voice lacked any enthusiasm or conviction.

"Yes." Deborah sighed. Before today this announcement would have delighted her, so why did she now feel the prick of tears at the back of her eyes?

Still, nothing had changed, really. "Yes, it will."

"Are you trifling with her, or are you going to offer for her soon?" Alexander stood head to head with Henry. He had seen Sarah return with Fort from their tête-à-tête and was determined to know his friend's intentions.

"Don't rush me, damn your eyes. If you would only make up your mind about Anna-Marie—"

"Why should that signify? I'll not cut you out with Sarah. I've already told you I wouldn't grieve her by separating her from her father."

"Truth is, she's still very aware of you. Well, she as much as told me so. I don't think she'll be able to take another man's suit seriously until your fate is decided."

Alexander groaned. "If that's true, I am robbing her of the chance to select a husband her father will accept. I don't want that."

"Then perhaps, if you aren't going to marry Anna-Marie, you ought to leave for India and set both those young women free to find eligible husbands." Henry lowered himself into a straight-backed chair and crossed his legs, swinging the right over the left in seeming nonchalance, but his eyes were intent and serious.

Alexander paced to the window and stood with his back to Henry, moodily staring into the evening gloom. At last he growled, "You are right, of course. But I want your word of honor you won't—"

Jumping from the chair, Henry grabbed him by the arm and spun him around. "You can't seriously think my intentions dishonorable?"

"No, you'd never get your hands on either fortune that way."

"Damn you! And I thought we were friends. But no friend of mine could suspect me of such a thing. Say what you might of me, I've never harmed innocent females!"

Alexander dropped his eyes first. "You're right, of course. It is jealousy that makes me speak so."

"Especially would I not harm Sarah, Alex. You are right about one thing. She would be very easy to fall in love with."

Alexander shrugged off the hand on his shoulder. "I am glad to hear it, for if you ever hurt her, I'll see you regret it . . ."

"Then you'll marry Anna-Marie?"

"That wouldn't be fair to her. I feel nothing for her but a wish to be kind. And I believe Lord Eberlin might court her if I were not in the picture." Alexander sighed deeply. "I will go to India. I'll wind up my affairs, visit my parents, and set sail as soon as may be."

Henry's shoulders slumped in relief. With Alexander out of the way, he would have an excellent chance of engaging Lady Sarah's affections.

"I hope you come back a nabob." Henry clapped his arm around Alex's shoulders. "Come, let us crack a bottle of brandy together to salute the future."

Alexander shook his head. "Sorry, Fort. I wish you well, indeed, but I cannot toast these painful prospects."

"Good morning, Jennifer. How is your mother today?" The duke gave his hat and gloves to the Cornwall butler as he greeted Jenny, who was coming down the stairs, dressed in a bright blue walking dress. Her maid was following her.

Jenny smiled and gave him a respectful curtsy. "She is doing very well, sir, but has elected not to go out today, for this wind would surely irritate her eye."

The duke glanced upstairs. "Is she receiving?"

"She is in her office, and I know she would be glad to see you." Jennifer gave him a cheery smile as she turned toward the door.

She is acting like her old self, now, the duke thought. *Glad to see she got over that nonsense of flirting with me.* Then a thought sent his pulse tripping. *Perhaps Deborah told her what happened yesterday. Perhaps she even confided a change in attitude toward me.* Hastening up the steps, the duke allowed the footman barely time to announce him before hurrying into Deborah's cramped little office.

"Justin!" Deborah had been staring out the window. "You must have just missed Jennifer. She was . . ."

"I saw her on her way out."

"But . . ."

"She was taking her maid; no need to fret yourself. I want to see that eye." By this time the duke had reached Deborah where she stood in the brilliant morning light. He took her chin in his hand and turned her head so he could study her eye.

"Look up!" He gently touched the upper lid, holding it in place. "Now look down. Good. It is red, but no sign of infection that I can see."

Deborah slid from his grasp. "Thank you for your concern, sir. It feels much better this morning."

"What is this 'sir' nonsense? Yesterday we were using first names." He smiled and attempted to take her in his arms.

Eluding him, she exclaimed, "No. You mustn't. That is, I don't understand why Jennifer left. She was coming to see . . . that is . . ."

"How prettily you color up when embarrassed. No, Jennifer was conducting herself very sensibly this morning, I am pleased to say. I supposed you had told her—"

"There was nothing to tell her." Deborah's voice was sharp, almost panicky.

"Now, Dee. I am sure you know that our kiss put an end to all this nonsense of courting Jennifer."

"No!" Deborah put her hands to her mouth.

"It showed me my heart, my love, not that I really had any doubts. I had hoped it did the same for you."

"You presume much too much from a kiss. You took me by surprise, and I was vulnerable, and—"

"Deborah!" The duke's mouth firmed. "I am getting out of patience with you. I love you, and that's an end to it. And I think you love me, if you will only admit it. There is no question of courting Jennifer, for I plan to marry you. We will find some other way to deal with Vincent."

"You love me?" Deborah walked away, taking refuge behind her desk. "That is very unfortunate, sir, for I can never return your love. And as for marriage, never again!"

Harwood's expression slowly changed from one of poorly suppressed excitement to one of somber thoughtfulness. "You feel that way still? I think it is time and past that you told me about your marriage, Dee."

She shook her head. "It wouldn't matter."

"Did he beat you?"

"Yes." She hung her head, her voice faint. "I couldn't draw a breath without thinking how it might affect him, set him off. Always guessing: Would this action bring me a beating? Would that action cause me to be locked in my room? How long would I have to go hungry to pay for his friend's attempting to steal a kiss from me?"

Deborah's voice began to shake with suppressed rage. "I never knew one moment of real peace. I can never put myself in that position again. I want to be *free*!"

"I would not fetter you in that way, my love, and I think you know it."

"As for a wife's . . . marital duties . . ." She clenched her hands into fists. Her voice rose. "I abhorred it. Even when he wasn't trying to hurt me, I found it disgusting and humiliating. You want kisses and . . . and more. I would make you a terrible wife."

Harwood stared at the agitated woman before him, and despair settled in his heart. "It would not be that way with a man you loved, Dee. But obviously that man is not me, or you would have some awareness of the truth." He sighed and turned to the window, staring out wordlessly for several moments. "Very well, Deborah. I won't importune you. I shall make up my mind to be lonely."

Deborah's heart twisted at the bleak words and his strained, unhappy countenance. A little sob escaped her lips. "I never meant to hurt you . . ."

"No." He turned and forced a little smile to his lips. "Forgive me for wallowing in self-pity. I shall do better." Visibly straining for control, he asked, "How are the plans for your ball coming?"

Gratefully, she grasped at the change of subject. "Almost ready." She picked up a piece of parchment from her desk with shaking hands. "I've received word this morning that Vincent and Winnifred will arrive day after tomorrow, to replenish their wardrobes."

Deborah yearned to ask the duke if he would still pretend to court Jennifer, but didn't dare. It seemed too cruel after what had passed between them. Her own thoughts and feelings were in such turmoil she could hardly have told *how* she felt.

After another moment or two of studying the uninspiring view of the garden below, Harwood turned toward her as if coming from a trance. "Then I had best leave you to your work. I will keep my promise to stand your friend, you know, yours and Jennifer's. I will show myself out."

Before she could even respond, Harwood was gone, leaving Deborah wondering why, when she had succeeded in discouraging the duke so thoroughly, she should feel so wretched.

Determined to overcome his unhappy state of mind, the duke strode up the steps of his town house, concentrating on the plans he had for his new secretary, who was to report for work later in the day. He would allow himself no time to brood over this latest setback in his pursuit of Deborah.

He charged into the office, and then stopped short, shocked by what he saw.

In the window embrasure, entwined in one another's arms in an intimate embrace, were Jennifer Silverton and John Warner.

"My God, John! What are you about, man?" The duke closed the distance in three strides and stoutly grasped John's shoulder. So involved were the pair that the duke had to shake him forcefully to make them end the passionate kiss.

Breathing deeply, Jennifer and John lifted identically dazed eyes to his.

"I cannot believe you have so far forgotten yourself as to compromise . . ."

"It is my fault, sir. I threw myself at him."

"It is not what you think, Justin. We are engaged to be married."

"Huh! A most unusual engagement. Neither Jennifer's mother nor her guardian will countenance the match!" But the duke's expression of outrage cleared somewhat. He took the young girl's hands in his.

"I am most sorry that my kinsman has so far forgotten himself."

"I am not, sir. I love him, and he loves me. I decided late

last night that I could no longer pretend otherwise. We will be wed, with or without my uncle's approval."

"You do realize that if you run away to marry against your guardian and your parent's wishes, the scandal that ensues will surely end all hope John has of rising in politics?"

Jennifer bit on her lower lip. "Oh, Mama said so, but why—"

"Why? Because disobedient children strike at the heart of the family, which strikes at the heart of society, at least in the conservative viewpoint of most adult men. And men are, after all, who make the laws, as your mother pointed out once when we were discussing the subject." The duke smiled kindly at her. "I don't say it is fair, but it is the way of the world."

"As if I care for a political career at the expense of my darling's happiness." John thrust his jaw out. "We shall live on my estate in Scotland, and be happier on a pittance than either she or I can ever be on a fortune, apart from one another."

"Bowled over, aren't you, lad?" The duke studied his determined young cousin. "Well, just so you both know and clearly accept what you will give up if you lose the game."

"What do you mean, 'lose the game,' sir?" John eyed the duke warily. "We've just said we give up the game."

"I mean that Lady Cornwall may think Vincent holds all the cards, but she may be surprised. I am willing to help you play the hand, if you both are quite sure you are prepared to make the sacrifice of the loss of your fortune, Jennifer, and your career, John, if we lose."

"I care naught for my fortune, sir, compared to a life with John. But . . ." She looked miserable.

John's eyes narrowed. "But you do not care to give up my political career?"

"Not for my sake! For yours. For England's! I would never wish to deprive you of your rightful place, which is surely in the government."

John dropped a quick kiss on her nose. "My rightful place is at your side as husband." He turned to the duke.

"Tell us what cards we hold, sir, for we both are willing to risk the stakes." John pulled Jennifer into the circle of his arm, in defiance of the duke's disapproving glare.

"Very well, but to begin with, you must cease and desist this sort of unlawful expression of affection. For the next two weeks, until Jennifer's ball, your behavior toward one another must be impeccable, and I must continue to be seen courting her."

"Still, sir?" Jennifer studied the duke with amazement.

"Yes, still. Not a vigorous pursuit, you understand, but an interest sufficiently noticeable that Vincent may begin to imagine himself as part of my circle of friends and relatives. I intend to show him just how influential I am. I'm hoping he will ponder well the advantages to himself and his daughters of keeping my friendship and regard by allowing you to marry whom you wish.

"When the time comes, I shall attempt to awaken him to the *ton's* disgust should it learn of the ten thousand pound bribe from Morton. The Silvertons were always very concerned for their consequence. I think he will shrink from scandal as much as your mother does, Jenny.

"If need be, but only as a last resort, I will offer him the same ten thousand pounds that Morton offered, to let you marry John. I confess I have a strong dislike of seeing him succeed in his greed, but it may be unavoidable.

"Of course, for insurance against Vincent's bullheadedness, we will begin immediately to place my best cattle along the North Road to speed you on the way to Gretna if need be."

Jennifer threw herself into the duke's arms. "My mother has a wonderful friend in you. She will be so thrilled."

Patting her back soothingly, the duke shook his head. "No, say nothing to your mother as yet. She might be too fearful to take the risks this entails." He straightened and smiled down at Jennifer, chucking her chin lovingly. "She doesn't appreciate just how clever a fellow I am, yet."

"In fact . . ." The duke appeared to consider carefully. "In fact, we might let her think that my masquerade is becoming a reality."

John frowned. "Even more gossip will result if I appear to have stolen Jennifer from beneath your very nose."

The duke nodded. "Our public behavior must be very cautious. I was thinking of giving Deborah some more private hints. Sarah might be helpful here."

Putting one finger to her lips and cocking her head, Jennifer murmured, "Now I wonder what you are playing at? A double game, methinks."

"Minx." Harwood ruffled her hair before offering his hand to John. "Your fiancée is too clever by half."

Chapter 18

"Y ou have contrived a very elaborate scheme for decorating the ballroom, have you not?" Vincent frowned over the plans Deborah had given him.

"Compared to what other balls have displayed, particularly balls honoring girls in their first season, this one is quite modest." Deborah felt a creeping at the back of her neck. Vincent standing over her like this, scowling and rocking back and forth on his heels, reminded her too much of her late husband.

"And the guest list—is it not too long for our ballroom?"

"A ball must be a squeeze or it will not be seen as a success."

"Ah. And have most accepted?"

"Of course." Deborah lifted her chin proudly.

"Harwood has accepted, hey?"

"He was among the first. He has already asked Jennifer for the second dance."

Vincent scowled. "Not the first?"

Exasperated, Deborah snapped, "Of course not, Vincent. As her uncle and guardian, you are expected to lead her out."

"You needn't get hoity-toity with me, madam. I was only the second son, consigned for the most part to an army barracks or a grim battlefield bivouac while Seymour was learning all the finer points of society."

Flushing with embarrassment, Deborah apologized, adding, "You are twice the man he ever was."

After a brief struggle with himself, Vincent smiled at her compliment. "A sort of rough diamond, eh?"

Deborah smiled back, in charity with him for once. "Something like that."

"Well, you must show Winnifred and me how to go on. I never cared much for the social whirl, nor ever shall, but we want our children to take their place in society as the family of the Viscount Cornwall should. Wouldn't want them to be held back by some faux pas of mine."

Biting back the urge to tell him that his proposed betrothal of Jennifer to Lord Morton would be the worst sort of faux pas, Deborah continued going over the plans for the ball with Vincent.

Just then the door to the library opened. "The Duke of Harwood, my lord," Rayburn announced. "Are you in?"

"Of course, of course." Vincent's heartiness poorly masked his nervousness. "Should we receive him in the drawing room, Deborah?"

"No, you shouldn't, Lord Cornwall. I followed your butler here." The duke shook Vincent's hand after greeting Deborah politely but coolly. "Just came to pay my respects and invite you to a dinner I am giving tomorrow evening. Glad you came up to town early for the ball. Don't know if you are interested in politics . . ."

Vincent shook his head as they seated themselves. "I've never given it a thought."

"I've been little better, truth to tell, but some strong new currents are stirring the political waters. It behooves us as peers to be aware of them, help chart a course."

Flattered and a little over-awed, Vincent listened to the duke run through the names of others attending his dinner. The most influential members of the *ton* were included."

"I hope that your wife will be able to attend as well. Jennifer and Deborah have already accepted. Remarkable and very fascinating for a young girl to be as interested in politics as Jenny is."

"I can't say that I approve of such an interest. The female brain . . ."

"An intelligent, well-informed female makes a much better companion than one with more hair than wit," the duke insisted.

Vincent didn't wish to come to points with the duke. "To each his own," he allowed. "As for Winnie, I'm not sure she will be able to attend. She is at the dressmaker's today; says she hasn't a thing to wear."

Harwood favored him with a conspiratorial grin. "So say they all. But why isn't Deborah helping her? She would be an excellent advisor."

"Ah, to tell the truth, sir, Winnifred and I are such different types and have such different tastes that I doubt I would be of much use to her." Deborah avoided the duke's eyes.

"Nonsense. She would be proud to have you help her. I'll suggest it this evening," Vincent asserted, though both he and Deborah knew that Winnifred's refusal to shop with Deborah sprang from jealousy over her sister-in-law's superior figure and countenance. The current Viscountess Cornwall did not show to advantage next to the dowager.

The duke noted Vincent's attitude with satisfaction. The man was virtually fawning on him. His plan was going well in every respect.

"And is Jennifer with your wife, Lord Cornwall?"

"No, I believe she has gone riding with some friends. But I am sure she will return shortly," Vincent assured him eagerly.

"I am sorry to have missed her, but I look forward to discussing politics with her this evening."

Vincent came without Winnifred to attend the duke's political dinner. "Says she would be embarrassed to be so out of the fashion," Vincent confided as he made her excuses to the duke. "But I feel sure it is partly that she has no interest at all in politics. Indeed, I was quite surprised to find that you were right. Jennifer and Deborah both seem keen on the subject." Vincent's voice had a martyred tone to it as he glanced at the two women he had escorted.

"I am very glad you came," Harwood assured them. "Lady Holland is here, and she will be grateful for intelli-

gent conversation while we men are talking politics over
our port."

"Which you likely will do until all hours." Deborah
smiled indulgently.

Jennifer pouted. "You mustn't have all of your political
discussions over port, sir. Else I shall miss them."

"Quite right." The duke took her hand and patted it
kindly. "I shall see that we join the ladies in good time, my
dear."

Deborah darted a glance at Vincent, and saw a gleam of
pleasure in his eyes at this sign of partiality. *Now if pretense can only lead to reality,* she thought, not without a
sense of shame at her plans for Harwood.

The duke was true to his word. The men joined the ladies
surprisingly early. The duke came directly toward her and
Jennifer, who were enjoying a comfortable coze with Lady
Holland and Mrs. Rush, the American ambassador's wife.

A lively political conversation ensued. After a time the
duke suggested that Deborah play and sing for them. "For I
think music the perfect way to end such an evening."

Deborah readily agreed, noting that the duke took her
place at Jennifer's side. Jennifer gave him a coquettish
smile, an expression her mother had seldom caught on her
face. Her heart gave a little flip flop. *What man would be
proof against that?* she wondered. And then wondered why
she wasn't more pleased at the thought.

"Are you quite sure you and your lovely wife won't accompany us to the Barrymores' ball? The countess will
make any guests of mine welcome, you know." Harwood
looked from Vincent to Winnifred expectantly. He and
Sarah had just dined with the Cornwalls.

"La, no, Your Grace!" Winnifred plied her fan. "Until
my new gowns are ready, I must play least in sight, for it
would never do to appear in three-year-old fashions."

"You look quite charming," the duke assured her, before
turning to Jennifer. "And you, my dear. You look like
springtime itself. I hope that the night is not too chill for

that fragile muslin, however." He let his eyes slide down Jennifer's slender form appreciatively.

"She does look a treat, doesn't she," Vincent boomed. "But then, the Knollbridge line has always produced beauteous females."

"And you see how *ravissant* Mama looks tonight," Jennifer agreed. Deborah patted her hair self-consciously. She knew she was in her best looks, in a rich gold satin lavishly trimmed with lace.

But the duke barely glanced at Deborah before responding in a neutral tone, "Indeed. Lovely as ever, Lady Cornwall. Here, let me tuck this shawl around your shoulders, little one." Carefully, solicitously, he wrapped Jennifer in the pale green cashmere shawl that she was carrying.

Deborah was left to whirl her shawl around her own shoulders, whereas until recently Harwood had eagerly performed that office for her.

He is doing an excellent job of pretending, she thought, turning to catch the avaricious glow in Vincent's eyes. Clearly Vincent believed the duke's interest in Jennifer was sincere.

After they were all four seated in Harwood's carriage for the short drive to the earl's ball, Deborah expected the duke's marked attentions to Jennifer to cease. But even after the door was closed against Vincent's watchful eye, the duke fussed with Jennifer's dress and shawl. "Here, let me arrange your skirts. Don't want to wrinkle that beautiful dress. And tuck that shawl around you well," he ordered, his hands busy around Jennifer's person. "Once we are inside, you may display those beautiful shoulders to the world, but no need to risk a chill until then."

The duke had seated Jennifer beside him, surprising Sarah and Deborah by handing them into the backward-facing seats. Deborah was puzzled. *Why is he doing this, now we are alone? I thought Sarah was in on the deception?* But Sarah was watching the duke and Jennifer with a look of surprise that said his actions were a mystery to her, too.

Once at the Barrymores' home, the duke continued

showing Jennifer marked attention, leading her out for the first dance, and requesting the supper dance before anyone else had a chance to do so. Deborah watched them as they whirled through the steps of a quadrille. Jennifer was certainly obeying her mother's orders, flirting with the duke to the exclusion of all others in the set. Moreover, the duke was returning the favor.

On the way home the duke asked to take Jennifer for a drive the next day. Deborah agreed, of course. It was, after all, just what they had planned. They had *not* planned that he would keep captivated eyes trained on Jennifer's face as he asked. Again Deborah glanced at Sarah. Harwood's daughter turned her head to meet Deborah's eyes and beamed at her. As the duke assisted Jennifer out of the carriage, Sarah leaned forward and whispered in Deborah's ear, "It's as if he never really saw her before tonight. I think he has quite forgotten it is all a pretense."

It is what I hoped would happen, Deborah told herself fiercely. *It is what I want.*

The Dowager Duchess of Carminster's annual ball was in full swing. The strains of waltz music wove their way through the close air, while overhead, hundreds of candles sparkled in glittering chandeliers.

The duchess's ballroom was said to be the most opulent in all of London, excepting only the Prince Regent's. The eighty-year-old matriarch was, moreover, not one of the numerous elderly ladies occupying comfortable chairs along the edges of the ballroom. No, she was dancing this waltz, as light on her feet as ever.

"I admire her so," Jennifer whispered to her mother as she watched the white-haired lady move without apparent effort across the ballroom floor.

Deborah smiled. "So do I," she agreed. "And envy her some, too."

"For dancing with Harwood?" Jennifer cast a knowing eye at her mother.

"Not at all. For being so carefree." But Deborah's heart

convicted her of lying. All evening she had felt as if a stiletto had been buried in her heart as she watched her daughter flirt with the duke.

He had been true to his word, pretending so well to an interest in Jennifer that it would have fooled anyone. When he had helped her into the carriage this evening, for instance, his look had been so tender it caused a peculiar ache in the vicinity of Deborah's heart. Once again, this look had been unnecessary for convincing Vincent, as only Sarah and Deborah saw it. It seemed that the pretense was leading to love.

"Our plan is going very well, wouldn't you say, Jennifer?"

"He is a very fine man, Mother. I begin to think you had the right of it. And it does seem that his attentions are very particular!"

Deborah's fists clenched. She felt that sick sensation she was experiencing every time she contemplated Jennifer married to the duke. *What is wrong with me?* she wondered. *Surely, I am not jealous of my own child?*

Sarah whirled by just then on the arms of Henry Fortesque. "They make a lovely couple, don't they?" Deborah asked her daughter.

"Hmmmm?" Jennifer's eyes had strayed across the room, to where John Warner was conversing with the American ambassador. Quickly, she returned her attention to her mother.

"Oh, yes! I begin to think she may fix her affections there. After all, Lord Alexander isn't even here tonight, so it isn't as if she is trying to make him jealous."

"I wonder why he isn't here? Everyone is, simply everyone. And there is Anna-Marie. Lord Eberlin will cut him out if he is not careful."

"Did you not hear the latest *on-dit?* I declare Arnold Lanscombe took the greatest delight in telling it in front of Anna-Marie, probably hoping she'd cry or something. That little worm!"

Deborah pulled her attention from the tall, lithe figure of

the duke whirling his white-haired partner through the dance. "He is a little worm, but he always seems to know what is going on. What did he say?"

"Alexander has announced that he is sailing for India soon. He has gone into the country to bid his family farewell."

Deborah frowned. "And how did Sarah take that?"

"Oh, I was proud of her. What she felt I cannot say. She hasn't confided in me at all, and I haven't liked to pry. But if she was upset, she certainly didn't show it. She was standing with Mr. Fortesque. She just laughed and said that Henry mustn't take it in his head to join Alex, and he assured her in the most gallant fashion that he would never leave England while she was in it."

"That young man is a bit forward," Deborah said reprovingly.

"Yes, well, better than being quite a bit behind-hand, as Alexander has been!" Jennifer tossed her head, and Deborah got the impression there was some hidden message in the comment.

In the time leading up to Jennifer's ball, the duke conducted a careful courtship, not just of Jennifer, but also of Vincent. He took him to the best men's clubs, solemnly introducing him to the cream of society. He invited him to political dinners where the issues of the day were discussed frankly and knowledgeably by the king's ministers and loyal opposition alike. He fenced with Vincent at Angelo's, challenged his prowess with a pistol at Manton's, and accompanied him to Gentleman Jackson's boxing club, though not being an aficionado of the Fancy, he disdained to trade blows.

By the evening of Jennifer's ball, the duke had succeeded in his goal of convincing Vincent of the value of the Duke of Harwood's friendship. Deborah was startled, therefore, to hear her brother-in-law reveal that he was not convinced of Harwood's interest in Jennifer.

"I begin to think it is all a hoax," he informed Deborah

pugnaciously as they waited with Winnifred at the bottom of the stairs for Jennifer to make her appearance.

"By no means, Vincent. He is clearly fond of her."

"I had hoped to make the announcement at this ball. Bah!"

Winnifred fluttered nervously at his side. "It may yet happen, dearest. He may ask for permission this very evening. Only just look how lovely Jenny is tonight."

All three adults watched appreciatively as Jennifer, splendid in a white satin robe with a beaded gauze overdress, descended the stairs. The tiny white beads flashed and sparkled in the light as she moved sinuously toward them. The gown featured a bodice molded to the line of her high bosom and a skirt that fell straight from the gathered bodice, emphasizing her slender figure. She had never shown to better advantage.

"Quite so," Vincent allowed grudgingly. "There is not the slightest doubt Harwood likes to look at her. But does he want to marry her?"

Deborah shut Vincent out. Tears in her eyes, she hugged her daughter when she reached the bottom of the stairs. "You are looking magnificent, darling."

Jennifer's eyes were huge, her features solemn. "I shall be in high fidgets during dinner, lest I ruin my gown."

Laughing through her tears, Deborah took the girl's arm. "Shall I have Cook pin one of her giant aprons on you?"

Leading the way to the drawing room to await their guests, Jennifer flashed her mother a quick smile. "Perhaps I should have put a pinafore over my dress." They all laughed at the thought of such attire at the formal dinner they were giving before the ball.

No accident marred dinner. Jennifer acquitted herself well in the opening dance, too, when her uncle led her out to dance alone for several measures before other dancers joined them.

The second dance was a waltz, which Jennifer had finally received permission from the lofty patronesses of Almack's to perform. As she danced with the duke, she batted her eyes at him flirtatiously.

The duke smiled down at her benignly. "You are a treat to look at tonight, Jennifer."

"Thank you, sir. You are all that is kind. I should tell you, my uncle is growing impatient for our engagement."

"So that is the reason for this adoring look?"

"He is of a suspicious nature, not like mother, who I believe half expects you to offer for me." Mischief lit Jennifer's eyes,

"And is your mother as thrilled with that prospect as Vincent would be?" Harwood's grey eyes studied Jennifer anxiously.

"I am sorry, sir. I cannot say for sure."

Harwood's mouth took on a grim line. "I am not at all sure how to proceed, then. I thought to bring her around, and then, as your stepfather, wrest you from Vincent's control by persuasion, intimidation, or, if necessary, legal action. But now . . ."

"It *is* a dilemma!" Jennifer glanced to where her uncle stood, studying them dourly, and gasped, missing a step.

"What is it, Jenny?"

"Look who is with Uncle Vincent."

Harwood looked. "Ah, yes. Lord Morton, back from France. He's failed with Mrs. Smithfield, too. I heard she eloped with an impecunious French count. You need not fear him, Jenny. I made it quite clear to Morton that he pursued you or your mother at peril of his life."

Jennifer relaxed and flashed him a smile even more adoring than before, and much more genuine. "Thank you, sir. From the bottom of my heart."

She would have been less relieved if she could have heard the conversation going forward between the two men observing the couple.

Chapter 19

"It seems Harwood has taken a leaf from my book."

Vincent gave Lord Morton a sneering look. "I understand you attempted to have both mother and child. Very bad *ton*, Dolphus. Not what you represented to me, was it?"

"Never tell me he doesn't intend the same. Just because he is more subtle than I . . ."

Vincent shook his head. He had learned enough about society in the last two weeks to know just how low in its estimation Morton stood, and just how high the duke ranked.

"I cannot believe it of him. No, my concern is that he is not truly interested in Jennifer."

"Of course he isn't. He's stalking her for his cousin, John Warner."

"Rot! I've made it clear that he won't do. But neither will you, Morton, so you might as well be off."

Dolphus chewed on his drooping mustache. He lacked the courage to continue his pursuit of Jennifer and her mother in the face of the duke's threats, but his wounded pride urged him to put a spoke in Harwood's wheels if he could.

"Harwood won't plump down any ten thousand pounds for her. He's no need to pay for a bride."

Vincent glowered. It was the one drawback to his cherished scheme to marry Jennifer to the duke.

"On the other hand, Tarkington would pay and pay dearly. Wants an heir, at last."

Both men's eyes turned to the Earl of Tarkington, stand-

ing like an emaciated bird of prey at the edge of the ballroom, his glittering blue eyes avidly following Jennifer as
she moved gracefully in the duke's arms.

"Hardly a desirable match. He looks to be diseased. Consider his reputation." Vincent shuddered at the rash on the
corner of Tarkington's mouth and across his bald head.

"She'll be a countess, though. Not to be sneezed at."
Morton nodded sagely.

Vincent turned away as the music ended. "Not what I'd
choose for my ward, I thank you." But his thoughts toward
Jennifer were less benign. *I'm damned if I'll give up ten
thousand pounds for anything less than a duke, though.
And it's time Miss Jennifer was very clear about that!*

There was no opportunity to impress his determination
on his niece during the ball. It was just the squeeze that assured its being called a great success, and Jennifer was be-
sieged by admirers. Vincent was not pleased that she
granted one of her dances to John Warner, but the duke had
made it very clear that he expected his kinsman to be received wherever he was. There was nothing Vincent could
do but gnash his teeth as John led Jennifer out for a set of
country dances.

After the last guest had been bowed from the house,
though, when the exhausted ladies would have gone to their
beds, Vincent commanded Jennifer and her mother to attend him in the drawing room. Winnifred eyed him uneasily and followed along uninvited.

Flipping up his long tails, Vincent sat and motioned the
women to do likewise. "Well, Jennifer, do you feel that
your ball was a success?"

"It was a lovely ball, Uncle Vincent. Thank you so much
for . . ."

He waved aside her gratitude. "It was *not* a success, for
your information."

"Vincent, it is very late. Can't this wait?" Deborah refused to sit and confronted her brother-in-law tensely.

"No, it can't. I'm tired of waiting. You said the duke

would likely offer for her at this ball. Where is that offer, Deborah?"

"The duke is not in a rush to make a decision, but you saw that Jennifer was the only eligible *parti* that he danced with. And he danced with her twice."

"Nevertheless, I feel that you are his object, not Jennifer. I have seen the way his eyes follow you as you dance. Either he seeks to curry favor with the mother by turning the child up sweet, or there is some deliberate deception going on."

Deborah's heart almost stopped. She had not thought Vincent would guess the truth.

"And I sense that Jennifer has a *tendre* for John Warner, in spite of all I've said on that head!" Vincent looked from mother to child challengingly.

Jennifer opened her mouth and then closed it again.

"Well, missy? Cat got your tongue?"

"I can't *make* the duke offer for me, Uncle."

"Ah, but I say you can. Clever girl like you, running tame in his household. I've been thinking. It shouldn't be too hard to maneuver him into a compromising position."

All three women exclaimed as one. "No, Vincent." It was Winnifred whose protests first found voice. "That is not the way to go on. Have you forgotten you hope to count the duke your friend when our girls make their come-outs?"

Vincent scowled. "Well, then, I may just have to accept another offer. Tarkington has expressed an interest in Jennifer."

"Tarkington. You wouldn't!" Deborah shuddered violently.

"Wouldn't I?"

"No, you wouldn't," Winnifred asserted. "Think of our daughters . . ."

"Madam, have you considered what an additional five thousand pounds apiece would do to our daughter's eligibility?" Vincent pounded the arm of his chair. "In my desk in the library is a signed contract for that amount from Morton, and Tarkington would offer at least that. Now, hear me, Jennifer. Bring the duke up to scratch, or I find someone who can make it worth my while to bestow your hand in marriage. My gals don't have your fine looks or your fortune. I would be remiss as a father not to do all I can for them."

"Not Tarkington." Unexpectedly assertive, Winnifred faced her husband. "That is a connection I could not bear."

"You have said quite enough, madam. Go to your room now."

"No, Vincent. You mustn't . . ."

"Do as I say, or suffer the consequences." He stood, raising his fist menacingly.

Winnifred drew back before this evidence of his determination. As pale as Jennifer's dress, she stood and walked from the room.

Abruptly Jennifer stood up, too. "You are despicable. Mother always said you were a better man than my father, but you are not! I've lost all respect for you. I no longer consider myself bound to obey you. I . . ."

Deborah stepped between Vincent and her daughter and put her hand over Jennifer's mouth. "Hush, child. You are distraught. Go to bed and get some rest. We shall speak of these matters more tomorrow when we are all rested."

"I did not give her, or you, permission to withdraw."

"I hate you! I hate you!" Jennifer spun out of her mother's grasp and fled the room, her sobs resounding as she climbed the stairs.

"A good night's work, Vincent." Deborah turned scorn-filled eyes on her brother-in-law. "It seems I have misjudged you."

The light of battle in his usually noncombative sister-in-law's eyes unnerved Vincent. Still, he was determined to carry his point. "I suggest you get control of your daughter, madam, before I have to take measures . . ."

Deborah's eyes met and held his. "I shall be the one to take measures if you try to marry her to someone like Tarkington."

"What can you do, woman? Tell the duke on me? But he

won't dominate me as he did Morton, I can tell you. I am not afraid to meet him!"

A thrill of fear went through her at this hint of a duel. A sudden horrifying vision of Harwood pitching forward, blood spurting from his chest, almost paralyzed her.

"No. I see that you are not." Needing to ponder her course of action, Deborah called upon all her long experience at presenting a submissive appearance. She slumped her shoulders and dropped her eyes. "I must consider what to do about Jennifer's rebelliousness. May I be excused?"

"You'd best consider how to bring the duke up to scratch."

"Yes, Vincent." Deborah kept her eyes downcast, a study in meekness.

At last, satisfied that she was in a properly submissive mood, Vincent dismissed her with a wave of his hand. He sat up late, nursing a brandy bottle, reassuring himself that he was in charge of things, and that this feminine revolt had been quelled.

Deborah hurried to Jennifer's rooms. She wasn't surprised to see light under her door, but she was surprised upon entering her bedroom to find clothes strewn everywhere and Jennifer, eyes bright with unshed tears, determinedly packing.

"Jenny, darling. Where do you think you are going?"

"Anywhere that is away from here."

Deborah rushed to her side. "You mustn't despair, love. Vincent doesn't mean it, I am sure. He was only trying to maneuver you into compromising the duke. When he sees we won't cooperate, he'll give way."

"Will he, Mother? What then? Will you expect me to continue trying to attach the duke?"

"He has seemed to grow more affectionate toward you, even in situations in which no one but ourselves could observe. I still have hopes that he . . ."

"Well, I don't, Mother. The duke doesn't love me, nor I

him. In fact, I love John, and the duke loves you, so it would be immoral for us to marry one another."

"The duke obviously does not love me, or else his constancy is in serious doubt, for his manner to you has been quite warm the last two weeks, as I am sure you well know!"

"Oh, Mother! It is all a pretense. You *know* that!"

"It began as a pretense, but it is as I hoped. The better the duke knows you, the more he can see that you would be a perfect wife for him."

"Do you really hope and believe that is what is going to happen?"

Deborah steeled herself, finding it unexpectedly difficult to look her daughter in the eye. "You know I do. What May game are you playing?"

"If I could prove the duke loves you?"

"If he did, it would not do him any good, for I . . ."

"Yes, I know. You are incapable of loving a man, because of my father's villainy. Well, do you know what I think, Mother?" Jennifer turned from her agitated folding of clothes to face Deborah squarely. "I think you are immoral. Immoral—and a coward as well! Your marriage plans for me are as immoral as Vincent's!"

"Jenny!" Deborah took a step back, horrified.

"Yes, immoral. You want me to trick a dear man into marrying me, who really loves you, and turn my back on the man I really love."

"Not trick, precisely." Deborah wanted to defend herself, but her actions suddenly seemed shabby in her own eyes.

"Yes, trick—fool—deceive. For it would be a deception to say that I want to marry him. And you are a coward for being unwilling to even entertain the notion of marrying the duke! He loves you. He has been pretending to be truly attracted to me to make you jealous. And your indifference has hurt that dear man's feelings terribly, I can tell you! You should forget the past, Mother, and marry the duke!"

"Jennifer!" Deborah's hands flew to her cheeks in shock

and mortification. "How can you? You know what I suffered . . ."

"Spare me, Mother." Jenny flung away from her in disgust and began thrusting clothes into a carpetbag. For several moments there was nothing heard in the room but the sound of both women breathing deeply, raggedly.

Finally, in a low voice throbbing with emotion, Jennifer said, "If you wish never to recover from my father's pernicious influence, that is your choice. But don't ruin my life because of it." She continued with her packing, leaving her mother stunned by Jennifer's unexpected defiance and bitterness.

At last Deborah managed to murmur, "Promise me you won't run away into the night alone. This is dangerous, Jenny. We must have a plan. There is still America."

Jenny looked up into her mother's face, her expression inscrutable. After a moment's thought she nodded her head. "I won't go alone, Mother. But I won't go to America, unless John goes with me."

Deborah watched her child a few more moments before slowly walking from the room. She was losing her daughter. This alienated, determined young woman was a stranger to her.

Long and long Deborah sat in her dark room, thinking. As she thought, she grew progressively angrier at the situation, at Vincent, at male-dominated society in general. At last she turned her anger on the one who she now realized bore the brunt of the responsibility.

Toward morning she emerged silently into the hall and crept down the stairs. Ascertaining that Vincent was no longer in the drawing room, she stealthily entered the darkened library and made her way to the desk in which he kept his papers.

Chapter 20

The next morning, having slept very little during the night, Deborah awoke later than usual. Surprised Betty had not aroused her, she dressed herself. She tucked the product of her night's labors into a reticule and entered Jennifer's room, only to find it empty. On her pillow was a note.

> Mother:
>   I have kept my word not to go alone. Betty agreed, reluctantly, to accompany me. I make no secret of my destination. I go to convince my love to elope with me before my cruel uncle sells me to the highest bidder. If you love me, you won't try to stop me.
>
> Jennifer

With a little cry Deborah turned and, clutching the letter to her bosom, fled downstairs and out the front door, heedless of the lack of a maid. She arrived at the Duke of Harwood's home scarcely a quarter of an hour later. Timmons solemnly put her in the gold salon and asked her to wait.

In a few moments Harwood was with her, his brow wrinkled with concern. "Deborah! I was expecting you." He stepped forward and took her hands. "You are as pale as a ghost."

"Is Jennifer here?"

"She is, safe and well."

"Where . . ."

"Having breakfast just now. Will you join us?"

Eating was the last thing on Deborah's mind, but she desperately wanted to assure herself her daughter was not already winging her way toward Gretna Green. She nodded and took his arm as he led her to the breakfast room. There she found Jennifer, rosy with happiness, chatting cozily with John.

The sight of those roses fading from her daughter's cheeks as she turned to her mother rekindled the anger that had kept Deborah up half the night. "Please finish your meal," she urged the three. "I feel like the uninvited guest at the wedding. I shall go back to the drawing room to wait." She turned on her heels and left.

Ignoring her instructions, the other three followed her, abandoning their plates. Once they were settled, Deborah gave John a piercing look. "I believe you have something to say to me, Mr. Warner."

The vertical frown line between John's eyebrows deepened. "I realize you can't give your permission, so I hadn't thought . . ."

"But I can, and I will!"

At Jennifer's gasp, Deborah spread her hands, revealing three sealed packets of parchment. "I spent a great deal of time last night thinking about what you said, Jennifer, and growing progressively more angry as I thought."

"I am so very sorry, Mother. I shouldn't have spoken to you that way. But I still cannot . . ."

"Please, hear me out. I was not—am not—angry with you, nor with Mr. Warner. I am angry with myself, mostly. You spoke the truth last night. I have been a coward. All during my married life I put up with your father's brutality rather than risk a public scandal by insisting on a separation. I should have taken you and fled, not let him tyrannize you as he did me."

"It wasn't your fault, Mother. Grandfather wouldn't help you. He talked you out of it."

"True, but others would have helped. My Grandfather Knollbridge was still alive then. He would have stood by me. No, I lacked courage, just as you said. And I still do.

But now I am tired of cringing before my brother-in-law. I am tired of letting the fear of what others may say ruin my life. I am through, forever, with being the pawn of any man."

She turned to the duke. "I believe you told me you are holding the letter Vincent wrote to me, ordering me to permit Lord Morton to pay his addresses to Jennifer?"

The duke nodded. "It is safely locked away."

"I have something here I wish you to lock away with it. It is the promissory note that Vincent took from Morton in exchange for that letter."

Deborah bowed her head a moment. "Before you agree, I should warn you it is stolen. I purloined it from Vincent's desk. I hope you can forgive me, sir, but I intend to engage in a little blackmail. You see, Vincent cares about three things: money, his reputation, and his children's future. I intend to show him that he cannot force Jennifer to marry where she does not wish to, without injuring himself in all three regards."

Since the duke did not shrink from her at this announcement, Deborah held one of the three packets out to him. He took it, an approving smile enlivening his features.

"These other two packets are copies of the originals, with a detailed account of some of my late husband's activities, things which Vincent either does not know or prefers to forget. All of them were immoral, and one or two items in this account are, I believe, hanging offences.

"You cannot hang a dead man, more's the pity. But the *ton* will be scandalized by them, and will find it easy to believe Vincent is cut from the same cloth, once they read the documents pertaining to his sale of my daughter. One copy will go to my solicitor, with instructions to make it public if I so direct him, or if anything happens to me. The other I intend to take to Vincent now. He will read of his brother's deeds in black and white, with no quavering voice nor weak feminine tears to distract him from the disgusting story."

"Oh, Mama!"

"You see, Jennifer, it infuriates me to think that you should be deprived of your fortune, and your husband of his rightful career, in which he can benefit so many, because of Vincent's greed and snobbery. I shall see that it doesn't happen. So promise me you will give no more thought to eloping."

Jennifer slid her hand into John's. "We promise, don't we, John?"

"Of course." John's craggy face creased in a delighted grin. "But Lady Cornwall, I would like to ask that you permit Jennifer to remain here with us. I think any underhanded tricks might be harder for Vincent to pull with Jennifer in the duke's household."

Deborah looked questioningly at the duke, who nodded. "Thank you," she breathed. "I will feel braver for knowing she is protected, though I think by the time I have finished with Vincent, he will be prepared to escort her down the aisle of St. George's to give her as your bride with all due ceremony!"

"Brava!" The admiring, adoring look the duke gave her warmed Deborah to her toes. "Shall I go with you to beard the lion in his den?"

"No, I thank you, but I have things to say to him that can be said only in private. I owe Vincent at least the chance to keep this scandal sealed. Will you see that my solicitor receives this document?"

"Gladly." The duke took the packet from her, tucking it and the first one into an inner pocket of his morning coat. Then he caught up her hands to bring them to his lips for a kiss that seemed scorching even through her gloves.

Deborah drew back as if he had dropped live coals on her. "Then I shall go without further delay to confront him. I shall return as soon as I know his response."

Eyes dark with pain at her obvious rejection, the duke escorted Deborah to his front door. "I wish . . ."

She lifted troubled brown eyes to meet his charcoal gaze. "Say no more, Justin. I must stand on my own two feet, now and in the future."

He bowed and let her go, motioning a footman to escort her. *If she is not back within the hour, I will follow her*, the duke promised himself as he returned to the drawing room, to find the young lovers in an intimate embrace. Sighing, he hesitated between separating them and returning to his abandoned breakfast. Suddenly, Sarah's maid hurtled in the door.

"Oh, Your Grace. 'Tis terrible. You must stop them. I did not know what to do." And she burst out crying.

Harwood grabbed the weeping maid and shook her sternly. "Stop this useless weeping, Mary. What has happened. Where is Sarah? I thought she was still abed."

"No, Your Grace. She was up early and wanting to walk. You know how she likes to walk and walk when she is upset. She refused even to wait for a footman. I tried to get her to, I really did!"

"Yes, of course you did. Where . . ."

"We was in Hyde Park, walking along the carriageway. She walks so fast I can't keep up, you know. I was a block behind, half running. Never did understand how her short legs could move so fast and—"

"Have done, Mary. What has happened to Sarah." The duke grasped the maid's fluttering hands in a painfully tight grip.

"Well, a young man drove up to her, the one with the matched greys, you know."

"No, I . . ."

"Lord Alexander's greys, they was, only isn't he blond? I thought this man had dark hair. Could have been that Mr. Fortesque. Anyway, she got up next to him and waved to me, and then he turned the curricle and left the park instead of proceeding around the carriageway as he should have. She looked back over her shoulder at me and called out something but I couldn't hear her. I waited and waited, but they didn't come back."

The duke's expression was grave. "How long did you wait?"

"Not having a watch . . ."

"When did you leave the house?"

" 'Twas early, sir. Around eight."

The duke consulted the watch tucked into his vest pocket. "It's ten now. Would you say you waited an hour?"

"Not quite that long, I don't think, sir. We had been walking quite a while before this happened."

Fighting panic, the duke thought quickly. "John, you heard? Sarah has left. Eloped, or been abducted. Probably by Meade, damn him. You have his address, haven't you?"

John was already up and moving. "In my office. I understood Meade was going to India."

The duke and Jennifer trailed after John as he hastened to his office. "So did I. 'Twas why Sarah was so blue-deviled, I'm sure. Apparently, he's changed his mind. Though it's just barely possible it was Fortesque. But why would he abduct her when I had made it clear I would look favorably on an offer from him?"

"Can't understand it myself, sir," John responded, rifling through his papers. "Jennifer?"

She shook her head. "Sarah hasn't been confiding in me much lately. She seems lost in thought much of the time."

John handed the duke a piece of paper. Harwood tucked the address into his vest pocket. "You wait here, in case they come back. I'm going to Meade and Fortesque's lodgings, see if I can at least determine whom I am chasing."

"Yes, sir. I'll have your valet pack a carpetbag for you, shall I, and ready your carriage?"

"No, I'll ride Tuppence instead. I can catch up to them on a good saddle horse, no matter how fast those greys are." He didn't wait for an answer, but disappeared toward the servants' quarters, through which he could proceed directly to the mews.

Alexander looked around their living quarters with disgust. He had returned after a farewell visit to his family, to complete his packing. He found his flat in disarray, Henry's belongings thrown about as if someone had gone through them one by one. Cushions were tossed from chairs, drawers were standing open, and heavy chests were thrust away from the wall.

"Mason," he called, hoping to question their servant, but received no answer. He was picking his way through the mess to check on his own room when he heard a violent pounding at the front door. He reversed directions and opened it, astonished to find that the Duke of Harwood, looking like Zeus about to launch a thunderbolt, stood glaring at him.

"You! Where is my daughter!"

"Something has happened to Sarah? Come in, sir."

The duke entered, taking in the chaos around him. The signs of a struggle struck terror in his heart. Suddenly he lunged forward, grasping Meade about the throat. "Where is Sarah? If you've harmed one hair of her head, I'll kill you."

Alexander wrenched free, no easy task, for the duke was a powerfully built man. "I haven't seen Sarah in upwards of two weeks, sir. Please tell me what's happened, and why you suspect me of involvement."

A silent, impassioned study of Alexander's concerned features convinced the duke. "She went for a walk early this morning in Hyde Park. She got into a curricle and left. Her maid thought it was with you. She recognized your team."

"Mary?"

"Yes, Mary," the duke snapped impatiently.

"Mary accompanied us one morning when I was driving Henry's team of greys."

Bewildered, the duke rubbed his furrowed brow. "Why would Henry Fortesque have abducted my daughter? They both know I would have countenanced the match."

Alexander's nostrils flared. "Oh, yes, you made it quite clear whom you would and would not permit to court your daughter!"

The duke growled, "You are too easily discouraged, young man. I asked Sarah only to go slow while I had some reports to your detriment investigated. At the first sign of hesitation on her part you turned elsewhere."

"Not true, sir. I had it from your own lips that you wouldn't consider an untitled country squire of little fortune for your daughter, and since that is my fate if I remain in England . . ."

"Had it from my lips?"

"At the opera. You were informing Arnold Lanscombe of how you ended Sarah's understanding with her country swain."

"Oh!" Understanding dawned in the duke's eyes. "I was trying to keep her from being mortified in front of her friends because she had been jilted."

Alex shook his head. "I thought sure you knew I was listening, that your words were meant for me."

Harwood gestured impatiently. "This is not finding Sarah. Do you think Fortesque has eloped with her?"

"I wouldn't be surprised." Alex surveyed the mess in the flat. "It looks to me as if some of Fort's havey-cavey financial dealings have brought the duns down on him."

He bent and picked up a bloodstained shirt. "And playing rough, too."

Comprehension dawned. "So Fortesque's financial house was not as well in order as I was told."

"I'm guessing he's mortgaged every dime he can hope to inherit from his father, probably with the cent-per-centers. They must have become impatient."

"Then he clearly feared I would find out his financial situation and refuse him permission to marry Sarah. I must go after her." The duke turned on his heel.

"Do you . . . do you think she went willingly, sir?"

Harwood turned around and saw the pain and fear in the young man's eyes. "I don't think so, but she has not confided in me as much as she was wont to do."

"May I go with you, sir?"

The duke hesitated.

"I've fast cattle posted along the Great North Road," Alexander said. "Or rather, my brother and father have.

They keep their own horses *en route* from home as they traverse it so often. I can commandeer them in an emergency.".

"I'll have no problem catching them, that is if they are making straight for Gretna. Still . . ." The duke nodded. "I may need a second, anyway. If he's harmed her . . ."

· "I claim the first challenge. I warned Fort if he harmed Sarah I'd have his guts for garters."

"Then you had some inkling . . ."

"I was concerned he might try something like an elopement, but he told me he was falling in love with her, and wouldn't wish to do her a wrong. I thought he meant it. And it's possible he might have. In fairness to Fort, never having known a father's love, or any sort of decent family life, he didn't grasp the pain estrangement from family could mean to someone like Sarah. If he was convinced she loved him, he would feel quite justified . . ."

"He obviously thinks I'll rescue him from the duns once they are wed," the duke growled. The two men were charging down the steps as they spoke. "But unless Sarah truly loves him, which I doubt, I'll make her a widow before I'll let her stay married to a villain like that."

"Not if I beat you to it, sir." Alexander's grim expression told the duke he was in deadly earnest. "My horse is waiting. I was on the way to my ship, which sails at the next high tide."

Side by side the two men rode with single-minded purpose. They had no difficulty tracking Sarah and Henry. The matched greys and maroon curricle were notable enough, but their cargo of a grim-faced young man and a beautiful, tearstained blond maiden made them even more memorable to the turnpike gatekeepers.

Expecting a long, hard chase, the duke and Alexander were astonished when, at the third stage, they were told that the couple had not appeared. Backtracking, they found a nearby coaching inn where they were informed that the couple they sought had engaged a private parlor shortly before.

The duke burst into the parlor with Alexander hard on his heels. Sarah and Henry had been standing at the window, looking out into a kitchen garden. When she saw the duke, Sarah sprang from Henry's side and launched herself into her father's arms.

"Oh, Papa, Papa. He forced me. Henry forced me!"

Chapter 21

The shaft of pain Sarah's tearful wail sent through the duke almost destroyed him. His precious daughter, ruined by this vicious scoundrel!

"I'll kill you! You'll marry her in the morning, and by afternoon you shall meet me," the duke snarled over Sarah's shoulder as he crushed her to him.

"He's mine first!" Alexander charged past the pair and straight at Henry, who didn't defend himself from the hard right fist that crashed into his face.

The blow dropped the dark-haired young man to the floor. Dazed, he raised a shaking hand to wipe away blood from his nose. It was then that Alexander and the duke noticed that Henry's visage bore evidence of more blows than the one just landed. Both eyes were purple, and his lip was badly split.

To their astonishment, Sarah tore herself from her father's arms and thrust between Alexander and his victim.

"Oh, poor Henry. Don't get up. I shan't let him hit you again." She rounded on Alexander. "Don't you dare. Can't you see how much he has suffered already?"

"All I can see is how much he deserves to suffer for what he has done to you." Alexander startled everyone, including himself, by jerking Sarah into his arms. "My precious love. I won't let you stain your name by uniting it with his. I shall marry you! That way, whoever wins, you'll have the name of an honorable man."

Sarah tilted her head up, joy coursing through her. "You . . . you care for me, Alexander?"

"I adore you. You are my one and only love!" Alexander dipped his head and kissed her fervently until the duke, recovering from his astonishment, clapped him on the shoulder.

"Good lad. And if the worst happens, never fear, Sarah. I shall avenge your husband as well as yourself."

Sarah felt torn. In Lord Alexander's arms was where she had so often dreamed of being. But Henry was struggling to his feet with great difficulty, and both men looked as if they'd prefer to murder him on the spot.

"No, you shan't, either of you! He doesn't deserve such a terrible fate. He's been punished enough. And he knew he was wrong. He had already agreed to take me home. We were resting the horses when you came in. With any luck at all we can be back in London before tea time, and no one the wiser."

"Sarah!" The duke's anger warred with astonishment. "You can't treat ravishment as if it were a harmless prank."

"Shock has affected her thinking, sir." Alexander stepped around her, drawing his glove off to slap Henry in the face. But Sarah caught the length of soft leather in her hand and jerked it away.

"No, no, no! You've misunderstood, both of you."

Her father and Alexander stared expectantly.

Beet red with embarrassment, Sarah cast her eyes anywhere but where they would meet the blue or grey ones trained so intently upon her. "I didn't mean . . . he didn't ravish me. He just abducted me. I didn't want to come with him, but it took me quite a while to convince him that I didn't love him, and never could."

Three men exhaled as one. "Precious child," the duke murmured, drawing the blond head against his chest as he cradled Sarah in his arms. "Thank God!"

Alexander glared at Henry, still angry. "You gave me your word . . ."

"I can explain." Fort touched a careful finger to his battered eye. "My creditors paid me a call last night. They had gotten together and compared notes. They realized my debts exceeded even my father's plump pockets. The only way I escaped was to convince them I was about to marry an heiress."

Fort looked sadly at Sarah. "I had convinced myself she loved me, or soon would. Since you announced you were going to India, Alex, she had been most encouraging. I suppose I couldn't believe that any woman could long resist me. I felt under the circumstances I was justified in taking drastic action. I felt, too, sir, that you would forgive me and help me once you saw what a good husband I meant to be to Sarah."

"He also thinks he can win the derby this year with Demon, you see," Sarah interjected. "If he does, he can come about."

"It is a villainous proceeding, young man, and you know it." The duke shook a fist in Henry's face.

"Yes, sir." Henry hung his head. "I realize that now, sir. Alex tried to tell me how it would be, but I didn't understand until I saw how distraught Sarah was over your feelings and over how the scandal might affect your chances of marrying Lady Cornwall . . ."

"It was partly my fault, Papa."

"Nonsense, Sal."

"But it was. You see, I didn't want to admit to anyone, not even myself, how hurt I was when Alexander dropped me. I let Fort think I was enamored of him. I really tried to believe it myself. But the minute he took off with me, I knew I had been deceiving us both. If I'd behaved as I should have, if I hadn't let pride get in the way of honesty, he never would have done such a thing."

"I think I need to sit down."

The duke led his daughter to a sofa and dropped down, holding her hand as if he'd never let it go. "I'm too old to go racketing around the countryside like this, daughter."

The two young men took chairs, Henry tentatively, Alex dropping down with much the same exhausted relief as the duke. For long moments they sat silently contemplating each other and the events of the morning.

It was Meade who stirred first. "Sir, if it is true that you no longer object to my courting Sarah . . ."

"I think after that display of a few moments ago, I must insist upon it." Harwood's smile was genuine. "Besides, any man who announces his intention of marrying a woman he thinks has been ruined is truly in love. If my daughter returns your affection, I would be honored to have you for a son-in-law."

"You know I do, Papa."

Harwood looked down at her pretty, round face. He stroked a long finger caressingly down her pert nose. "Even so, I want you two to take some time to get to know one another really well before finally committing yourselves, for marriage is a permanent connection that can lead to great misery with the wrong person."

"Yes, Papa!"

"I agree, sir."

"Oh, poor Henry." Sarah pulled away from her father's encircling arm. "What will you do? Those dreadful men will kill you if you return to London not having married an heiress."

"I've been thinking. Alex, you won't be needing that ticket to India now . . ."

"Most definitely not!"

"Perhaps you would trade it for my greys. It is time I learned to do something honest with my life."

"What about Demon?"

Henry sighed. "He's capable of winning the derby, but I'm sure the duns would have him away from me to settle part of my debts long before I could see him through the race."

"Perhaps I could purchase him from you?" The duke smiled. "I've always fancied owning a derby winner. And you'll need some cash to get you started in the business world."

The three men stood and began shaking hands. Sarah watched them fondly, particularly Alexander. *Would Fa-*

ther think six months a long enough time to get to know one another? she wondered. *For I am sure I know, right now.*

Once Sarah and Alexander had departed for London in Henry's curricle, and a post chaise had been engaged to convey Fort in privacy to Alexander's ship, Harwood mounted and rode slowly, contemplatively, back to London. *Sarah's second season just may turn out well for her, after all,* he thought. Alexander Meade looked to be just the sort of young man he had wished for as a husband for Sarah.

His thoughts then turned to Jennifer and Deborah. *All will be well with Jennifer and John, too, even if I have to intervene on their behalf.*

But for himself the duke was not so sanguine. Deborah had asked for his help, showing that she trusted him with her friendship and would turn to him for assistance. But the way she had jerked away from him this morning still stung. She was no nearer feeling any of the softer emotions for him, and probably never would.

Not for the first time Harwood regretted that the dead could not be called to account by the living. He was not by nature a violent man, but he would like nothing better than to have pummeled Seymour Silverton to a bloody pulp.

These profitless musings occupied him until he made his way wearily up the steps of the ducal mansion just before sunset. Here he found a lively game going on in the foyer. Alexander, Sarah, Jennifer, and John were rolling a hard ball that looked suspiciously like one of his pool balls. Mittens, her toenails clicking on the tile as she barked ecstatically, was chasing it while her human friends cheered her on.

"All done in by your distressing day, I see," Harwood greeted his daughter as she ran to hug him.

"I feel wonderful. Better than I have in months!" Sarah seemed literally to glow as she beamed up at him. "I am determined to accompany Jennifer to the Bentons' ball tonight, in case anyone might have seen Henry and me driving out of town today."

"That might be best to keep gossip at a minimum," the duke agreed.

"John and Alexander are planning to escort us."

"I expect I must attend, too," the duke sighed, "though I should like nothing so much as to sit before my own fire with a brandy. But tell me, Jennifer, what I already think I can see in your sparkling countenance. Was your mother successful in her bid to talk your uncle around?"

Jenny nodded her head eagerly. "She said it was partly because you had done such a good job of convincing him it would be better to be with you than against you."

"Ah!" The duke rocked back on his heels, satisfied. "Then those tiresome two weeks of taking him about were worth it. Where is your mother? Does she go with us tonight?"

Jennifer frowned. "I'm not sure. She was extremely upset when she heard about Sarah, and particularly when she learned you had taken dueling pistols. She began to cry and then raced from the room. I think she must have gone home, for I haven't seen her since."

"Hmmm. Should I see this as a hopeful sign, do you think?"

Jennifer shook her head. "I wish I could say yes, sir, but I doubt it. She cares for you in her own way, but I fear my mother will never be able to love as she ought."

The duke patted Jennifer's cheek. "I fear you are right, my child. Well, I must go and change for dinner." Slowly, feeling every one of his forty years twice over, the duke climbed the stairs to his bedroom.

"I must bathe," he told his valet. "I am covered with dust from the road."

Boynton had a peculiar look upon his face. "I tried to get her to wait elsewhere, Your Grace, but she insisted."

"What are you talking about, man?" Irritably, the duke peeled off his cravat.

His valet cast a significant look toward the duke's bedroom door, which was closed. That in itself was unusual, as the door was normally open unless Harwood had retired for the night. Mystified, he thrust it aside and strode across the room to examine the long, curving mound on his bed. It was a woman's body, curled in a fetal position, facing the center of the bed. Honey gold curls spilled across the pillows.

Joy and a melting tenderness almost undid the duke. *Are those tear tracks on her cheeks?* he wondered. *For me?*

"Deborah! Dee!" Whispering, he eased himself onto the bed to sit beside the sleeping woman. "Whatever are you doing here, my love?"

Slowly Deborah came awake. As soon as awareness returned, she sat up abruptly. "You're here! Are you injured? Are you all right?"

To the duke's intense pleasure, Deborah threw her arms around his neck. "I've been so worried. I was terrified that young monster would do you an injury. Your valet told me you are a famous shot, but I made sure in that case he would choose swords."

"But I am also a famous swordsman, love." The duke moved so that his back was braced against the headboard, and pulled Deborah across his lap.

"Oh! But still . . . you're unhurt then?"

"There was no duel. Thanks to Sarah's peace-making, Fortesque is on his way to India, and Alexander Meade is below, courting my radiant daughter."

"Oh, thank God," Deborah breathed fervently.

"I hear you had success, too."

"Yes! I was amazed at how quickly Vincent retreated after reading the list of Seymour's misdeeds. He stopped blustering, heard me out, and then had the nerve to act as if John were his very own choice for Jennifer!"

"I am very pleased. Your daughter is delightful, but I confess I am tired of dancing attendance on her when my heart is elsewhere."

A tiny frown angled Deborah's eyebrows downward.

"You very nearly had me convinced you were about to offer for her."

The duke chuckled and kissed her palm. "It was a ruse, my sweet. I was hoping to make you jealous."

"Well, you succeeded," she snapped.

He grinned as he lightly abraded her palm with his stubbled cheek. "I really should shave first, but I can't wait," he murmured before lowering his head for a kiss.

Deborah received his kiss passively at first, then tensed. He lifted his head. Obviously, the battle for her trust was not entirely won. He began gently stroking her, smoothing her hair, tracing her ear, cupping her chin in his hand, then repeating the process until she had relaxed again. He traced her lips, top and bottom with a gentle finger, over and over until they parted. When he kissed her again, instead of tensing, she relaxed against him, and even returned the pressure of his mouth with her own.

"Ah, Dee. How I've dreamed of this moment. But as late as this morning I despaired of it ever coming true. What has happened, my love? Though I suppose I shouldn't ask, just thank my lucky stars."

Deborah laid her head against his shoulder, tilting it so she could look into his eyes. "I despaired, too, when I learned you'd taken your dueling pistols. This day has been one hundred years long, Justin, and in every one of those years I've died over and over, when I thought of losing you. I realized how precious you'd become to me.

"But, oh! Justin. I don't know if I can ever give you what you want . . . what every man wants. I know you won't hurt me as Seymour did, but still, I find that . . . that act so disgusting . . ."

Harwood kissed the top of her head. "Did you find my kiss disgusting just then?"

She let out a long sigh. "No, it was magnificent."

"Yet only a few minutes before, you tensed as if you wanted to escape."

"I . . . I guess I was waiting for it to hurt."

"As it did when Seymour kissed you?"

She hung her head. "Yes."

"But it didn't."

"No, but . . ."

"The act you fear will not hurt you nor disgust you, when you let me love you as you deserve."

Deborah wasn't exactly sure what Harwood meant, but nestled in his arms, with the pleasant glow of his kiss still warming her, she found that she trusted him to know what he was talking about. She snuggled closer to him. "I love you, Justin."

"Dee! My darling Dee!" Harwood hugged her to him, tears standing in his eyes at her declaration, "I love you, too. I shall never hurt you, my darling."

"I know you won't."

They sat thus, holding one another, savoring the moment, for a very long time. But, gradually, the duke could tell from Deborah's posture that her mood had changed. Once again she grew tense, and her shoulders shook. Her head dropped down so that he could not see her face.

"Are you crying, dearest?"

She lifted tear-filled eyes to him. "I just remembered. I can't marry you. Not that you've asked me, but . . ."

He put her away a little bit and gave her a gentle shake. "Of course you'll marry me! And soon."

She shook her head. "You don't understand. I can't give you an heir. After Jenny was born, I almost died. The doctors said the fever had quite destroyed any hope of children. And indeed, in spite of Seymour's determined efforts, there was never . . ."

Suppressing the profitless lurch of fury at her dead husband, Harwood shifted her closer and kissed her forehead. "My love, I have a nephew who is fully twelve years old, and another who is ten. An heir and a spare, thanks to my brother. He sends Andrew to me for a part of every summer and holiday, that I might train him in his future duties. The boy would doubtless be quite aggrieved to be replaced."

Hope lit Deborah's features. "Then we can . . . ?"

"We can, and we will, and that quickly. I may preach

caution to our children, but you and I are going to cast it to the winds. As soon as you can organize a wedding to your liking . . ."

"Tomorrow?"

His kiss was her answer.

Epilogue

"I don't see how they can do this to us!" Deborah waved a perfumed letter about indignantly.

"What is it, Dee?" Harwood looked up in puzzlement from the perusal of his own mail.

"This morning I've had two letters, one from Sarah and Alex, and one from Jennifer and John."

"I noticed. Bad news?" A worried frown crossed his brow as the duke rose and started toward his wife.

"No, wonderful news. But really! What shall I do?"

There were tears in Deborah's eyes. Harwood took her in his arms. "What is going on?"

"They both write me that they are expecting a child."

Harwood's eyes lit up. "Both!"

"Both," Deborah wailed.

"But I thought you would be pleased. Do you dread being a grandmother so much?" Harwood's voice spoke more of amusement than irritation because of his wife's paradoxical reaction.

"Don't be a goose. I'm thrilled to tears for both of them. After all, it's been three years, and we'd begun to worry."

"So?"

"But how shall I go to London to be with Jennifer, and to Hampshire to be with Sarah, all in the same month?"

"They're both due in the same month?" Harwood laughed gleefully. "The minxes! But that is easily solved, love." The duke grinned at Deborah. Sliding his hands up under her arms, he swung her in an exuberant circle.

"We shall simply insist that they all come here to stay for the last months of their pregnancies."

"Do you think they will?" Deborah's brow cleared. She clung to her husband joyfully.

"Of course. Where better to have the newest additions to the family born than at the family seat?"

"I'm sure John won't mind. He will want Jennifer out of London's unhealthy air anyway. Thank goodness Parliament will be in recess then, so he won't be missing any important votes. Even with a baby on the way, it would be hard for him to pry Jennifer away from politics with unfinished business on hand. But Alexander? He's so involved with improving Sarah's dower estates, I wonder if we can tear him away?"

"*We* can't, but he'll do anything to please Sarah, you know, and she'll insist on being with us, I am sure."

The last day of August, 1822, was clear and hot, even in the early morning, as a happy family party made its way to the chapel of Harwood Court.

Along with the duke's brother, his wife, and hopeful family of two girls and two boys, the party included Mrs. Augustus Warner, John's mother; and Lord and Lady Cornwall, their son and two daughters, and the older daughter's new husband. Also present were the Marquess of Hanley's large family.

John's sour-tempered mother had an uncharacteristic smile upon her face this morning as she beheld her only grandchild.

The duke had never cut Vincent or Winnie, but he had not sought their company out, either, so the Cornwalls' smiles reflected their sense of good fortune at having been invited to this family gathering.

The marquess and marchioness were by now grandparents for the third time, yet their smiles were no less broad than the other members of the party.

"This is surely the noisiest christening on record," Deborah whispered into her husband's ear as they took their places around the baptistry.

"Justin Colby Meade seems in unusually good voice today." The duke looked fondly across the baptistry at his daughter and grandson, his glance encompassing Alexander, who was fussing with the baby's lace-edged blanket.

Next to them newly-made knight Sir John Warner took his red-faced son from his lady wife, who looked to be tiring.

"Stanton MacTavish Warner," Jennifer whispered warningly to her son as she handed him over to his father, "you do not have to try to outdo Justin at loud crying. There'll be time enough for rivalry in the years ahead!"